SILENT WITNESS

SILENT WITNESS

Nigel McCrery

POCKET
BOOKS

LONDON · SYDNEY · NEW YORK · TOKYO · SINGAPORE · TORONTO

First published in Great Britain by Pocket Books, 1996
An imprint of Simon & Schuster Ltd
A Viacom Company

Simon & Schuster Ltd
West Garden Place
Kendal Street
London W2 2AQ

Simon & Schuster of Australia Pty Ltd
Sydney

A CIP catalogue record for this book is available
from the British Library

ISBN 0-671-85506-9

Typeset in Sabon 10.5/12.5pt by
Palimpsest Book Production Limited,
Polmont, Stirlingshire FK2 0NZ
Printed and bound in Great Britain by
HarperCollins Manufacturing, Glasgow

For Gill with love.
Without you I could do nothing.

My thanks to **Helen Witwell**, Home Office Pathologist and my inspiration, for all her help, advice and patience; **Bernard Knight**, Home Office Pathologist, for all his help, time and advice; **Peter O. Rose**, for his advice on ivy and the use of his learned book, *Ivies*; **Mike Lucas**. (Mike Lucas Yachting) for his advice on knots and use of *The Ashley Book of Knots*; **The National Training Centre** for Scientific Support to Crime Investigation, Durham; **Peter Ablett**, Director; **Keith Fryer**, Assistant Director; **Sue Thornewill**, Head of Fingerprint Training; **Sandy Bushell**, Instructor; **Dr Z. Erzincglioglu**, entomologist; **Amanda Burton**; actress; **Vicki Featherstone**, script editor; **Catherine Reed**, book editor; **Kevin Hood**, writer; **Ashley Pharoah**, writer; **Caroline Oulton**, executive producer BBC Drama; **Tony Dennis**, producer BBC TV; **Patrick Spence**, script editor; **Nick Webb** of Simon and Schuster; **St John Donald** of Peters Frazer and Dunlop; **Sue Hogg**, executive producer, BBC TV; **Colin Ludlow**, producer, BBC drama. And for all those who may not have been included, many thanks.

PROLOGUE

Nothing ever happened in Northwick. It was that sort of village; quiet, predictable. A place you passed through en route to somewhere more enticing without even registering its existence. Even its church, in a county famous for its churches, was dull and uninteresting, and attracted few visitors.

After months of drought the storm, when it came, was a welcome relief. The heavy droplets bounced off the red, slatted roofs and gushed along the drains and gutters, dragging with them the soot and dirt which had built up over the summer months, before finally spilling out on to the roads and pavements and reflecting the street lamps in pools of shimmering light.

PC Morris Jay stood impassively under an ancient yew whose branches stretched out over the cemetery wall, offering him a temporary sanctuary from the relentless downpour. As he watched the water drip from the tip of his helmet, the church clock struck the quarter hour. He looked down at his watch; one forty-five. There was just enough time to check the last few shops on the high street before making his way back to the station to dry out and investigate the mysteries of his sandwich box.

Despite working shifts for almost twenty-five years PC Jay still hated nights, there was something unnatural about them. Nights were meant for warm beds and soft women, not hard roads and wet feet. As the lightning forked across the sky and the thunder rolled overhead, he pulled the collar of his raincoat tightly around his neck, secured his helmet strap, and left his leafy refuge.

Any energy Mark James had left in his body was knocked out of him by the fall. He lay on his back, peering through the rain, letting it splash over his face and along his lips, taking in deep gulps of air, his rib-cage rising and falling with each rasping breath. Fear had dried his mouth and he was suddenly very thirsty. He licked his lips, picking up the droplets on the end of his tongue and letting them trickle to the back of his throat, providing momentary relief. He needed time, time to think, time to sort out what had happened. Everything had gone so well. How had he been found out so quickly? He wondered now whether he had made a grave error in crossing Bird for a second time. He normally knew when to quit, but this time he seemed to have made a big mistake, gone too far, and now he was running for his very life.

He had felt no sense of apprehension when the car had arrived. It had followed the agreed procedures to the letter. Stopped, flashed its lights twice quickly and then once slowly, just as arranged. The only thing he had found a little unusual was the location. He was a bit of a moth and liked to hover around the bright lights of the city.

Despite living in Cambridge all his life he'd never heard of Northwick. It was a cold, isolated place in the middle of nowhere, the kind of village to which people came to retire and die. He hoped he'd never see it again. Still, the man must have his reasons, and whatever they were it was fine by him.

When the initial approach had been made Mark had been surprised, the man didn't seem to be the type to be involved in the drugs trade but then, who was. The merchandise was top quality, though – the best he'd seen in a long time. It was cheap too, so he expected to be able to move it on quickly and still make a tidy profit.

Feeling secure, Mark had stepped out of his hiding place and made his way through the rain towards the vintage sports car. Nice car, he'd thought, big and old-fashioned. Mark liked old cars, he'd owned an ageing Spitfire for years and, although its seats were ripped and its bodywork falling apart, he loved it.

He had been only yards away from it when its engine suddenly roared back into life, and the car accelerated towards him. He had leapt sideways, narrowly avoiding the nearside wing, and crashed into a row of dustbins. The car's reversing lights had flashed on and, realizing the driver was preparing for another attempt to squash him against the nearest wall, he had scrambled frantically to his feet and made a dash for an ancient sandstone wall. Half climbing, half jumping, he had begun to scramble over the wall when the car, still desperate for its prey, collided heavily with the sandstone blocks sending Mark crashing to the ground on the other side.

Recovering quickly, Mark wiped the rain from his eyes and tried to focus on his surroundings. Strange dark shapes seemed to rise unnaturally from the ground, silhouetted for a instant against the black sky as the lightning turned night into day, before disappearing again into the darkness. With a sense of overwhelming dread, Mark realized where he was; a cemetery. His mind raced as he tried to calculate his next move, his eyes searching for his best line of escape. His concentration was broken by the sound of his pursuer beginning to scale the wall. Whatever he decided, he would have to act quickly. He forced himself to his feet and made his way deeper into the graveyard, slipping and falling on the wet grass and mud, as he made his last frantic bid to escape. Finally, exhausted, he threw himself behind a tall, flat headstone, pushing his back into the smooth slate monument, trying to blend into his surroundings and hiding his face in his hands in his desperation not to be seen. Mark had no choice but to sit and wait. He was disoriented and too breathless to do anything else. Fear had robbed him of rational thought, but he knew his life was important to others and he was determined to survive, if only for their sake.

He tried to focus his mind, to rationalize his situation and understand where it had all gone wrong. Instinctively, for the first time in his adult life, he prayed.

*　　*　　*

PC Jay's radio suddenly crackled into life. 'Control to 784, over.'

PC Jay fumbled through his clothes trying to get to his radio.

'Control to 784, over.' The message came over the radio again, only this time the voice was more impatient.

Jay was annoyed at their persistence. 'Hold your horses,' he thought. 'Bloody office men, what do they know about life at the sharp end?' Finally, forcing his raincoat to one side, he got to his radio. '784 to control, go ahead, over.'

'There's a Mr Typhoo at the police station to see you. He says you've got to deal with him.'

'Yea, ten-four control, I'll be right in.'

He recognized the shift code. It meant the tea was in the pot and the cards were on the table. Only one more building to do, he would have to be quick.

He was late and Frances Purvis was becoming concerned. She glanced at her watch again. The last train had gone and the station had become a strange eerie place.

A couple of drunks had ambled past a short while before, their carrier bags stretched to capacity with numerous cans of strong lager. They'd settled themselves down on one of the porter's trolleys and quickly began to drink the contents of their bag dry. They'd made a few lewd comments, but so far hadn't bothered her unduly. However, she wasn't sure how much longer that situation would last. It wasn't the kind of place a solitary girl should hang around late at night. She began to wonder if she hadn't asked too much of Mark. He wasn't the brightest of people but his devotion to her was touching, and he was the obvious choice when she had felt so desperate. Perhaps Bird, or one of his strong-armed employees, had got hold of him, then she would be in trouble. She'd have to deny everything, of course, and hope Bird believed her. Just five more minutes, she thought, and then she'd have to make her way back to the house and hope she got there before Bird returned. She'd pretended to be ill, making her excuses not to go to the club. As soon as Bird had driven off, she'd packed and caught a taxi to the station. It had seemed the logical place to meet, but now, in the dark, with the two drunks becoming bolder with their comments she wasn't so sure. Where on earth was Mark?

Mark looked up towards the sky, as if to ensure his prayer would be heard. It was then that he saw her, looking down at him, smiling, her face white and beautiful, illuminated for a moment by the moon, as it found a brief gap between the rolling clouds. One arm stretched out towards him while the other pointed to heaven, as if offering an escape from his torment. In the madness of desperation, Mark found himself reaching out to her, and grasping at her small, white, marble hand. Then, without warning, something struck him full in the face. The force, although not great, sent him crashing backwards, screaming with terror and thrashing out with his hands as he tried to ward off the unseen presence attacking him. The cat had been *perched, hidden, at the angel's feet, sheltering beneath her marble shroud. The storm had frightened it and, seeing Mark, she had jumped into his outstretched arms, searching for some human comfort. He looked down at the giant black shape which was now lying across his lap, its green eyes glaring up at him. Mark normally liked cats. Frances had two and he always made a point of playing with them when he was visiting her. But he didn't like this one; this one had probably killed him. He grabbed the cat violently by its scruff and threw it away from him, watching it land awkwardly several yards away before it disappeared quickly into the darkness of the cemetery.*

Mark strained his ears for the sound of approaching footsteps, there were none. Perhaps his pursuer hadn't heard his screams, perhaps he'd stopped searching and Mark was safe after all. He got to his feet slowly, peering over the top of the headstone for any sign of movement.

The sheer power of the blow that struck him down from behind sent him sprawling into the wet grass and mud of the cemetery. He lay there for a second clutching the back of his head, searching for the source of the pain which shot through his neck and down his spine. He didn't wait for the second blow to arrive, nor did he look behind to see who his assailant was, too afraid of what he might see. He began to run, almost on all fours, using his arms to keep his balance as his feet slipped on the wet earth. He tried to keep low, running stooped and hoping to use the other headstones as cover, in an attempt to shake off his pursuer. He ran quickly towards the safety of the village's street lights. He knew once he reached them he would be safe.

Finally, he reached the cemetery gates, his last obstacle to freedom. He pulled at the handles and shook them violently hoping they would give way, but although the iron gates rattled loudly against his assault, they remained firmly locked. Looking out along the village street for any sign of help he saw him, his saviour, his knight in blue armour. Mark had never thought he would be pleased to see a policeman, but now he was. He smiled with relief, forced an arm through the gate's railings and drew breath to call out.

PC Jay crossed the road towards the post office. Pulling his torch from his pocket he shone it through the shop's front window. Everything seemed to be in place, nothing tipped over, nothing broken and the windows were all intact. He walked over to the front door, grabbed its handles tightly and gave them a firm shake. They were locked, it would take a bulldozer to get through those doors. PC Jay breathed in deeply with a sense of relief, it had been a quiet night, and those were the ones he liked best. He was already visualizing himself sitting in the police canteen, his feet up, eating his sandwiches while his uniform dried out over a hot radiator. He turned deliberately and started to make his way back towards the police station.

Mark knew his mouth was moving. He could feel it, couldn't he? His mind told him he was shouting, but he heard nothing. The policeman didn't react either, *just pulled on a door, and flashed his torch into a building. He tried again, his eyes bulging and his face reddening with the effort, but now he felt far away, his world spinning towards the bottom of a long black tunnel and there was nothing he could do to stop it. He realized he could no longer feel his mouth, his tongue would not react to the messages from his brain. As if a great weight was pushing him down, his legs buckled and he fell heavily to his knees. He tried to steady himself by grasping the gates, but his arms felt heavy and his strength was gone. Finally, he fell sideways on to the grass. Sheltered from the street by the cemetery wall, Mark lay motionless, looking up at the sky through the leaves of an ancient yew. He felt strangely calm, almost as if he were at peace with himself. He began to wonder what Frances would think when he didn't turn up; it would be the first time he'd ever let her down in his life. A dark shadow moved slowly across his face and Mark realized his nemesis had arrived.*

The commotion disturbed PC Jay. He turned and stared back through the rain towards the church but could see nothing. He looked at his watch, five to two, if he went back now he'd be late, they'd start without him, and the tea would be stewed. He convinced himself there was nothing wrong; probably an animal of some sort, it nearly always was. Nothing serious had happened in the village for years, not even a burglary, so it was unlikely to be anything important. He stared along the street towards the church one more time, just to salve his conscience. Then he saw it. Its large black shape jumped quickly on to the cemetery wall under the tree where he had been sheltering, it crouched low and stared back along the street towards him. Jay knew it was the sexton's cat but was surprised to see it was still out, he thought it was cleverer than that. PC Jay smiled to himself, turned and walked away.

Mark James was dragged slowly back into the cemetery. His eyes were still open, allowing the rain to bounce off his unprotected pupils, obscuring the face of his killer, and run along the channels of his twisted face.

CHAPTER ONE

Samantha Ryan looked around the old magistrates court at Ely. It had been over a month since they'd found Andrew Stringer's body at the back of the Cromwell Library at St Steven's College and now she was about to pronounce judgement on his rather bizarre death. She enjoyed her visits to Ely, much preferring them to the make-shift inquests which were organized in committee room number three at the Park Hospital, with its plastic and chrome fittings. Here was a court worthy of the law. Its beamed ceilings and wooden benches oozed justice from every grain, while ancient paintings of long-dead judges hung from the oak-panelled walls, looking down imperiously on the innocent and guilty alike.

Sam scanned the room, looking at the faces of other witnesses. She moved from face to face examining each in detail before moving on to the next. She wondered what part each of them had played in Stringer's life and, more importantly, his death. Detective Superintendent Harriet Farmer was there, next to her was Dr Richard Owen, the police surgeon, followed by Detective Inspector Tom Adams. As her eyes drew level with his, he looked across at her. Their gaze lingered for a moment before Sam looked away, slightly flustered. Adams was amused at her embarrassment and continued to stare at her for a few moments longer.

He had first met Sam when she'd turned up at the Ross murder a year before. It had been a tricky one and if it hadn't been for her evidence they would probably have lost the case. He'd never really understood why she'd moved from the bright lights of London to a comparative criminal backwater like Cambridge, but that was her affair, and he was sure he'd find out in time. He'd liked her from the moment they'd first met, but she'd always kept the relationship strictly professional, and at times was even offhand towards him. The squad called her the 'ice maiden' but he wasn't convinced. She wasn't stunning in the 'accepted' sense, no long, blonde hair or silicone-enhanced breasts but there was something about her. Some women, he thought, simply possessed an indefinable attraction. She wasn't tall, but she was slim and beautifully proportioned, with an attractive face and the most memorable, soft, brown eyes he'd ever seen. She was also intelligent and he'd always found that appealing. He'd attended one of the old secondary modern schools in which intellectual ability was under-estimated and frequently stifled. Future employment prospects for most of the boys had relied upon one of the many apprenticeships on offer at that time. He hadn't fancied any of those and so had joined the police cadets. He had seen this as a step up, it made him feel middle class, respected, part of the establishment, and he'd always enjoyed the work. The ultimate 'pull'

during his school-days had been to go out with one of
the grammar school girls and he had, quite often, but it
had never come to anything. They had usually gone on
to marry the boy who became the local bank manager,
accountant or company executive. Still, he thought, he
could dream. He'd been ambitious and astute enough
to take advantage of the opportunities offered by the
Open University since those days, and had found that
education was more enjoyable and rewarding the second
time around. Suddenly, realizing he'd been looking at
her longer than he'd intended, he turned his head and
focused his stare back into the court.

George Allan's firm voice suddenly cut across the
court, 'Dr Ryan, would you like to give your evidence
please?'

Sam, still feeling slightly disconcerted and annoyed
by Adams' persistent stare, hadn't been paying attention
to proceedings and was taken by surprise. She moved
quickly, collecting her notes together and walking across
the court to the witness box. She knew the procedure
well. Picking up the Bible she read the oath aloud. She
had done this a hundred times before and needed no
prompting. When she'd finished, she looked across at
the coroner, he nodded and she continued.

'Dr Samantha Ryan. I am a Bachelor of Medicine,
and a member of the Royal College of Pathologists. I
am the holder of a diploma in medical jeoprudence, a
consultant Home Office pathologist and senior lecturer
at Cambridge University. I am currently employed at the
Park Hospital as a consultant in forensic medicine.'

Allan looked across at her, 'Thank you, Dr Ryan.'

He studied his notes for a moment before peering back at Sam over his half-rimmed spectacles. 'The police surgeon, Dr Owen, has stated in evidence that because of the advanced state of rigor mortis, he concluded that the deceased must have been dead between . . .' As if forgetting his lines, he looked down at his notes again and, reading from them, continued, 'between six and eight hours.' He looked back at Sam. 'I see from your notes, Dr Ryan, that you don't entirely agree with Dr Owen's findings. Perhaps you could elucidate?'

He sat back and waited for Sam's reply. She opened her notes and began to give her evidence. She didn't really need them, it was one of those cases which she was unlikely to forget easily. In her fifteen years as a forensic pathologist, Andrew Stringer's death was probably one of the most bizarre and difficult cases she'd had to deal with.

From the moment she arrived at the scene she'd felt the sense of disquiet amongst the investigating team. She'd arrived early for once, which was unusual for her. The time needed to arrive at a scene could vary considerably, depending upon the time she was contacted, where she was, what she was doing, where she'd left her car keys, and, most importantly, where in the county the body was located. Just travelling to a scene could sometimes take over an hour. This time she was lucky, the body had been discovered behind one of the old colleges, close to The Backs, making it easily accessible, especially during the early hours of the morning. Despite her punctuality, however, everybody still seemed to have arrived before her and there was the normal commotion and organized chaos which seemed to accompany every murder scene she attended. Uniformed and plain-clothed police officers scurried to and fro, while white-suited Scene of Crime Officers, SOCOs, carried both mundane and suspicious-looking objects away in a variety of plastic bags. The whole area was illuminated by high-intensity mobile lights which gave the scene an almost surreal perspective. Parking her car on the grass verge behind St Steven's College she left her car keys with a surprised PC on the main gate, before making her way the hundred yards along 'Fellows Lane' towards Old Bridge and the back of the college. Half-way across the bridge she noticed two CID officers talking to a couple of bowler-hatted porters. Both looked pale and shaken, and she assumed they had been the ones to discover the body. As she reached the far side of the bridge she turned left, crunching her way across the gravel path running between the River Cam and the Cromwell Library, and made her way towards the murder tent.

At first she had thought it was some kind of peculiar joke but the faces of Farmer and Adams told her it wasn't. The victim was sitting bolt upright on a wooden bench, his body and face turned slightly to one side. A small stream of blood ran from beneath the bench forming a sticky pool by the victim's feet. She walked around to the front of the body, bringing the man's face slowly into view. It was alabaster white, the half-open eyes staring blankly ahead. His mouth was wide open and fixed in a giant, soundless scream. A large metal-handled knife protruded from the left side of his chest about six inches below his armpit, twisting his arm unnaturally upwards as if someone had forced a coat hanger inside his T-shirt. Sam stood back for a moment. Murder it certainly seemed to be, but there was something about the entire scene that puzzled her.

'When you're ready, Dr Ryan?'

The coroner's inpatient voice interrupted Sam's thoughts and she began to give her evidence.

'For rigor mortis to have advanced to such a degree I would have expected the body to have been both stiff and cold. However, the deceased's body was still warm and had, in fact, hardly cooled by the time I arrived at the scene. From that, I concluded that the deceased had only been dead for a short time.'

Allan interrupted her, 'About how long is "a short time"?'

'It's impossible to be absolutely precise about these things, but I would certainly have thought less than two hours. I also examined the deceased's legs and found no evidence of hypostasis,' – Sam glanced across at the press gallery and noticed several reporters looking up at her expectantly; she took the hint – 'the settling of the blood downwards due to gravity after death.'

The journalists started to write again. Allan noticed the glance and was irritated by what he interpreted as Sam playing to the gallery. He continued with his questions.

'How, then, do you explain the presence of rigor mortis, Dr Ryan?'

Sam waited for a moment, scanning her notes to make sure her explanation was clear and accurate.

'It wasn't rigor mortis. Well, not in its true sense, anyway.'

Allan suddenly sat up with renewed interest. He knew Sam well, and was aware of her professional competence; he even found himself looking forward to her evidence. It was always clear, precise and well presented with no flights of fancy. This was certainly a deviation for her and he was already intrigued.

'It is a condition known as cadaveric spasm.' Sam looked across at the press gallery again. 'The instantaneous contraction of the muscles at the time of death.'

Allan pulled her attention back to him. 'I'm well aware of what cadaveric spasm is, Dr Ryan, but in fifteen years in this court I have never before come across a case of it. Are you sure of your facts?'

'Yes,' Sam replied firmly.

'In fact, isn't there a certain school of thought which believes that the condition doesn't even exist, or if it does, it's only likely to be found on battlefields and the like?' This time *he* looked across at the press gallery and, with a certain amount of satisfaction, watched them note down his every word. 'But you clearly think it does exist?'

'Yes, I do.'

'Then how do you think he died?'

Sam looked into his face, waiting for his reaction when she made her announcement.

'Suicide. It is my belief that Andrew Stringer took his own life. We know that the emotional state of a person in these circumstances is important. We also know that the deceased was in a highly charged state due to the recent engagement of his former girlfriend, and had, in fact, threatened revenge. This, I believe, was his revenge.'

'That's a bit elaborate, don't you think?'

'Not if you wanted the authorities to think you were murdered.'

Allan, leaning back in his chair, waited to see how her arguments developed. Sam continued, confident of her facts.

'We now know the knife he used was stolen from his former girlfriend's flat some days before he died. It is my belief that he arrived at the college fully intending to kill himself and hoping the blame would fall either on her or her fiancé. Sitting on the college bench, he carefully positioned the knife between the top of the bench and the soft tissue area under his left armpit. This would explain the unusual position of his arm at the time he was discovered. At first I thought he might have been trying to pull the knife out, but he wasn't, he was trying to ensure it went in. The scratch marks found on the top slats of the bench were consistent with a metal-handled knife being scratched across the surface of the paint. Once the knife was in position he pushed his body back on to it with such force that the knife passed between the deceased's sixth and seventh ribs before penetrating both his heart and one lung. Death would have followed almost immediately.'

The court was now totally hushed and Sam continued with her evidence.

'The pain and the shock of the knife entering his body, combined with his emotional state at the time, almost certainly brought on the spasm. Had it not been for the spasm, preventing the body falling to the ground, an innocent person might now be facing a murder charge, and the deceased would have had his bizarre revenge.'

Although captivated by her testimony, Sam had stepped beyond the bounds of her expertise and Allan interjected quickly, 'I think that's for the court to decide, don't you, Dr Ryan?'

Sam, also realizing she might have gone a bit far, nodded and closed her file.

Reg Applin had been the church sexton for as long as anyone could remember. He enjoyed the status, but knew his time was short; rheumatism was stiffening his knees as the ageing process took its inevitable toll. If he'd been in any other job he'd have been retired by now, but the parish, not surprisingly, were having problems finding a replacement and had asked him to stay on for 'a while'. He had hoped they'd buy him a mechanical digger to take the strain out of the job, but there wasn't enough money in the parish fund. They bought him a new type of spade instead, by way of compensation, but it wasn't much use. The new spade had a sort of lever at the back and was supposed to take the effort out of the digging, but it broke after a week and he was forced to use his old one again and that had finished his knees off. And the work wasn't as rewarding as it once had been. People either didn't tip him or if they did, it was hardly enough to buy a couple of pints at the Black's Head. Besides, most people wanted to be cremated these days and there was nothing for him in that job. It was funny, really, he'd known most of his 'clients' when they were alive; they all thought themselves better than him, but here he was still alive and throwing dirt on to most of them. He'd already picked out his own spot and been promised it by the vicar. It was under the old yew tree at the back end of the cemetery. He liked it there, it was cool and shaded from the extremes of the weather and the kids seldom ventured that deep into the cemetery, so he hoped to be safe from the vandalism which had desecrated so many of the graves in recent years. He propped his bike up against one of the numerous old tombstones which littered the graveyard, unravelled his bag from the handlebars and, with his terrier, Scruff, marching by his side and his spade over his shoulder, made his way into the cemetery to start preparing another grave.

Sam emerged from the court into the daylight. It was mild and muggy and the air lay heavily over the town. The sky was black as the storm clouds began to roll in from the east. Stretching her shoulders, she looked out across the old town's roofs towards the cathedral. Although much of the building was hidden, it was a majestic sight all the same. The great mass of stone rose above Ely like a forbidding glacier, its amber, grey and pink colourings standing out against the black sky, illuminated by the final rays of the rapidly setting October sun. She visited it from time to time, wandering around the various chapels and reading the inscriptions to the great and the good. She felt that it helped to add a spiritual dimension to her otherwise clinical life, even though she wasn't sure about God any more. She used to be, when she was child, but that was before her father died.

She had seen it happen, had watched as one moment he waved goodbye and the next exploded into a ball of flame and light. They never caught the people responsible, they seldom did, it was all too political. He knew he was under threat, a Catholic and a policeman was an almost certain recipe for disaster. Dozens of his friends had already died or been seriously injured, which was why he had been such a careful man. He normally checked everything at least twice and she could remember playing with the mirror on the long pole which he ran under his car every time he went out. She'd being playing with it on the day he died. She had left it at the end of the garden when her mother called her in for lunch. Her father had been called out in an emergency and had taken a chance. The IRA were blamed, but later when Sam was old enough to ask questions of her own she had doubted that conclusion. Catholic policemen weren't trusted. All her daddy wanted was a peaceful Ireland. She knew his death was her fault, her mammy had told her. Mammy had stood by his grave holding Sam's sister close to her and refusing to acknowledge Sam's presence. So God and the church had become Sam's scapegoats and all her anger was directed at them as her mother's had been directed at her. Fifteen years as a pathologist had only confirmed her atheism, exchanging what remained of her spiritual awareness for the cold clinical analysis of the dissecting table and the laboratory.

Now, for some inexplicable reason she found herself being drawn slowly back, examining all her past assumptions. The cathedral had been the first church she had entered for over twenty years. It had been a difficult process and she had found herself hanging about outside the main entrance trying to summon up the courage to enter, walking up and down and looking at the door as if it were the gateway to hell. Finally, tagging along with an organized group, she had been swept anonymously into the vast interior.

Her thoughts were interrupted by the police surgeon, Richard Owen. 'Quite magnificent, isn't it?'

Sam looked at him, confused for a moment.

'The cathedral, magnificent.'

She collected her thoughts. 'Yes, it is.'

'I always like to come to the cases I've been involved with, especially when they're heard at Ely. It's such a beautiful place.'

Sam nodded. 'Yes, it's lovely, isn't it?'

'You were quite brilliant in there. Made me look a bit of a chump though.'

'That wasn't the intention, Richard. It's an extremely rare condition, it's the first time I've ever seen it. There's no reason why you should have spotted it.'

'*You* did. If I'd bothered to take his temperature properly then I might have realized something was wrong. It just seemed so obvious.'

She looked into Richard's face and found herself feeling quite sorry for him. 'Well, you'll know for next time,' she said awkwardly.

'Yes, I certainly will.' He paused for a moment.

'Listen, Janet and I were wondering, if you have a spare evening over the next few weeks, whether you'd like to come and have some supper with us. Give you the chance to get to know her, you're about the same age. I'm sure you'll have a lot in common. Perhaps we could swap a few ideas as well?'

It was the first time Owen had really spoken to her since she'd come to Cambridge a little over a year ago. They'd swapped notes occasionally but it had always been on a strictly professional basis, she wasn't even sure he liked her very much, so she was surprised by the invitation. She was pleased that her display in court hadn't alienated him. Owen was one of the old school and set in his ways. He'd been the local police surgeon for almost thirty years and had been dealing with murders while she was still in pigtails and running around in blue serge knickers. The problem was that he was finding it difficult to adjust in a rapidly changing world.

'I'd love to.'

Owen appeared pleased, 'Good, good. I'll ring you next week to make arrangements.'

Their conversation was interrupted by the approach of a young girl. She was about twenty-two years old, slim and pretty with a sweep of long blonde hair. Sam had seen her in court. She spoke to Sam.

'Dr Ryan? I wonder if I could have a word with you?'

Richard Owen took the hint. 'Look, I must be going, I'll catch up with you later.'

Sam smiled, nodded and watched him leave. She returned her attention to the young girl.

'I'm Rebecca West, Andrew's old girlfriend. I'd just

like to say thank you for what you did. I knew Andrew was a mad sod, that's why I left him. I just hadn't realized how mad.'

'Well, he certainly won't be causing you any more problems.'

'No.'

Sam noticed a young and rather handsome young man standing a few yards along the street, watching them intensely; they clearly belonged together.

'He looks nice.'

Rebecca glanced at him and smiled, the boy smiled back as only young lovers can.

'He is, best thing that ever happened to me really.'

'Fresh start.'

The girl smiled broadly at Sam. 'I hope so. Well, thanks again.' She put her hand out. Sam took it and gave her a gentle squeeze. She'd been through a difficult ordeal for one so young and Sam found herself hoping that everything would now work out for her. She watched with a certain degree of jealousy as Rebecca rejoined her boyfriend and they disappeared hand in hand along the road. She envied their youth and their fresh start.

'Penny for them?'

Detective Inspector Tom Adams' question made her jump. She turned around and looked up at him.

'They're worth more than a penny.'

'I expect they are. Well, that's another one we've lost.'

Sam was irritated by the remark. 'You didn't lose it, you never had it in the first place.'

'Try telling Superintendent Farmer that, she's chalked it up as lost glory and guess who she's blaming?'

'She can suit herself,' Sam replied.

'Clever stuff though. I was very impressed.'

Sam felt flattered and slightly embarrassed. She was attracted to Adams, who was tall and broad with a crop of dark black hair that seemed to enhance his blue, twinkling eyes. He was different to most of the police officers she had to deal with, and although he was a bit rough around the edges she always felt he was only playing a part and that in fact there was far more to him. He never gave the impression that he considered women to be in any way inferior to him. His manner suggested that he was at ease in and comfortable with the company of women. A very attractive trait, Sam thought. Their conversation was interrupted by a call from the opposite side of the road. Superintendent Harriet Farmer was standing by the side of her dark blue Escort, staring across at them. She seemed annoyed.

'Do you want a lift back or are you walking?'

Sam glanced across at Farmer. She looked every inch the police officer. Although tall and slim and not unattractive, she had a hard face which expressed years of struggling, not only against criminals, but also against a system which had difficulty dealing with career-minded women. Her hair was long and brown and she kept it in a smart ponytail. This she pulled back so tightly that it seemed to stretch her skin like a cheap face-lift. Sam always imagined that when she let it out at night her face would crumple into a thousand crinkles and lines. Farmer was watching the two of them impatiently, waiting for Adams to break off his conversation and join her. Adams looked down at Sam. 'Got to go, conspiring with the enemy and all that.'

Sam looked across at Farmer. 'She who must be obeyed.'

Adams laughed quietly before turning on his heel and walking off. As he did, the two women's eyes met for a moment before Sam finally turned and made her way towards the cathedral.

It was late, and the storm was raging overhead. Reg was sheltering under the branches of the old yew, sitting on his spade and watching the rain bounce off the church roof and pour down its walls. If they didn't get the drains repaired soon, he thought, there'd be no more St Mary's. It was the season for storms, and this was the second bad one in a month. He reached into his bag and retrieved his flask. Pouring the last of his tea into a small plastic cup he slurped it down. It was almost cold, but he didn't care. The grave he had just finished was already an inch deep in water and he wondered if the deceased had realized he was going to be buried at sea. He was exhausted. All the digs seemed far longer and harder than they used to. He'd have finished this job hours ago if he'd been younger and fitter, then maybe he would have missed the storm. He would have to stop, they'd have to find a younger man, he wasn't up to it any more. One day, he thought, they'd find him dead inside one of his own graves and then they'd have some explaining to do. He stood up, secured the cup on to the top of his flask and emptied the contents of his sandwich box on to the ground before slipping on his jacket and slowly making his way through the rain towards his bike. It wasn't until he reached it that he realized his dog was no longer with him. Probably sheltering under some bush or headstone, Reg thought, he wasn't stupid. He glanced at his watch, the pub had already been open over an hour and he was keen to get in out of the wet. He called out, 'Scruff, where are you, boy, time to go, come on, pub's open!' He peered through the rain for any sign of his dog. Suddenly the small terrier came bursting through the wet grass and ran towards him. As the dog came closer Reg noticed that he was holding something firmly in his mouth.

'What you got there then, boy, eh, what you got there?'

He crouched down and tried to pull the object away from him but Scruff was keen to hang on to it and fought fiercely for his prize. Finally, Reg managed to tear it free, leaving only a small part in the dog's mouth which he chewed and swallowed quickly, fearful of losing that as well. Wiping the rain from his eyes, Reg stared down at what he'd retrieved. At first he wasn't sure what it was and thought it might be just a piece of rotten meat, or perhaps the remains of an animal. However, as his eyes began to focus, he realized it was none of those things but was, in fact, a person's hand, or rather what was left of one. Half of it was missing and three blackened fingers dangled loose from a disembodied palm. Scuff had brought a few bones back in his time and that was bad enough, but a human hand, and one that hadn't been dead long, shocked and surprised him. Almost instinctively, Reg threw it across the graveyard, not wanting the object near him. It travelled for several yards before colliding with a headstone and splashing into the mud in a crumpled, blackened heap. Scruff, having lost his prize, raced back into the cemetery looking for another. Reg, shaken, called after him, 'Scruff! Come on, lad, let's have you, I'm getting soaked!'

Normally, he would have left him in the cemetery and let him find his own way back. It wasn't the first time he'd disappeared, but he was concerned about how Scruff had come across the hand and fearful of what his dog might bring back next. Reg hung his bag over one of the old headstones and pushed his way through the wet grass following the sound of his dog's barking. The trail led him into one of the older, overgrown sections of the graveyard. He looked around. The barking was coming from the seventeenth-century tomb of Sir Jasper Case. He knew the tomb well. It was one of the more interesting in the cemetery, but it was old and falling apart. He'd done what he could, but as fast as he repaired it the bloody kids came in and smashed it again. It was a sort of contest and the kids were winning.

'They've no respect for nothing these days,' he mumbled.

The lid, like the rest of the tomb, was broken and a large piece was missing. It was clear that Scruff had managed to squeeze inside the tomb and had got himself trapped.

'Silly beggar,' Reg shouted at his dog. 'Should have more sense.'

He peered into the darkness of the tomb searching

for his dog. As the sky flashed cobalt blue he was just able to make Scruff out. He was sniffing around something lying in the bottom of the tomb. The light wasn't good enough for Reg to see what it was so, in the half light, he leaned in and, cupping his hand under the dog's stomach, started to pull him clear of the tomb. The job, however, wasn't as easy as Reg had hoped and Scruff was resisting. Pull as he might he just couldn't seem to move the small dog. He looked down into the tomb searching for the cause of the problem.

'Come on, you daft beggar, we'll be here all night.'

He pulled again with no result, so he waited for another flash of lightning. He didn't have to wait long, a particularly powerful fork crossed the sky lighting up everything for a moment in a brilliant blue flash. Reg looked deep into the tomb. It was only then that he realized he wasn't holding Scruff. The head twisted towards him in his hand, causing the face to stare up at him. It was only half there, the flesh dropping from its bones. The lips had already disappeared, exposing the teeth and producing a sort of grizzly smile. One eye was missing, leaving a black void, and the other bulged out of the skull, red and bloated, the skin surrounding it having been eaten away. Reg screamed and dropped the head, staggering backwards. He looked down and noticed that part of the scalp had stuck to his hand. Shuddering, he frantically wiped it off on the long wet grass and ran from the cemetery.

✤　　✤　　✤

It had been the same dream, the one she'd had for the past month. The one that woke her in the middle of the night leaving her body and bedclothes soaked with perspiration. She lay there for a moment trying to come to terms with it, staring into the darkness of her bedroom, her chest heaving up and down as she strove to recall the images that only moments before had invaded her dreams. As usual, however, they were gone, like will-o'-the-wisp, disappearing into the dark recesses of her subconscious only to reappear the following night to terrify her again. She knew her dreams were vivid, she did have momentary flashes of them, all in glorious Technicolor. But the faces were alabaster blank and smooth, appearing and then disappearing again, floating off into a void. The ringing of the phone by her bedside finally brought her back to reality. She propped herself on one elbow, turned on the bedside light and picked up the phone, almost dropping it as she brought it to her ear.

'Hello, Dr Ryan.'

She fought against the slurred tiredness in her voice but it was impossible. The voice on the other end of the phone was young, confident and awake. These facts alone told her it was a policeman.

'Sorry to bother you, Dr Ryan, but they've discovered a body at St Mary's Church and we were wondering if you could come out. It's a bit of a dodgy one.'

Sam couldn't help but be impressed by his clinical interpretation of a suspicious death as being 'a bit of a dodgy one'. He must have got that from one of the many police series which had invaded TV of late. Besides, what did they expect her to say, 'No, sorry, it's my day off and I'm going shopping'? She could feel her bad mood and she tried to control it.

'I thought Dr Stuart was on call?'

The answer came back crisply, 'Yes, he is, but we can't find him, he's not answering his bleeper. That's why we're a bit late phoning you.'

Probably interfering with his love life, Sam grumbled to herself. She was beginning to recover.

'Yes, of course I'll come . . . just a moment, let me grab a pen.'

She leaned across the bed and opened the drawer in her bedside cabinet. Fumbling around inside she found a small, black notebook and pen. She sat up, resting the book against her legs, trying to focus on its clear white pages. 'OK, I'm ready now. Where is it?'

His voice was so sharp it made Sam wince. 'St Mary's Church, Northwick. It's just off the B381, about twenty miles outside . . .'

Sam cut in, 'Yes, I know where that is, thank you.'

He was only trying to be helpful but she didn't need his efficiency right now.

'There'll be a policeman on the gate to direct you to the scene. Superintendent Farmer is already there.' He said it as if it were some form of warning for her to hurry. She wasn't about to be intimidated by Farmer or anyone else. 'Yes, thank you. I'll be about an hour.'

She put the phone down and looked at her alarm clock, twelve twenty-eight a.m. She made a note of the time in her book before dropping it on the bedside table and swinging her legs out of bed. She calculated that, by the time she'd got dressed and ready, it was going to take her longer than an hour to get there. Northwick was on the other side of the county and not the easiest place in the world to reach, but the police liked a time, it gave them something to look forward to.

Shuffling across the room to the window she pulled back the curtains and threw open the window. The storm had passed, but she could still hear the distant sound of thunder as it rolled on across the county. The mugginess that had seemed to linger for weeks had gone and been replaced by fresh, clear air. It raced unchecked across the East Anglian countryside from the North Sea before pouring through her open window, cooling and reviving her naked body. The heavy rain had filled the air with the smells of the night and she loved those. It reminded her that her sense of smell was still intact and hadn't, yet, been totally destroyed by the aromas of the mortuary. She looked down into her garden. The storms had been a welcome break from the long hot summer the county had just experienced. The garden had burst into life again as it drank deeply. She looked forward to the season's work. Closing the window and securing the latch she made her way back across the bedroom towards the shower.

She was surprised to find herself musing with some pleasure that if Farmer was dealing with this case, Adams was almost sure to be there too.

Samantha was late as usual. She'd managed to lose her car keys yet again and was finally forced to use the spare set which she kept for just such an occasion in a kitchen drawer. She imagined Farmer pacing up and down, waiting impatiently for her to arrive and pass judgement on the deceased. She turned into the village. The church wasn't difficult to find, she only had to follow the blue flashing lights which were illuminating the whole area. The press were there already, milling around the graveyard looking for their lead story. They were only stopped from invading the cemetery and destroying the scene by a thin piece of yellow and black police tape and a single police officer's vigilance. The press always seemed to find out quickly about major cases, tipped off no doubt by some friendly detective within the murder squad. It wasn't strictly allowed, but it always happened. She drove through the throng of reporters slowly, masking her face with her hand from the camera flashes and ignoring the numerous taps on the side-window of her car.

As she approached the church she was stopped by a young constable who shone a torch irritatingly into her face. He looked cold, but then he'd probably been there several hours already. By the time every police officer and his dog had travelled out to the scene and expressed their opinion on the situation, it could take hours before somebody finally made the decision to call out the pathologist. She flicked open the glove compartment and rummaged through the collection of chocolate papers, discount vouchers and maps which littered the inside, searching for her identity card. Finally, locating the piece of drab plastic, on which was an even drabber photograph of herself, she held it up for the constable's inspection.

'Dr Ryan, Home Office Pathologist.'

He nodded, and after making a few quick notes on the pad he had secured to a clipboard, directed her to her parking place by the side of the church. She thanked him, dropped her ID card back into the mess of her glove compartment and drove steadily along the road towards a small gap in an apparently unending line of police cars.

The police swarmed around the site. Some in uniform, with their black woolly hats pulled tightly around their ears, carrying long poles, the SOCOs in their white boiler suits, and the CID wandering around talking earnestly to each other but not, apparently, doing very much.

She climbed out of her car and made her way through the church gates, following the taped path to the scene. Half-way along the path she was approached by the crime scene manager who handed her a white boiler suit. This, of course, was for the protection of the crime scene, preventing contamination of the evidence, but it was also invaluable for protecting her own clothes. She was always careful about her appearance. Smart but practical, with just a hint of make-up. She remembered turning up to one scene looking like death warmed up. She'd been out to a late dinner the night before and hadn't bothered making her usual effort after the phone had rung at five in the morning. Her greatly reduced concentration had been focused on getting to the scene. Unfortunately, the press had been tipped off and were everywhere. Newspaper reporters, photographers, television crews, the works. She had found herself pushing through a wall of flashing lights and unanswerable questions before emerging into the field in which the body was lying. She'd seen herself the next day on both the national and local news looking dreadful, like a bag lady, pale faced and scruffy. But most humiliating were the phone calls from friends who had also seen her. Farmer, on the other hand, had looked her usual cool, confident self, dressed smartly in trousers and a rather expensive-looking black winter coat. Sam had made a promise to herself that she would never be seen in that condition again, even if it did mean turning up at a scene a few minutes late.

She was approached by Richard Owen. He looked every bit the prosperous country doctor in his dark wool blazer and unprotected green wellingtons, which, after all, she thought, is what he was. A police surgeon's main function in life, as far as Sam was concerned, was to pronounce life extinct, and that at a suitable distance if possible. Some, she found, fancied themselves as latter day Sherlock Holmeses, and would often interfere far beyond their brief and, more irritatingly, their competence. Owen had learned, when dealing with Sam, to keep his opinions and diagnoses to the minimum. She was surprised and a little annoyed to see that he wasn't wearing his white protective boiler suit and wondered how he'd managed to get around the crime scene manager, as they were normally sticklers for procedure. He greeted her with a half smile, 'Evening, Sam. Managed to fight your way through the circus, then?

Sam nodded. She rubbed the edge of his jacket between her fingers. 'Nice smart jacket, Richard, very in keeping with the situation.'

Owen looked down at his uncovered jacket and brushed it with his hand.

'Do you like it? Present from the memsahib. Got to show willing, haven't you?'

'You could have covered it up with a set of white overalls. It's the first thing I teach my new students.'

Richard remained unrepentant. 'Hardly worth the effort, I was in and out in a trice.'

Sam did her best to hide her annoyance at this lack of procedure but found it difficult. 'Have you never heard the saying, a person can be murdered once, but the scene can be murdered a thousand times?'

Owen changed the subject. 'Thought Trevor Stuart was on call?'

'He is, but they couldn't find him; probably stuffed his bleeper under some unfortunate's mattress.'

'Perhaps they should have tried some of the female student blocks, always a good bet during his student days.'

'Well, it's time he grew up. Anyway, what have we got?'

'White male, late teens, early twenties, been dead a few weeks I would think.'

Sam listened politely but took little notice, preferring to make up her own mind about what she found at the scene.

Owen continued, 'Church sexton found him a few hours ago; he'd been strangled. The cord's still around his neck. He's in a bit of a state, I'm afraid, animals got there before we did.'

'No identity on him?'

'No, nothing. He's naked and there's no sign of his clothes at the moment.'

Sam considered what he had just told her for a moment. 'Sexual motivation?'

'Not sure, but then you're the expert on these things, not me. I'm just a jobbing police surgeon.'

Knowing he was aware of her feelings on police surgeons, she smiled across at him.

'I've told them they can take the body out of the tomb if that's all right? Wasn't enough room to swing a cat in there.'

As much as she disliked people 'mucking about' with the body before she got to the scene, Sam knew he'd made the right decision and it would certainly help her get on with the initial examination. She nodded, acknowledging his help. 'No, that's fine. I suppose I'd better go and see what I can do. Thanks for the help.'

Picking up her bag and looking back across at Owen, she couldn't resist having one more swipe at him about his failure to follow the rules. 'Hope the smell hasn't stuck to your jacket, Richard, or Janet will be upset, won't she? See you later.'

Sam turned and walked away along the taped path towards the centre of the cemetery, a wicked smile across her face. Owen waited until she was out of sight before grabbing the bottom of his jacket and bringing it up to his nose. He winced, Sam was right, the smell of the body seemed to have clung to every fibre, it would have to be cleaned. He dropped the jacket back into place and, shaking his head, made his way towards the cemetery gate.

The body wasn't difficult to find, broadcast by the presence of arc lights and the commotion surrounding it. Sam spotted Farmer and Adams, surrounded by SOCOs, standing by the side of a tomb. One SOCO was already inside the tomb taking various samples while others combed the surrounding area and yet another took photographs. They all looked cold and Farmer and Adams were drinking steaming coffee from cardboard cups. She made her way towards them.

She noticed that the lid from the tomb had been removed and now lay in three pieces on the wet grass. The body lay next to it on an opened-out bodybag. Owen had been right, the tomb was small and she certainly couldn't have worked inside it. Farmer looked up as she approached, clearly surprised at her presence.

'I thought Trevor Stuart was on call?'

Sam was becoming tired of the question. 'They decided this one should be done properly,' she snapped.

Farmer and Adams looked at each other, detecting a problem. Sam crouched down by the body, opened her medical bag and searched through the array of bottles and instruments for her dictaphone. It wasn't there. Then she remembered. She had been using it at the Park Hospital to copy up some notes and had left it on her desk. She took out her pad but was unable to find the pen. Awkwardly she asked, 'Can anyone lend me a pen for a moment?'

Farmer and Adams exchanged an amused glance before Adams felt inside his pocket and handed Sam a biro.

'Make sure I get it back,' he joked, 'that's how I got it.'

Sam thanked him but was too annoyed with herself

to smile. She jotted down the time and location of the initial examination of the body into the book, as well as a list of those who were present at the scene. She looked down at the body, it was a mess, there wasn't much she could do with it at this stage. Owen seemed to have been right about most things. She began to make her notes.

'The body is that of a white male, probably in his late teens or early twenties. It is badly decomposed and naked. The right hand is missing . . .'

Adams spoke up, 'We've found that; the sexton's dog had it.'

'There are also three fingers missing from his left hand . . .' She looked up at Adams. 'Don't suppose the dog has those as well?'

'No, sorry. We didn't find his hors-d'oeuvre.'

'Half of one foot has disappeared and there are superficial injuries to both arms and the torso. The injuries to the torso seem a little unusual. They consist for two cuts, one vertical and one horizontal. The cuts intersect at the lower stomach, in an approximation of an upside-down cross.' Although intrigued by the injuries she knew there was little more she could do until she had the body back at the mortuary. 'A ligature has been twisted tightly around the victim's neck. There is a small metal pole on the left side of the neck to which the two ends of the ligature have been attached and which was clearly used to twist the cord tight, forming a garrotte.'

Sam turned her attentions to Colin Flannery, the Crime Scene Manager. 'Have we got the air temperature yet?'

Colin had been with the scene of crime department most of his working life and found himself resenting the question. It was almost as if Sam was challenging his competence. He nodded. Sam continued.

'What about inside the tomb?'

Colin nodded again.

'We'll need to get on to the weather bureau to establish the mean temperature for the last few weeks.'

Colin could feel himself becoming annoyed. He disliked the feeling, it didn't sit well with the cool, calm image he liked to project at any scene.

'It's all in hand, Dr Ryan, you don't have to worry.'

Sam wasn't sure what it was, the tone of his voice or the sharpness of his reply, but she realized she'd offended him.

'Telling my grandmother how to suck eggs here, aren't I, Colin?'

He gave a sort of half nod but didn't respond. Sam returned to the body. The maggot infestation was extensive and seemed to make the body move as they wriggled to and fro just below the remaining skin. An average fly could lay more than three hundred eggs each and this body had been visited by a lot of flies.

'I'd like samples of these maggots. Have we sent for an entomologist yet?'

'We're still trying. Having trouble getting hold of one.'

'Would there be any objection to me taking a few?'

Colin shook his head. 'I'll get you some formalin.'

The samples would be important if there was to be a chance of establishing, with any accuracy, the time of death. Contrary to popular perception, establishing time of death is a very inaccurate science and she would need any help she could get, insect or otherwise. Sam delved into in her bag and emerged with a small specimen jar. Plucking several of the small white creatures off the body, she dropped them into the glass container before sealing it and handing it to one of the SOCOs.

Colin quickly returned with a second jar containing the formalin. He crouched down beside her and plucked several more maggots off the body before dropping them into the jar, watching them sink slowly to the bottom. Sam then took the thermometer from her bag and shook it before pushing it into the mass of maggots which surrounded the body's neck. She had to establish the temperature at which the maggots had developed. The cooler the temperature, the slower they would develop, the warmer the faster; it all helped. When she had finished she asked Colin to roll the body carefully on to its side. He did this quickly and professionally, taking care to cause the minimum of disruption to the remains. After a quick glance along the back of the body, and seeing no further injuries, it was rolled back into place. Sam looked at her watch and stood up.

'Initial examination concluded at one fifty-eight a.m.'

Farmer and Adams examined their watches and nodded.

'PM at ten a.m. if that suits everyone?'

They nodded again.

'Right, well, see you there then.'

Sam began to walk away from the scene, followed by Farmer and Adams. Farmer spoke first.

'What can you tell us?'

'Not much more than you already know. He was certainly strangled and there appear to be other injuries to both his body and arms. But whether they were caused by our killer, or because he's been out in the open for a while, I won't know until I get him cleaned up at the mortuary. Have his clothes been found yet?'

'No, not yet, we're still looking for them. Do you think there could have been a sexual motive, being naked?'

'It's going to be difficult to tell after all this time.'

Farmer continued with the cross-examination. 'How long has he been dead?'

Sam shrugged. 'A few weeks maybe. I'll try to get it as close as I can but don't hold your breath. I might have a better idea when I've finished the PM and the entomologist's had time to do his dirty work.'

As Sam began to peel off her white boiler suit, Farmer looked across at her. 'Dr Owen did a bit better than that.'

Sam, annoyed at having her judgement challenged, snapped back, 'Really? Well, as far as I'm concerned if you want it any closer ask a gypsy.' She finally kicked off the boiler suit and handed it to a passing SOCO before making her way towards the cemetery gate, leaving Farmer impotent and annoyed.

CHAPTER TWO

As Sam reversed her car into her allotted spot she noticed that the hospital had finally managed to erect a name board officially reserving her place. It had only taken a year, she thought, not bad. The board was dark green with black lettering informing uninvited guests that this was her space. **RESERVED. DOCTOR SAMANTHA RYAN. PATHOLOGY.**

She parked her car and clipped the anti-theft device around the steering wheel. It was only there for show, she'd lost the keys months ago, but still, she hoped, it might put people off.

Climbing out of her four-wheel drive Land-Rover, Sam stared down the long, dark alleyways of the concrete maze they called a car-park. It was a forbidding place, even during the day; badly lit with pillars and alcoves which cast irregular shadows across the concrete floor. At night it assumed an almost sinister quality, making even the short trip from the lift to her car an unnerving experience. She'd often complained about the security but it made little difference; other priorities claimed the hospital's limited budget and the general consensus was that it would take a rape or murder before any changes were made. Sam hurried across the car-park to the lift, fingering the anti-rape alarm which she kept concealed in her coat pocket. She wasn't sure how effective it would be against a determined attacker, but it was the one small concession made by the hospital to help calm the female staff's increasing concern.

Stepping out of the lift at the fourth floor, Sam began to feel relaxed and comfortable again. Here it was warm and light and full of people. As she approached her office door she noticed her secretary, Jean Carr, making her way purposefully towards her. In one hand she held a steaming cup of coffee, while in the other was the rest of Sam's week, cunningly concealed inside a large brown desk diary. Her strong Norfolk accent caught up with Sam first.

'Morning, Dr Ryan!'

Jean was a short, stocky woman with a large face and deep-blue eyes which were exaggerated by a pair of heavy-rimmed spectacles sitting uneasily on her nose. She was always smartly dressed, if a little old-fashioned, but had always resisted Sam's attempts to bring her wardrobe up to date. Jean had worked at the Park Hospital for over twenty-five years, with only a short break to bring up her family. She was one of the great unrewarded assets of both the department and the hospital and Sam was aware that life would be impossible without her. As Jean finally caught up with her, Sam lifted the mug of freshly brewed coffee from her hand and began to sip at it, smiling wickedly with her eyes.

'Thanks, Jean, mother's milk, my caffeine level is right down.'

Realizing that any protest would be useless, Jean just sighed and shook her head. She liked Sam and was fiercely protective of her. It was the first time she had worked for a woman and despite Sam's persistent attempts to try and change her, she was enjoying the experience. They entered Sam's office together. It was a large room with a homely feel engineered by the inclusion of numerous pot plants and a discriminating selection of prints adorning the walls. It contrasted sharply with her grey, clinical office in the mortuary which was about as appealing as the interior of a prison cell. At the far end of the office behind her desk was a large window which looked out over the back of the hospital and gave her a clear view of the mortuary. This allowed her to keep an eye on its various comings and goings.

As Sam reached her desk Jean's interrogation began. 'What's all this about you being called out last night? I thought it was Dr Stuart's turn?'

'So did I. Haven't seen Trevor this morning, have you?' There was a casualness about Sam's voice that Jean often found a little irritating, as if her mind was elsewhere and not concentrating on the present.

'No, I don't think Dr Stuart's in yet. Probably still in bed.'

Sam looked down at the pile of paperwork and unopened correspondence that littered her desk and casually flicked through it, searching for anything new or unusual which might stimulate her interest. There was nothing. Finally, her curiosity satisfied, she looked up and returned to the conversation.

'Probably, but with whom?'

Jean was aware of Trevor's predilections and had a reasonable idea where he might have laid his head.

'I'd check the female student blocks if I were you. That's where he normally turns up when he goes missing.'

Sam smiled. 'Jean, whatever are you implying?'

'I'm implying nothing, I'm stating. A middle-aged man like that. I don't know what they see in him.'

Sam was amused. Jean was probably the straightest person she had ever known, and although as aware as other women of Trevor's attraction, she heartily disapproved of him. Jean returned to the point.

'Where did they find the body?'

'The graveyard at St Mary's Church.'

'In Northwick?'

'Yes, do you know it?'

'I was married there.'

'It's got a lot to answer for then.'

Jean frowned at her but the mischievous look on Sam's face quickly calmed her and she smiled back.

'You've had quite a few messages.'

Sam slumped into her seat taking a final sip of her stolen coffee and awaited the onslaught. Jean opened her diary and began to outline the messages.

'Your sister called, it's your mother's birthday and she expects to see you this evening, but call first to say what time you're coming.'

'What? Oh God, it can't be a year.'

'I ordered a "With much love on your happy day" bunch of flowers which should be delivered this morning.'

Emerging from behind her hands, Sam looked up at Jean with a sense of relief. 'Thanks, Jean, how could I forget?'

'You're busy. The bill's on your table, they'd appreciate an early settlement. Nothing was too good for your mother, I thought.'

Sam picked up the bill and looked at it, her eyes widening when she read the price.

Jean continued. 'The Murphy case has been brought forward to . . .'

Sam interrupted. 'Not the Murphy case? I thought that had been sorted out.'

'Apparently not, so you've got to hold yourself in readiness for Crown Court.'

'Which one?'

'Norwich, I think.' Jean flicked quickly through her papers, searching for confirmation of her last statement. 'Yes, Norwich.'

'Who's defending?'

Jean ruffled through her papers once again. 'Mr Atkinson.'

'Not "I put it to you, Dr Ryan",' she intoned in an affected upper-class accent. 'He hates me. I'll be in the box for hours. Better get the file out, I'll have to be ready for that one. Anything else?'

'Mr Chambers of Walter, Chambers and Pilkington wants a meeting about the appeal as soon as possible. Their client's case is going to be heard at the end of the month and they want to make sure they agree on some of the more salient points of the case.'

'They do, do they? I don't know why I bothered

becoming a pathologist, it would have been easier to be a barrister, I spend enough time in court.'

A short, sharp knock on the office door interrupted Jean before she had time to finish her list. The two women looked up to see Trevor Stuart's smiling face appear around the door.

'I hear I owe you one?'

He strode into the room as confident and as dapper as ever. Although short, he was slim and wore an attractive air like an expensive suit and looked younger than his forty years. He was one of those men to whom women are inexplicably attracted and he knew it, using his attraction to its best advantage and taking great care with his appearance, from the tip of his Gucci shoes to the top of his carefully styled head. The one woman who had exhibited no sign of succumbing to his charm, however, was Jean Carr and today was no exception. She glared across at him before turning back to Sam.

'I'll give you the rest of your messages later, Dr Ryan,' she looked pointedly at Trevor Stuart, 'if you're not too tired.'

As she left the room she eyed him icily, but Trevor was not intimidated.

'Morning, Jean, any chance of a coffee?'

His cheek made Jean's mouth drop for a moment but she quickly composed herself and, making her displeasure clearly felt by the tone of her voice, she responded with a curt, 'I'll see what I can do,'

When he felt it was safe to do so, he turned towards Sam. 'Exit the Demon Queen. Don't think she'll put anything in it, do you?'

'Bromide if she's got any sense. Have you come to apologize?'

Trevor smiled and sat uninvited on the opposite side of Sam's desk. He liked Sam and had been attracted to her since she'd arrived. He thought she quite liked him too, she certainly flirted with him, especially with those eyes, but he wasn't sure if this indicated any serious intent or whether she was playing him at his own game. Although these doubts made him keep their relationship as professional as possible, he was always looking for opportunities to take it further.

'Sorry about last night. Spent the night at a friend's and my bleeper didn't go off.' He unclipped his bleeper from his belt and waved it in front of Sam in a feeble attempt to prove his point. 'Jap crap.'

Sam was singularly unimpressed. 'I thought it was your sense of smell you'd lost, not your hearing.'

'I'll take over the PM if you like, give you a chance to finish your list.'

Sam was having none of it. 'No, it's all right, Trevor, I'll do the PM, *you* finish my list.'

Trevor nodded reluctantly. 'Where did they find him?'

'Graveyard at St Mary's Church, the one in Northwick.'

'Body found in cemetery. There's a novelty. Natural causes?'

'There was nothing natural about this one. Strangled, been dead a few weeks too.'

'Anything else?'

'Not much. He was naked, there was no sign of his clothes and no identification on him. So we've got absolutely no idea who he is.'

'No old wounds, tattoos?'

Sam shook her head. 'Nothing obvious, but there was an odd-shaped cut down the front of his body. A sort of upside-down cross.'

'Naked men in graveyards with crosses cut into their bodies. All sounds a bit kinky to me. What time's the PM?'

'Ten.'

'Really? You'd better get a move on then, it's ten past now.'

Sam glanced quickly at her watch, jumped up and made for the door. 'Damn!'

As she opened the door she looked back at Trevor who was flicking casually through her private papers. 'Don't forget to do my list. All of it.'

Trevor nodded, holding his hands up reassuringly. Sam wasn't convinced. 'It'll be "Bobbit" time if you don't.'

Trevor winced and moved his hand between his legs. Sam smiled and shook her head before closing the door firmly behind her.

The trip to the mortuary, which was situated in the hospital basement, wasn't a long one. A short descent in the lift, followed by a brief walk, the whole exercise taking no more than five minutes. Today, however, the lift appeared to be stuck on the sixth floor and after slamming the lift-call button several times, Sam finally gave up and ran for the stairs, jumping down them two at a time. She could smell the remains as she descended the stairs. Despite an efficient extraction system, the smell still seemed to escape from the mortuary and drift its way slowly through the lower floor of the hospital. To be fair, the hospital had done what it could, but the foul smell of a rotting corpse was very pervasive.

Finally, hot, out of breath and flustered, she arrived at the mortuary fifteen minutes late. Sam changed quickly into her green surgical gown before scrubbing her hands and snapping on a pair of protective latex gloves. When she entered the dissection room it was already crowded; SOCOs, various detectives, and Mr Palmer, from the coroner's officer, were all there awaiting her attendance. The mortuary at the Park was always very bright with powerful ceiling lamps bouncing their light off the white tiled floors and walls which reflected back into the room. Sam noticed Superintendent Farmer standing with Adams glaring across at her disapprovingly and glancing pointedly at her watch. Sam ignored her and looked across at Fred Dale, her mortuary technician.

'Everything ready, Fred?'

Fred had been with Sam since she had arrived at the Park a year before and she trusted him completely. He was both efficient and loyal and seemed to guess her next move on every PM they did together. A gentle giant of a man, he stood six feet two inches in his stockinged feet with a large, round face which seemed to have a permanent grin playing over it. He was also a natural clown with the darkest sense of humour she had ever known, but which lightened the atmosphere of even the most harrowing occasions, and there had been plenty of those. Although younger than her, he looked years older. A former corporal in the Royal Green Jackets, he'd been badly wounded in the leg during a riot on the Falls Road in Belfast in which several of his friends had been killed. The wound had left him with a slight but permanent limp which had ended his career prematurely. After spending some time on the streets selling copies of the *Big Issue*, he had drifted through several civilian jobs and eventually ended up at the Park. He'd found a sort of contentment surrounded by death and, despite his appearance, Sam had noticed how gently, even reverentially he treated the bodies he worked on. It was probably his association with the troubles in Northern Ireland which made her feel close to him, an experience which, although never spoken of, was still shared.

Sam walked across to the long, black, plastic bodybag lying across the grey, stainless steel table. She nodded to Fred who began to unzip it, slowly revealing the decomposing body concealed inside. As he did so, the SOCO photographer stepped forward and began to take the first of a series of photographs which he would continue to take throughout the PM. Fred gently rolled the body on to its side and Sam pulled the bag carefully from underneath it before passing it to one of the SOCOs who folded it and placed it in a large plastic exhibits bag. Sam and Fred then stepped back while the radiographer X-rayed various parts of the unknown corpse, conducting a full skeletal survey as he searched for any unseen fractures, foreign bodies or wounds.

The body, or rather what was left of it, was now lying

black and naked in front of her. Fred placed the head on to a curved wooden block and removed the black plastic bags covering his feet and one of his hands. The other hand, which had been retrieved from the sexton's dog, lay twisted in a plastic bag by the side of the body. This was also unwrapped and laid carefully at the bottom of the arm. It wasn't going to be an easy PM due to the advanced state of decomposition and clues, if there were any, were going to be difficult to spot. She began to speak her way through the PM.

When Sam began any PM, especially a forensic one, her concentration was total and her world closed in around her. It was as if her consciousness changed in both time and space and nothing existed or mattered except the body on the table.

'The body is that of an unknown, white male in his late teens or early twenties. It is well developed and nourished. One eye is missing and his hair is fair, although it seems to have been dyed, the roots being either black or dark brown.'

Sam picked up a chart from the end of the bench and read from it. 'The body is sixty-eight inches long and weighs a hundred and forty pounds.' Despite all the recent changes, Sam still preferred to work in inches and pounds when it involved the larger measurements, only reverting to centimetres for the small marks and injuries she found on the body. 'The remains are in an advanced state of decay as a result of lying out in the open. The maggot infestation is severe. I am going to take several more samples for examination by the entomologist.'

Fred, picking up Sam's direction, held out a small, dry glass tube.

'Pity I'm not a fisherman, I could clean up.'

Sam scowled at him but Fred, undaunted by this silent reprimand, smiled back and labelled the two maggot-filled jars before passing them to the exhibits officer.

Sam continued with her examination. She lifted the right arm. 'There is a crude, possibly self-inflicted, tattoo on the right arm. Fred, could you clean this up a bit?'

Fred stepped forward with a bowl of warm water and a small sponge and cleaned the area of the tattoo quickly. Warm water was the only thing he could use at this stage; any form of chemical could destroy evidence secreted on the body. Sam returned to the table and measured the tattoo.

'The tattoo is six centimetres long and consists of seven letters.' She spelled the letters out as she identified each one, 'F.R.A.N.C.E.S. Could we have a photograph of this please?'

Sam held the arm while the photographer took several photographs of the tattoo. When he had finished, she put the arm down and examined the rest of the body for other tattoos, marks or injuries that might help identify the anonymous corpse. There were none. She moved on.

'A cord has been pulled tightly around the deceased's neck continuing around the neck for a full 360 degrees, without a gap, before being tied off on the left side of the neck to a hollow metal tube, forming a garrotte or Spanish wind-lash. This tube has been twisted tightly, possibly causing stangulation; will confirm later in the PM.'

Without prompting, Fred passed Sam the scissors from the steel tray by the side of the body. Sam cut the cord, taking care to avoid the area around the hollow tube. As she gently eased the cord away from the neck, a layer of decomposing flesh came away with it. The cord and the pieces of flesh were dropped together into the exhibits bag which was being held out by one of the many SOCOs littering the mortuary. Sam returned to the body, and took swabs from both the mouth and nose, forcing the swabs deep into the body's nasal cavities before passing them to Fred. It wasn't an easy job as the nose had been all but eaten or rotted away. She moved down the body.

'There are superficial and unusual injuries to both the chest and abdomen. These consist of two linear incised wounds. One running vertically from the base of the neck to the suprapubic region. The other running horizontally across the abdomen forming a cross, an upside-down cross.'

Fred passed her a tape measure and she took the measurements of the injuries.

'The vertical cut measures forty-two centimetres and the horizontal cut twenty-eight centimetres.'

She passed the tape back to Fred who exchanged it for a dissecting knife. Pressing down firmly with the scalpel, she opened up the two cuts.

'The cuts are superficial, and not deep.'

She looked across at Fred and nodded. He rolled the

body gently on to its side and Sam ran her eyes carefully over the body.

'There appear to be no obvious injuries to the rear of the body.'

Sam nodded again and Fred lowered the body back into position. Picking up the dissecting knife once again she began to cut into the body.

'I am now commencing my internal examination.'

Adams knew what was coming next, the cutting of the liver, removal of the bowel, samples for toxicology. He'd already seen enough and looked away as the first incision was made.

Frances looked at her face in the mirror, paying special attention to her left eye, examining the fading bruise that had only just calmed down sufficiently to be covered with make-up. He'd never hit her before and she was determined that he would never do it again. He'd apologized but, although it was completely out of character for him to do so, she was still very wary of him.

It had been a month since her failed attempt to leave Bird. She'd finally given up waiting and had just reached the war memorial at the bottom of Station Street when she'd heard the familiar roar of a sports car engine. At first she had thought it was Mark and was angry and delighted at the same time. Dropping her suitcases on the ground she'd jumped up and down waving wildly at the car lights as they approached. The car had come to a sudden halt in front of her. She couldn't see the car clearly through the lights, but she had smiled broadly at the windscreen. The car door had clicked open and the dark shape of a man began to emerge.

'You took your time, didn't you?'

'I'd have been here earlier if I'd known.'

It wasn't Mark's voice. Frances had felt her body freeze as Bird's tall figure emerged from behind the lights and walked towards her.

'Remarkable recovery. When I left, you were at death's door, now look at you, all fit and well again. Amazing what a couple of aspirin can achieve, isn't it?'

Frances had just looked at him, not daring to move or speak. He moved his arm quickly, grabbing her face in his large hand, squeezing her cheeks against her teeth, forcing her to cry out.

'Hasn't he turned up then, your lover?'

The menace in Bird's voice had terrified her and she could only look at him, waiting to see what he would do next.

'When will you ever learn, you stupid bitch? He didn't want you, he just wanted the money and now that he's got it you'll never see him again. Nobody crosses me and gets away with it, not you, and certainly not James.'

The blow, when it had come, was not held back or controlled. The back of Bird's hand hit her full in the face, knocking her backwards and sending her sprawling across the road before she felt her body hit the concrete with a thud. The next thing she remembered was waking up back in Bird's bed the following morning.

It was odd really, he'd never mentioned Mark or the money since that night. She knew Mark had stolen it and managed to get out of the club via the fire escape at the back, just as they'd planned; the staff told her that much. But nobody had seen hide nor hair of him since. Probably living it up on some beach in Spain, she thought. She couldn't understand why he'd taken the money and left her behind. If anything, she'd have thought it would have been the other way around, given how he felt about her. She obviously didn't know him as well as she thought, but then, she considered, she had always been a poor judge of character; how else would she have ended up with Bird?

That money was hers and the baby's. Bird had always made it plain that he had no interest in children and there would be little chance of him paying maintenance, so she'd decided to take a small advance against the baby's future and Mark had offered to help her.

Staying with Bird despite his behaviour was her only real option at the moment. She'd visited a local women's refuge but that was worse than staying with Bird and she really didn't fancy bringing her baby up under those conditions. She was unsure of her father's response if she suddenly turned up now on his doorstep looking like Little Nell with an illegitimate bundle. She wasn't sure she would be able to take her father's rejection as well, especially after Mark's.

Bird's behaviour towards her had been impeccable, although he'd also made it quite clear that if there was one more incident like the one with Mark she'd be extremely sorry, and she believed him. She looked down at her tight-fitting evening dress, which had become a little tighter-fitting recently as her stomach began to swell. She would have to tell him soon or find somewhere else to hide. Bird shouted up the stairs.

'Come on, Fran, it's time to go!'

Grabbing her bag from the bed she made her way down the stairs to meet him.

The day had passed quickly, that was the way of it when the work was interesting, which it wasn't always. As usual, the police were screaming for her report and had actually sent, at great public expense no doubt, a traffic car to collect it as soon as it was finished. She moved the cursor to print and clicked the top of her mouse, sending her printer humming into action. As she watched the paper emerge from the other side of the machine something was bothering her. She'd gone over and over the report but still, she felt, there was something amiss, something she had missed, not realized. As she bit into her tuna sandwich, which had to suffice as lunch, a voice from behind broke through her thought pattern.

'Finished already?'

She didn't need to turn around to know who it was, the voice was familiar enough.

'Twice in one day, Trevor; this *is* an honour.' She turned to face him. 'And what can I do for you?'

'Just thought I'd pop in and see how things were going.'

Sam turned back to her word processor. 'OK. There are a few odd points, but I'm sure I'll resolve them, *without any help*.'

Trevor nodded and eyed Sam's spare sandwich. 'Is

that sandwich going spare? I'm absolutely starving, no breakfast.'

She looked at him for a moment and, despite her better instincts, found herself giving in. 'Go on. Perhaps you should consider having an affair with someone who can cook?'

Trevor took the sandwich and bit into it. 'I heard *you* were a bit of a Delia Smith.'

Sam ignored the comment, though she was flattered by it.

'Discovered who he is yet?'

Sam shook her head. 'No, his clothes are still missing, and there wasn't enough skin left on his fingers to get any prints.'

'Odontologist had a look at him yet?'

'He's just about to have a look. Depends whether there are any dental records to make a match, of course.'

She picked up the photographs which were lying by her side and handed them to Trevor. 'What do you make of those?'

Trevor stopped eating for a moment and picked them up. 'You've got your photographs back already, you're obviously well in.'

Trying to retrieve PM photographs was a bit of a standing joke amongst the pathologists at the Park. If they came back at all they came late and usually ended up in someone else's in-tray. Trevor examined them casually. 'Decomposed corpse of a young male, been dead a week or two by the look of him.' He bit into his sandwich again, flipping the photographs on to the desk.

'Look harder at his torso, can't you see it? Look at this one.' She handed him a close-up photograph of the body's torso and a magnifying glass. Trevor put down his sandwich and studied the photograph under the lens.

'I see now. You want me to confirm your theory about the cross. Mmm, might be a cross I suppose.'

'What do you mean *might be*? That's the last sandwich you get off me.'

'Might be lots of things.'

Sam could feel herself getting annoyed with him. 'Like?'

'Defence wounds, or perhaps he was tortured before they killed him; it happens.'

Sam felt that he was being deliberately awkward. 'Since when do you get defence wounds on your stomach?'

Trevor shrugged. 'You might have a signature killer on your hands, somebody who wants you to know it was them. It wouldn't be the first time. Happens quite a lot in the States apparently.'

'It's the first one they've found.'

'He's got to start somewhere. Worrying isn't it?'

Sam nodded. 'I thought there might be some sort of ritualistic element to it, otherwise why a cross, why not something else?'

'Like what?'

'I don't know, I'm just grabbing at straws I suppose.'

Trevor contemplated her for a moment. If there were two things he'd learned to trust during the time he'd known Sam, it was her judgement and intuition.

'Can I have a look at the body?'

'If you think it will help.'

The two pathologists left the office and made their way into the mortuary. The body had already been laid out on one of the many mortuary slabs. Fred was standing outside the door while Dr Clive Gilbert, the department's odontologist, X-rayed the skull. Sam and Trevor waited while he finished.

Although not routinely used, the PM radiography would reveal details unavailable by any other means: root structure, arrangement of sinus cavities, structure of any bony areas and such like, and it was therefore very useful when identification was difficult. It was certainly one of the most accurate and reliable methods of identification, but still relied, like fingerprints, on a comparison with ante-mortem information. More recently a new development in X-ray technology, xeroradiography, was being used. This produced an image of both soft and hard tissue on the same exposure. By this means, non-metallic invading bodies such as wood, plastic and glass could be seen. The principle behind it was quite simple. Charged selenium particles, when exposed to the X-ray beam, become photoconductive, producing an electrostatic image. Since they had miniaturized the equipment, making it practical for use in forensic dentistry, it had become the eighth wonder of the world in that field. Sam was pushing hard for the funding to enable her to have the new technology available in the mortuary but had, as yet, met with little success. Under certain circumstances, and to make it easier for the odontologist to make his examination, Sam would remove the entire jaw and put it to one side. In this case, however, she hadn't had the chance, but Gilbert was coping.

Gilbert finally finished and left the mortuary without a word. Sam had always found him a bit of an odd fish but good at what he did, which was all that mattered, really. Fred began to pack away the equipment while Sam and Trevor walked across to the body and began to examine its unusual injuries.

'Very peculiar, it's certainly a cross and it's definitely deliberate, single-stroke incisions. I can see why you think there's an occult angle to it.' Trevor walked to the top of the table and looked down over the body. 'On the other hand he might have been tortured or it might have been done as a warning to others. I understand street gangs and drug dealers do that sort of thing to each other?'

'This is no Colombian necktie, there's far more to it than that. Upside-down crosses, graveyards at midnight.'

'Like I said, it all looks a bit kinky to me. Told Farmer yet?'

'It's in the report, but God knows what she'll make of it. "By the way, superintendent, I think he might have been murdered by a witch." I don't think she'll be impressed.'

'Yes, I see your problem.' Trevor paused for a moment. 'Could be a religious nut, there are plenty of those around.'

'Trouble is, they all work for the church.'

Trevor laughed out loud. 'True enough. There might

be someone worth talking to, though. A chap I know, Simon Clarke, he's a psychologist, a fellow at St Steven's. I met him at some dinner or other, he specializes in serial crimes and killers, especially those with an occult angle to them.'

'Do you think he'd talk to me?'

'Oh, he'll talk to you all right. This is right up his street, probably end up writing a paper on it. I'll ring him, get it arranged.'

'Dr Ryan?' Jean Carr's voice, recognizable but muffled from the opposite side of the mortuary door, broke into their conversation. 'There's a police officer outside your office, says he's waiting for your report.'

Sam looked across at the door. 'It's ready, you can come and get it if you like, Jean.'

'No, thank you, I'm quite happy where I am. The smell's quite enough, but you'd better hurry, he seems in quite a rush.'

Trevor and Sam looked at each other smiling secretly.

Farmer scanned the faces of the expectant reporters in front of her like a teacher overlooking her class. It was a good turn-out with a number of national newspapers there as well as the locals. She was surprised that the nationals were taking an interest in such a local murder, there were so many of them nationwide these days. She hated the press and considered them social parasites. If they weren't after you for a story they were trying to turn you into one. Still, she considered, they did have their uses and this was one of them. They'd had the body just over a week now and were no closer to establishing its identity than they had been on day one. They couldn't take his prints and couldn't find a match for his teeth. The missing-from-home files had been checked for every force in the country but had proved fruitless. This really was their last chance.

Farmer looked at the E-Fit which had been developed from a photograph of the corpse's face and marvelled at the technology which could produce such a realistic image. The Electronic Facial Identity Technique used computers to create a full-colour image and was a huge advance on the old photo fit technique. She looked across at Adams, who was sitting at her right, before standing.

'Ladies and gentleman,' the sharpness of her voice stopped the general chatter that always accompanied these occasions and brought the reporters' attention back to the desk at the front of the room. 'First, I'd like to thank you for coming this morning. I am Detective Superintendent Harriet Farmer and the gentleman to your left is Detective Inspector Tom Adams.' Adams nodded. 'As most of you already know, the body of an unknown male was discovered in St Mary's churchyard in Northwich just over a week ago. Due to the body having lain out in the open for several weeks and the absence of any clothing or other means of identification, we have not been able to establish who he is, despite extensive enquiries. What we can tell you about him is that he was a white male, in his late teens or early twenties, approximately five-feet eight-inches tall, and weighing ten stone. Although his hair was fair this wasn't its natural colour which was dark brown. Probably the most important clue to his identity is a tattoo on his right forearm. This tattoo consists of seven letters in blue ink and spells the name Frances.'

One of the reporters suddenly stood up. 'Peter Bushby, the *Sun*. Is it true, Superintendent, that the murder of this young man has some sort of link to black magic? Especially with him being found naked in a church at midnight?'

Farmer was slightly unbalanced by this question. 'The body certainly wasn't discovered at midnight . . .'

Another reporter jumped to her feet. 'Claire Hargreaves, *Cambridge Evening News*. We understand that ritualistic markings were carved into the front of the victim's body, can you elaborate on that?'

Farmer could feel herself becoming angry. 'There were a number of injuries to the body, whether they were ritualistic or not is open to debate.'

A question came from the right of the room.

'Helen Blackmore, *Daily Mirror*. If it wasn't some sort of black magic killing how do you account for the presence of a dead cockerel and four black candles?'

'As far as I'm aware there were no . . .'

'Can you confirm for us that there is a connection with black magic?'

The room errupted with a cacophony of shouted questions. Adams had to raise his voice to its full volume to be heard above the confusion.

'I don't think we have anything more to say at this time. PC Gill Warren will hand out a brief press pack as you leave the room which will give you all the information you need on our unidentified body. Thank you.'

The two detectives left under a torrent of further questions from the reporters.

Farmer was fuming. 'Where the fuck did they get all that information from!'

Adams tried to calm her down. 'Most of it was wrong.'

'Some of it was right though. How the hell did they find out about those cuts?'

'Could have been anyone. Half the squad go drinking with the local press.'

'This is that bloody pathologist's fault, her and her half-baked ideas. You can bet your life that's where it's come from!'

'I can't see Dr Ryan getting herself involved with the press, she's far too professional.'

Farmer glanced up at him, surprised by his defence of a person he knew only slightly.

'Well, whoever it was, I want them found and found quickly!'

Frances looked at the clock beside the bed. It was ten to one. Early really, their days didn't usually start until two. They hadn't left the club until three that morning and when they finally did get home Bird had been keen to demonstrate his manhood. She was off sex but daren't admit this in case he started to ask difficult questions, so she had been obliged to make all the right sounds to reassure him of his sexual prowess. She wasn't sure how much longer she could hide the truth from him. She'd been lucky with the morning sickness and managed to explain it away, but now she'd started to put on weight and her normally flat stomach was expanding. He'd already mentioned it once, insisting she go on a diet, and had taken her to his training centre to get her back into shape. Frances knew she'd have to tell him soon. She had no idea what his reaction would be and that caused her further anxiety. She threw her legs out of bed, slipped her short satin dressing-gown over her naked body and staggered towards the kitchen.

She picked up the kettle and shook it, it was empty so she filled it from the tap while switching on the transistor radio on the window sill. While she waited for the kettle to boil she examined her face in the kitchen mirror. The bruising had almost gone and she wouldn't need quite so much make-up in future. She remembered the punch with a shiver, how it hadn't broken her jaw she didn't know, she must be tougher than she thought. The kettle began to steam and she walked across to the fridge to collect the milk. The one o'clock news began; she was only half listening to it when she heard the item.

'An appeal was made by the police this morning for help in identifying the body that was discovered in St Mary's churchyard, Northwick, just over a week ago. The body is that of a white male in his late teens or early twenties. He was about five-feet eight tall and weighed approximately ten stone. Although his hair was fair that was not its natural colour which was dark brown. Probably his most distinguishing feature was a small tattoo on his right forearm which spelt the word "Frances . . ."'

She hadn't really been listening up to that point, but

she recognized the description of the tattoo straight away. She remembered the pride on his face when he'd shown it to her. The report staggered Frances almost as much as Bird's punch had. She grabbed the side of the sink to try and steady herself, but the milk bottle slipped from her hand and smashed, sending glass and milk spraying across the kitchen floor. Frances' vision became cloudy and her stomach churned with shock as the realized for the first time why Mark hadn't been there that night. Bird had murdered him.

Bird's voice broke through her thoughts. 'Fran, what the bloody hell's going on out there!'

A sense of self-preservation now took over. She hadn't realized until then how dangerous her situation actually was. She would be a very important witness and Bird would be aware of that. There was also another feeling, one much more basic, one that she hadn't felt until now, the feeling of a mother protecting her unborn child. She ran quickly to the door, grabbing Bird's car keys before making a dash to his car.

Bird lay in bed for a moment collecting his thoughts. He called out again but still there was no reply. Suddenly the sound of the engine of his sports car being over-revved spurred him into action and he rushed into the kitchen to see what was happening. In his anger he'd forgotten that it had been the sound of smashing glass which had first woken him and as his naked feet reached the kitchen floor the glass cut deeply into them, making him scream out and grab the kitchen table to stop himself falling. Although in great pain, he managed to stagger to the wide-open kitchen door, his feet trailing blood behind him. He watched as he saw his beloved Porsche jump off the drive as Frances struggled with an unfamiliar gearbox. Finally managing to select the right gear, she sent the car roaring off along the suburban street and disappeared from sight. Bird watched her departure before falling to the floor to begin plucking large slivers of glass from his bloody feet.

Frances could not master the Porsche's gear-lever, the car was just too complicated and powerful. Her only experience of driving had been a rather shabby Ford Escort which spent more time in the garage than it did on the road. Her eyes were still red and bloated and tears streaked along the smoothness of her skin. She was also cold and the thin satin dressing-gown offered little protection. The combination of this and the shock of hearing of Mark's death made her shake uncontrollably. She couldn't stop thinking about him or blaming herself for what had happened. She'd played with him, toyed with the feelings that she knew he had for her, kept him at her beck and call like a pet dog she could whistle for at any time. He'd been worth more than that. And now, because of her selfishness, he was dead, murdered by her boyfriend. She wasn't sure she would ever get over the shock.

She brought the Porsche to a jerky halt at a set of red traffic-lights, pulling the gear-lever into neutral as she did. Almost as soon as the car had stopped, the lights changed to green and the cars behind began to rev their engines loudly, keen to get on. She fought to push the gear-lever back into first, pressing her foot down hard on to the clutch pedal, but despite her efforts, the lever would not drop into place. Several of the drivers behind her became impatient and sounded their horns, encouraging her to move on or get out of their way. Finally, with one last desperate push, the gear-lever slotted into place and the Porsche began to move forward. The sudden shock of the gearbox complying to her wishes took Frances by surprise and the car staggered forward into the junction before stalling. As it did the lights returned to red and cars from both her right and left began to move into the junction. Now, in a total panic, Frances fought to get the car started again but she flooded the carburettor and, try as she might, the car wouldn't start. Under a barrage of horns and the voices of angry drivers, she finally collapsed across the steering wheel and cried inconsolably.

Standing at the front of the lecture theatre, Sam scanned the faces of her young students and wondered how many of them would eventually become forensic pathologists. Probably not many, most of these were Thatcher's children and far more interested in the glittering prizes and bank balances which came with the various forms of surgery now on offer. She nodded to a student sitting at the back of the room and with a quick click of a switch he threw the lecture theatre into darkness. Sam pressed the start button on her remote control and a beam of light immediately pierced the darkness throwing a photographic image on to the wall behind her. She turned to face it. It was a photograph of a large sitting-room; on the sofa were the remains of a man. The left side of his head had been blown apart and large sections of his brain, skull and flesh were slashed across the wall behind him. The man's body was leaning slightly to the right and what remained of his brains hung flaccid from the skull's cavity. The right side of his face, the side still intact, held an expression of shock and surprise. It was a terrifying spectacle. The control she was holding emitted a small red light which she used to point at the various areas she was describing on the photograph.

'Crime scene, well, maybe. We see here,' she pointed to the victim's head with her red light, 'extensive head injuries. Anyone got any idea what might have caused them?'

After a few moments' silence, a voice broke through the darkness, 'Gunshot.'

'Good, any idea what kind?'

The same voice answered again, 'From the blast damage it looks like a shotgun.'

'Right, very good. Can anyone see any sign of the shotgun?'

The room remained silent.

'Then what do you think we might be dealing with here?'

A different voice this time, 'Murder.'

'OK, let's see.'

Sam pressed a switch on her hand control and the photograph changed. This time the picture was of the same room but taken from a different angle. Leaning against the side of a door was a double-barrelled shotgun. Sam pointed to it with her light.

'Here we have the "murder" weapon. A double-barrelled, Purdy shotgun. It's about ten feet from the body. Now, what do we think it is?'

This time several voices spoke up, 'Murder?'

'That's what the police thought and spent at least three weeks investigating it as a murder, they even had a suspect. But it wasn't a murder, it was a suicide.'

Expectant and muffled whispers filtered out from the dark.

'Anyone know how?'

'Shot himself and then staggered back on to the sofa?'

'After putting the shotgun neatly against the wall? And don't forget most of what's left of his skull has been blasted up against the wall directly behind him.'

Sam clicked the hand control again. This time the smiling face of a uniformed police superintendent appeared on the screen and Sam continued, 'Anyone recognize this man?'

The room was silent.

'You're lucky. He's retired now, probably the best thing he ever did for the police force. Superintendent John Munrow. Divisional Commander of 'A' division where the killing took place. Shortly after the body was discovered Munrow arrived at the scene. He entered, telling the hapless PC on the door not to book him in or out because he was only going to be a moment. The PC, not wanting to find himself posted to the outer reaches of Cambridgeshire, did as he was told and kept quiet. Meanwhile, friend Munrow, being a bit of a gun buff, recognized the shotgun which, by the way, was still being held by the deceased. So he decided to pick it up and examine it. After satisfying himself that it was indeed a fine example of a Purdy, he left the room, carefully leaning the shotgun against the wall in case it was damaged further.'

Whispers of disbelief filtered from the floor. Sam touched the button on her remote control again and a close-up picture of the man's thumb was thrown up on to the board.

'What made the pathologist in this case suspicious was the position of the man's thumb. As you can see,' she circled the man's thumb with her red light, 'the thumb is in an unnatural position, twisted around; in fact, in the kind of position you would have expected to find had we been dealing with a suicide. After this was pointed out to the investigating officer, a few more enquiries were made. This time a bit closer to home. Three weeks after the man's body had been discovered, the young PC who had been on the door finally admitted that Munrow had been in the room and the full story came out. Munrow retired on a medical pension a few months later.'

Sam flashed her light to the back of the room. One of the students switched on the lights and Sam continued, 'So what does this tell us about our profession?' She looked at the students, waiting for an answer. One spoke up.

'Never assume the obvious?'

'Good. Anything else?'

Their faces remained blank.

'No matter how good, or how clever the science, never ignore the possibility of human error, and always build it into your equation when dealing with any crime scene or corpse. So remember . . .'

The orchestrated voice of the students replied, 'Never say never, never say always!'

'Right.'

Frances finally managed to arrive at her destination; a large Georgian townhouse. For a while she had thought she wouldn't make it, but the sight of a beautiful young girl, scantily clad and in some distress, had brought the male drivers of Cambridge to her rescue in droves and thus she'd managed to limp her way here. She looked up at the impressive building. Here, contained within these bricks and mortar, were all her happiest memories. Here she had grown up happy and secure with her mother and father. She longed for those times to return. She'd been stupid, immature and selfish. She remembered how, at seventeen, she had screamed at her father to stop treating her like a child and to give her some space. When she finally left, she knew she was causing her father pain, but she was young and more than a little stupid. She considered that she had managed to hurt just about everybody who loved her. She desperately wanted to go home, but she wasn't sure if she would be welcomed back.

Suddenly, there was a loud knock on the driver's side-window. Startled, Frances looked quickly towards her right. She saw her father's familiar face, large and strong, though time had certainly taken its toll on his hair, which was receding rapidly. As he opened the car door Frances just looked at him, scared to move, like a naughty child waiting for its punishment. Suddenly, she was unable to stand it any longer and she threw her arms around her father's neck and sobbed, 'Oh, daddy, I'm in trouble, I'm in so much trouble.'

Her father did not say a word, just patted and stroked her back gently before lifting his dishevelled daughter from the seat and carrying her into the safety of the house, closing the door quietly behind him with his foot.

CHAPTER THREE

He parked his car a good distance from the entrance of the large double-fronted house. Although it stood back from the road it still managed to dominate the local area. He was always careful and had been watching the house for about a quarter of an hour; the last thing he needed was to be caught before his work was finished. It was still very early but the world had begun to stir and people on the early shifts, their collars turned up against the wet and the cold, were already making their way to work. A battery-powered milk-float hummed and clattered its way into view, the driver stopping every few yards to deliver his white cargo to customers' doorsteps. As the float drove past he pushed himself deeper and lower into his seat, trying to keep himself from view, but he needn't have worried, the driver was far too busy checking his next drop to pay any attention to him. Adjusting his scarf so that it covered both his nose and the bottom part of his face, and making sure his hat was pulled low over his forehead to completely obscure his face and hair from view, he picked up the large, brown paper parcel lying on the passenger seat next to him, opened the car door quietly and made his way towards the building.

Although he was dressed warmly against the weather, the cold seemed to penetrate through every layer of clothing and bite deep into his body almost as soon as he stepped from the car. He was thankful though. Had it been mild, he might have looked out of place and people would have remembered him, but on a morning like this he was just another cold person making his reluctant way to work and covered up against the weather. After only a few minutes he'd arrived at the front gate and made his way along the path towards the door. Fortunately, the door was surrounded by a large wooden porch which protected it against the extremes of weather. The parcel was far too large to go through the letter-box, so he placed it against a wall, covering it with the door mat. Content that it was out of sight and secure he turned and made his way back to the car. Although his journey had been short and only taken minutes he was still surprised that he hadn't seen another living soul. He began to realize the truth, that this was a holy mission, that God was on his side and clearly wanted him to finish the work he'd begun.

Sister Veronica Butler had been at the convent now for three years. She enjoyed the work but was ready to move on. She hoped this time she'd get her long-awaited posting to Africa. There, she thought, she was really needed. Running a home for single and destitute mothers was all well and good but none of them was starving or suffering from the multitude of rare and unpleasant diseases which seemed to plague Africa.

Despite their sad situation, they and their children were well fed, well clothed and would eventually do all right. The people in Africa, on the other hand, had nothing, not even a Christian belief to sustain them through their hardships. There was a lot to do and she felt that she was the woman to do it. Still, she thought, those decisions were in the hands of others and if God did not want her to go, then she would have to be content with what she had. She picked up the mail from the floor and flicked through it, bills and unsolicited advertising mainly, as if they hadn't got enough to contend with. She opened the front door and picked up a bottle of milk. There were twelve bottles in all but she only wanted to make herself a quick mug of tea and would bring the rest in later.

She almost missed it, concealed as it was behind the doormat. But the corner of the brown paper envelope poking out from one corner of the mat caught her eye and, pulling it to one side, she found the large paper parcel. Why the postman hadn't knocked as he normally did when there were large parcels to deliver, she didn't know, probably a new boy who wasn't aware of the system. Lucky it didn't get stolen, they were like that around there. She looked up and down the street as if to reassure herself that she wasn't being watched and then stepped back inside, closing the door behind her. She carried the parcel into the kitchen and dropped it along with the other letters on to the table before going across to the kettle and switching it on.

'That smells good.'

Sister Veronica turned to see Father Edward Farrar smiling across at her.

'There's no smell yet, it's only boiling water.'

'Ah, but there will be and I'm full of anticipation.'

She laughed. 'So I'd better make it tea for two then.'

'Very kind and not a single hint dropped.'

Sister Veronica turned and continued to make the tea while Father Farrar picked up the mail and began to flick through it.

'Bills, bills and more bills. Here's an interesting one and addressed to me.' He opened it, pulled out its contents and read it with amusement. 'Ah! All our troubles are over.'

Sister Veronica, pouring the tea, looked across at him quizzically.

'According to this I've won £10,000, a trip around the world and a sports car. All I have to do is fill out this small form, send it off and the riches of the world will be mine.'

'And what would you want with a sports car?'

'To help me carry the £10,000 to the boat for the around the world cruise.'

She handed him the tea and took the letter out of his hand. 'Sounds like wishful thinking to me. Oh, I see, all you have to do is subscribe to a year's worth of dull magazines.'

'Our girls might like them.'

'Not unless it was *Just Seventeen* or *Cosmopolitan*.'

'They're not still reading *Cosmopolitan*, are they? And us with a library full of the great classics. Modern times, modern times.'

'It would take a miracle before anyone in this place was given something for nothing.'

Father Farrar looked at her sadly. 'I'm sure you're right, sister, and miracles, like money, don't grow on trees. See you later.'

Putting her mug of tea down on the kitchen surface Sister Veronica began to open her mail. She'd been right, they were either bills or circulars. Finally, she got around to the large parcel she'd found behind the mat. It had been well wrapped and needed to be cut open with a large pair of kitchen scissors. Finally, the top removed, she emptied the contents on to the work surface.

Her scream could be heard all over the convent. It was loud, piercing and unrestrained. Father Farrar was the first on the scene. Having heard the scream and thinking one of the girls was being murdered he ran the length of the house into the kitchen. When he arrived he saw Sister Veronica, her hand clamped firmly over her mouth and pointing at the kitchen surface with a trembling finger. Father Farrar's eyes followed the direction of her hand. Lying across the kitchen surface and spilling out on to the floor were hundreds of five- and ten-pound notes. Father Farrar looked at them in amazement as he picked up the typewritten note which had also fallen from the large envelope.

'I thought this might help the convent's good work. A Well Wisher.'

Father Farrar picked up a handful of banknotes and looked up towards the ceiling. 'That was quick. Now, about this sports car.'

When he finally returned home it was light. Parking his car in the garage he made his way quickly to his study at the back of the house. Although the study door looked wooden it was, in fact, a security door made of tempered three-inch steel. He unlocked it and pushed the door slowly open before slipping inside and locking it firmly behind him again. Walking across to his desk he opened one of the side drawers and pulled out a large blue cardboard file which he quickly began to flick through. The first photograph he came to was one of Mark James standing by his beloved Spitfire. Next to it was a brief synopsis of James' life and a day-by-day account of his movements. Across the front of both the synopsis and the photograph, a large red cross had been drawn. He lingered on it for a moment smiling, content at a job well done, before turning the page and examining the next photograph. This time it was of a beautiful young girl. She was walking along a Cambridge high street peering in at the shops. He looked across at her profile and her day-by-day activities before running his finger across her name at the top of the sheet, Frances Purvis.

Samantha Ryan made her way briskly along the grimy corridors of the forensic science laboratory in Scrivingdon. The large glass windows facing out into the corridors gave Sam a clear view of most of their interiors. Each of the rooms was characterized by white-topped benches punctuated to a greater or lesser extent by various pieces of high-tech equipment. Ghost-like, white-coated scientists and technicians drifted between the benches or sat hunched over a particular experiment. Scrivingdon was one of six regional laboratories scattered around the country and dealt with most of the forensic investigations in the eastern region. Tucked carefully away amongst the trees at the back of the local general hospital, Scrivingdon not only dealt with forensic evidence from its particular area but also with firearms enquiries from all over the country, making it possibly the busiest and most prestigious in the group. Over recent years it had become more independent and, although still controlled by the Home Office, now also accepted work from the prosecuting and defending side of an investigation. This change in attitude had been manifest when the board, displaying the helmet badges from every police force in the country, mysteriously disappeared from the laboratory's front entrance hall where it had been proudly displayed for many years.

Sam finally arrived outside the door she had been looking for. She knocked and peered into the lab through the glass panel, searching for her friend, Marcia Evans. She finally spotted her at the far end of the room, her eyes glued to a Nikon microscope, while her right hand delicately adjusted the focus as she changed each slide. On hearing Sam's knock she turned and looked up at the window. She quickly recognized her friend and, smiling, beckoned Sam in before returning to her microscope. Sam pushed down the grey handle of the door and entered the spotlessly clean, white lab. Marcia heard her come in but didn't bother looking up again.

'To what do I owe this honour?'

They had been friends since Sam arrived in the county a year before. Although Marcia was much younger than Sam, their friendship was strong and was matched by the mutual respect of fellow professionals. Marcia had only been qualified for a few years but she was naturally gifted with a quick, analytical mind and an even faster eye. Because of her ability she had already been marked out for early promotion but had so far resisted it, preferring life in the laboratory to one of paper-pushing bureaucracy.

'I thought I'd come and see how the workers were coping. And see if you were free to join me for lunch. I want to pick your brains about a new hairstyle, I'm fed up with mine.'

'A new hairstyle? Do I detect a romance? Is there a new man in your life you haven't told me about?'

'No such luck, Sherlock, I just need a boost to my flagging ego.'

'Flagging ego? That'll be the day, but a change of image does sound interesting, perhaps I'll join you.'

'Great. In the meantime, have you discovered anything interesting?'

Marcia gave a wry smile. 'Not much to go on without his clothes and they're still looking for those. I've found a couple of interesting bits on the body though. Want to have a look?'

Sam nodded and they walked across to the far desk where several binocular microscopes sat impassively on the top of a long white work-bench. Marcia lowered her eyes on to the top of one of them and adjusted the focus slightly to create a sharper image before looking up again. 'Take a look at that.'

Sam peered into the microscope. Under the glass she observed a single, dark blue fibre. The scale pattern on the fibre presented itself as a series of parallel wavy lines which made it a natural fibre, probably wool, she thought. Increasing the magnification from two to four hundred, she looked deep into the central core of the fibre to examine the broken black bands of the medulla. The bands were formed as the hair grew and the dying scales were replaced by minute air pockets which showed up as small black blobs. Sometimes the medulla could be very distinctive but this was not normally the case with wool.

'Dark blue, natural wool fibre.'

Marcia was impressed. 'From?'

'Either a blue jacket or pair of trousers.'

'That's what I think it looks like, but you have to be a bit careful with the colour. Under this intense artifical light it reveals its real colour, a very intense, dark blue. However, under normal circumstances and to the woman in the street, it looks black. So any potential witness would have seen our killer in a black jacket or trousers, not blue.'

Now Sam was impressed. Marcia continued. 'I'll be able to tell you a bit more about the colours when I've done the chromatography and spectrophotometry tests.'

Sam's eyes returned to the top of the microscope. As she looked, her mind was drawn back to the murder scene and her conversation with Richard Owen.

'Where did you find it?'

'Attached to the cord around James' neck.'

'Find any others?'

'A few. Why do I get the impression there's something you're not telling me?'

'Richard Owen was wearing a woollen jacket at the scene, it looked black to me. You'll have to get some fibres to be completely sure, but I bet . . .'

'What, Owen the police surgeon? Didn't he have a protective suit on?'

Sam shook her head. Marcia was furious. 'Well, that's it then, the police surgeon did it. Case solved!'

Sam frowned at her in mock seriousness. 'I don't think so, he's no street fighter. A bit too respectable to get his hands dirty.'

'Where the bloody hell was the crime scene manager? Has Owen never heard of Edmund Locard: "Every contact leaves a trace." This is bloody ridiculous, I thought I was on to something there.'

Sam interjected quickly, calming Marcia down. 'I'll have a word with him, you know what an old woman Owen is, bit set in his ways.'

'That's not the point, God knows how much time we could have wasted if you hadn't noticed his jacket.'

'You said there were a couple of fibres?'

Marcia changed the slide under the microscope, adjusted the focus again and Sam peered in. This time the fibre was long, coarse and dark, possibly brown, and had been cut at both ends.

'What's the magnification?'

Marcia took a quick glance at the microscope. 'Hundred and fifty.'

Sam nodded, increased it to two hundred and adjusted the focus to compensate. It made little difference. She still hadn't a clue what it was.

'You mean you don't recognize this one?' Marcia leaned down by her side. 'I feel secure again. Owen didn't have a horse with him, did he?'

Sam looked up, confused.

Marcia continued, 'It's a horse's hair, I found a few of them. All on his . . .' She picked up a clipboard lying by the side of the microscope, 'Right arm and hand.'

Sam looked back into the microscope. 'Unusual. How do you know it's horsehair?'

'By its look and structure mostly. It's too thick to be a man-made fibre, no uniformity to it. As you know, hair consists of three layers, the outer cuticle, the cortex and the inner core, the medulla. Have a look at the medulla. If you look closely you'll see that it is continuous. In human hairs the medulla is generally absent or at least fragmented except, that is, for mongoloids where it's continuous. Animals, on the other hand, tend to have differing and quite complex medullary structures but it's the cuticle of this hair which reveals it's animal and not human hair. Stop me if I'm boring you. Rabbit hair is pretty easy to identify through the medulla, but I had to check the structure of this one and then compare it with the pigment granules in the cortex. I compared the lot against some of the reference samples we keep in the lab. It could have been one of a few animals but I decided it was closer to horse than anything else.'

'Why horse?'

'Because the hair has been deliberately cut at both ends I think it's had some commercial use, stuffing for chairs, mattresses, that sort of thing. I know it's not used quite so much these days but horsehair was once used a lot. We'll have to have a good look around, see if we can't find a match for the hair. If the police could find his clothes it would help.'

Sam looked up at her, she was impressed with Marcia's meticulous analysis. 'They will. What about the cord and the tube used to garrotte him?'

Marcia walked across to a large table at the centre of the lab and opened one of the plastic exhibits bags lying on the top. She held up the metal pipe by the string which ran through a small hole at the top of the tube. 'It's a wind chime, I think it's been cut away from a group of chimes and then converted into a garrotte.'

'Any prints?'

'No, it's been out in the open too long. Odd thing to murder someone with though.'

Sam nodded, intrigued. 'Yes, it is.'

Marcia held the chime up and hit it with her pen, sending a high-pitched ring around the room. 'For whom the bell tolls?'

'Beware, it may toll for thee.'

Marcia smiled and shrugged. 'Well, I haven't "tolled" enough yet, so I'll see you later. Shepherd's at one and the drinks're on you.'

'Aren't they always?'

Marcia quickly put the chime back into the exhibits bag, and returned to her microscope, waving goodbye over her shoulder as she returned to her work.

Frances' bedroom hadn't altered, it was as if time had stood still in this small corner of the world. Her bedspread was turned down as if in readiness for bedtime and the assortment of fluffy bears, rabbits and dolls still sat on her pillow just the way she'd left them. Even her slippers sat neatly by the side of the bed where they'd always been. Frances looked up at her father.

'It's just the same, you haven't moved a thing. It's as if I'd never been away.'

Malcolm Purvis stared into the room. 'You haven't, not really, you're as much a part of this house as your mother was and she's still here, keeping an eye on things. I knew you'd come back one day, just a matter of waiting.'

Frances put her arms tightly around her father. She had hurt him deeply, yet he'd never stopped loving her, never stopped wanting her back. For the first time in a long while, and despite all her problems, she felt completely safe, even happy. She felt she could cope with anything.

'We have to talk, Daddy. I've got a lot to tell you.'

'I'm sure you have, but there's plenty of time for that. Get yourself a shower and get changed. I've kept all your old clothes in the wardrobe; they might be a little out of fashion now, not what you're used to, I expect, but they'll do until we can buy some more. If they still fit.' He ran his eyes along the length of his daughter's body, 'I think you've put a bit of weight on.'

Frances looked down at herself and a shadow of concern passed over her face. Her father noticed, 'Don't worry, it looks good on you, you were far too skinny.'

As he said it Frances could feel herself biting her lower lip anxiously, trying to stop herself from blurting out the truth. She'd have to tell him eventually, but this didn't seem the right place or time. At the moment she was daddy's little girl again, and she rather liked that. He was in charge and he would look after her. If she told him of her pregnancy it would break the illusion. She needed time to think, to calm her mind and allow her father's welcome to seep through her and strengthen her before becoming an adult once more.

Her father finally kissed the top of her head and walked back down the stairs. 'I'd better call the police and ask them to move that heap of rubbish outside the house. We don't want a little Bird calling, do we?'

Frances looked down at him, watching him descend the stairs, before turning and walking into the warm, friendly comfort of her old bedroom.

Wyn Collins pulled the curtains across her large sitting-room window, taking care to make them overlap in the centre, effectively shutting the outside world away for another evening. The nights were drawing in rapidly and the cold night air seemed to seep through every gap and crack in the frame. She turned back to her mother who sat uncomfortably in a large easy chair at the other end of the room. It was her mother's sixty-fifth birthday and Wyn was determined she should enjoy herself. Her trips downstairs from her bedroom, like her grasp of reality, were becoming less frequent. She'd dressed her mother in her favourite skirt and blouse and hired a mobile hairdresser to come and style her hair; the old lady had seemed to enjoy that. The girl who came couldn't have been much older than twenty, but she was kind and her mother had taken to her straight away. When the girl finally left Wyn used what limited skill she had to brighten up her mother's ageing and lined face with make-up, finishing off her efforts by placing a small colourful party hat on top of her head and pulling the elastic strip under her chin. The effect was to make her mother look like some grotesque clown, but she didn't seem to mind, only smiled inanely into the mirror which Wyn had propped in front of her.

'Well, Mum, what do think? You don't look a day over . . . sixty.'

The old lady smiled into the mirror and stroked her hands through her hair, she obviously liked what she saw. Wyn looked at her watch, 'There's no sign, so I suppose we'd better start without her.' Wyn placed her hand on her mother's shoulder, 'Never mind, too busy with her career I expect.'

Wyn walked into the kitchen and lit the candles on the birthday cake she'd spent the week preparing. She was proud of it. Mixed fruit in the shape of a giant sixty-five, topped with white icing and over thirty multi-coloured candles. She was determined to make this as normal a birthday celebration as possible, realizing that there would soon be little point in making any special effort on her mother's behalf. She had hoped that Sam would come and felt disappointed and annoyed that she hadn't rung.

She pulled a box of matches out of a kitchen drawer and lit each of the candles in turn. When she'd finished she carefully picked up the cake and walked back into the sitting-room singing, Happy Birthday. She put the cake down on a small table in front of her mother before kissing the old lady on the cheek. Her mother looked up at her and smiled but there was no recognition in her face, just mild confusion.

'Come on, Mum, we'll blow out the candles together.'

The old lady spoke for the first time that evening, 'Is your Dad back from work yet? Probably doing some overtime for Christmas. Do you still want a bike?'

Wyn shook her head gently. Her father had been dead for twenty years, but it didn't seem fair to remind her.

'No, Dad's not back yet, I think we'll have to start without him. Ready, one two three, blow . . .'

As Wyn began to blow out the candles, the front door bell rang. Wyn blew out the rest of the candles quickly not daring to leave her mother so close to fire, no matter how small, before answering the door.

Sam stamped up and down on the porch mat, trying to keep herself warm. A dense, freezing fog was descending over the area and it was becoming very cold. The front door suddenly opened flooding the porch with light and warmth from the house. Sam looked into her sister's face, 'Sorry I'm late, last-minute problems.'

Wyn found it hard to disguise her anger, 'I thought you weren't bothering. I told you to ring.' Wyn moved away from the door reluctantly and Sam stepped into the entrance hall.

'I've been really busy. I'm dealing with that murder at the church in Northwick.'

Wyn was not impressed. 'Really. Want a cup of tea?'

'Please, I'm frozen. Where's Mum?'

'Sitting-room.'

'Did she get the flowers?'

'I'm amazed you remembered.'

Sam felt a sudden pang of conscience but said nothing. Her sister continued, 'They're in a vase in her bedroom, they were very nice. You and your flowers, you're as bad as Dad was.'

Sam smiled, she liked the analogy. 'How is she?'

'Not one of her better days.'

Sam nodded and took her coat off, hanging it over the bottom of the stairs before walking into the sitting-room to see her mother. The sight which greeted Sam was not the one she had expected. With Wyn away her mother had decided to start without them and scooped out great portions of the cake with her hands in an attempt to feed herself. Unfortunately, she had managed to get most of the cake all over her. Sam looked down at her and smiled, 'Oh Mum, you're going to be popular.'

Her mother smiled up at her totally unaware of what she had done. 'Hello, dear, back from school already?'

Sam called into the kitchen, 'Wyn, can you bring a cloth out, Mum's decided to start without us!'

Wyn's anger didn't have to be spoken, it was written all over her face as she walked into the sitting-room and began to clean the mess from her mother's head and clothes with the cloth.

'It's worse than having a baby in the house.' Wyn grabbed her mother's face and looked at her, 'Do you know how long it took me to make that cake for you? Any idea how much it cost?'

Sam looked on, alarmed at her sister's treatment of

her mother. 'Take it easy, Wyn, she doesn't know what she's doing.'

Wyn was in no mood to be reasonable; she'd had such hopes for this evening and it had fallen apart so easily. She was tired and disappointment made her rub the cake off her mother's face all the harder as if she had a point to prove. 'She knows all right. Anything to make my life a bit harder.' She looked deep into her mother's eyes, 'True isn't it, anything to get at me?'

Sam interjected, 'That's rubbish.'

Wyn rounded on her instantly, 'Don't you tell me it's rubbish. When you start to pull your weight around this family *that's* when you can tell me it's rubbish. When you have to live with her day and night, week after week, listen to her constant moaning and insults while changing yet another soiled bed, that's when you can tell me it's rubbish!'

Wyn started to pull the large lumps of cake from her mother's hair while Sam, upset, and more than a little taken aback at her sister's verbal assault, struggled for a reply, 'I'll increase your allowance if that would help?'

It was the wrong thing to say.

'Everything's money with you, isn't it? No, I don't want any more of your money, I want you to take more responsibility for Mum. If it was Dad and not Mum who's still alive it would be different, wouldn't it?'

'That's not fair.'

Sam knew there was some truth in the allegation, but still, it hurt. She had always been closer to her father in much the same way as Wyn had seemed naturally closer to her mother. That was just the way things were in their family. She'd always been her father's 'good and clever girl'. When he had died, even though she was still young, the experience had shattered her. Most of her life since then seemed to have been spent trying to assuage her feelings of guilt and prove to his memory what a 'good and clever girl' she was.

Wyn turned angrily on her sister, 'Isn't it? Look, I've been on my own now for three years since John pissed off back to Ireland. I've got two kids and only a three-bedroom house. I've got her,' she pointed angrily at her mother who was picking off the last pieces of cake from her dress and eating them, 'who needs more attention than a baby and Ricky – who was seventeen last week by the way, thanks for the card . . .' Sam had forgotten and had no excuses. Her sister's onslaught continued, 'and who is sick of sharing his bedroom with his brother and wants his own space and seems to think it's fun to cause me as much grief as possible in an attempt to get his own way . . .'

Sam cut in quickly trying to calm the situation, 'What about a nursing home?'

'What about you taking her off my hands for a while!'

'I can't, you know that.'

'Interfere with your social life, would she, not quite nice enough to show to your middle-class dinner guests?'

Sam could see that Wyn was in no mood for compromise. 'I'd better go.'

Wyn folded her arms angrily and nodded. Sam leaned down and kissed the head of her rather dishevelled mother.

'Happy birthday, Mum, I'll come and see you again soon.' She stroked the old lady's hair gently and got her hand covered in fruit cake. Wyn handed her the cloth. 'Thanks.' She wiped her hands quickly, made her way into the hall and slipped on her coat. She turned to her sister, 'See you next time then.'

Wyn nodded, still angry.

'Tell Ricky I'm sorry I missed his birthday. I'll make it up to him.' Sam turned, opened the door and walked back along the path. She heard the front door slam behind her.

Wyn's attitude annoyed her. She'd never really been close to her sister, not even when they young, they were so different. It was sometimes hard to believe they had the same parents. To hear her talk you'd have thought she was the only one to have made sacrifices. The only reason Sam had left London was to be closer to her mother, Wyn seemed to have forgotten that. The allowance she gave her sister was generous too. Wyn certainly couldn't have coped without it, although she was reluctant to admit it. Despite Sam's anger though, they were all the family she had, and no matter how frustrated she might get, her sense of family loyalty was strong, so she would have to make the best of it.

Malcolm Purvis had just cracked another egg into the frying-pan when Frances entered the kitchen. He spoke to her without turning, 'Fancy some breakfast? I thought we'd have a fry-up.'

The smell of the greasy food made Frances feel worse than usual. 'No thanks. Shouldn't you be at work?'

'Taken a couple of days off, they'll survive without me. It's all legal aid stuff anyway.' He turned to look at his daughter. It was as if the past couple of years had never happened. She was wearing a white T-shirt and a long, blue denim skirt. He remembered it was the last thing her mother had bought her before she died.

Frances noticed the way he was looking at her and looked down at the slightly dated clothes. 'It's not the height of fashion but there wasn't a lot of choice.'

'I haven't seen you in that since . . .'

Frances cut in, 'I was twelve?'

'Not quite, I remember your mother buying it for you from C&A. You'd moaned about having one for weeks.'

Frances looked back at her father and judged the moment right. 'I'm pregnant.'

The short silence that followed seemed to last an age. Her father put down the pan and walked across to her, taking her hand. 'Are you sure?'

Frances nodded, 'Yes, I'm pretty sure. I'm getting morning sickness quite badly.'

'So did your mother. Sorry about the fry-up.'

'Are you angry?'

'Angry? How could I possibly be angry? My daughter's back home and she's about to make me a grandfather.' He hesitated for a moment, feeling presumptuous. 'That is, if you want to keep it?'

'Yes, I do,' she said vehemently.

Malcolm smiled and nodded back, 'What about the father? I take it it's Sebastian's?'

'I don't want him to know.'

'I think he might find out.'

'It'll be too late by then, he'll be in prison.'

'What for? He didn't hurt you, did he?' Malcolm asked in alarm, confused by his daughter's last remark.

'Not me. Do you remember Mark James?'

'Of course I do, I defended him, didn't I?'

'Do you know he's been murdered? It was on the news. The body they discovered in the graveyard, it was Mark.'

'Have you seen it?' Frances shook her head. 'Then how can you be so sure?'

'He tattooed my name on his right arm, did it with a pin and some ink. The body in the cemetery had the word "Frances" tattooed on its right arm. It's Mark, I know it is.'

Malcolm put his arm around her. 'Have you told the police yet?'

Frances shook her head.

'Don't you think you ought to?'

'It's more difficult than that. I know who killed him, it was Sebastian.'

Malcolm Purvis looked into her face, 'Are you sure, absolutely sure?'

Frances nodded. 'I'm frightened, I think I might be the next on his list.'

For a moment Malcolm was stunned and unable to think clearly, then he pulled his daughter to him and hugged her as if he would never let her go. 'No one will ever hurt you, not Bird, not anyone. We're back as a family and that's the way it's going to stay, I promise.'

* * *

Frances sat with her father in the interview room opposite Farmer and Adams. Farmer eyed her for a moment. Although she'd never met Frances, she knew her father, Malcolm Purvis QC, well. He'd both prosecuted and defended cases she was concerned with, and he was good. She passed Frances the E-Fit they had prepared for the press conference.

'Is that Mark James?'

Frances stared at the picture long and hard before making up her mind. 'It's very like him. The face is slightly the wrong shape and the nose is a bit big, otherwise I think it's him.' She pushed the photo-fit back towards Farmer. 'His eyes were blue by the way, dark blue.'

'Tell me about the tattoo.'

'He did it himself with a pin and a bottle of blue ink; trying to impress me, I think. He wasn't a bad person, just a bit stupid sometimes, that's all.'

'Has he got any family?'

'Not that I know of. His parents were killed in a road accident when he was young. He was brought up by his aunt after that, but she didn't really want to know. Anyway, she died a couple of years ago and left him on his own. He had his own flat . . .'

'Where?'

'On the Histon Road, number seventy-nine, I think. He let it go though, moved out on the day we were supposed to run away together.'

'From the little I know about Mark he doesn't really seem to be your type.'

'It wasn't a sexual thing, well not on my part anyway.

More like brother and sister. We've known each other since we were at junior school together, just great friends.'

'But Mark wanted to be more than "just friends"?'

'Yes, but he knew how I felt. He never tried it on, not in all the years I knew him.' She paused, 'Have you found his car yet?'

'What kind of car did he have?'

'A clapped-out old Spitfire, but he loved it.'

Adams turned to Farmer, 'There was a report of a burnt-out car being found just outside Northwick a couple of weeks ago, I think that was a Spitfire. There wasn't enough left to trace the owner with. The assumption was that it was down to joyriders again.'

'Everything he owned was locked inside that car, his entire life.'

'So why were you running away?' Farmer continued.

'I'm pregnant. Sebastian made it clear he didn't want children and I was frightened he might force me to have an abortion. He was becoming violent too.'

'He hit you?' Men who beat up women were Farmer's pet hate and she could feel herself becoming angry.

'Yes.'

'Often?'

'Just once, the night Mark went missing, but it was enough. It always starts with the first punch, doesn't it?'

'So why did you decided to run away with Mark?'

Frances looked across at her father, 'I thought he was the only friend I'd got left.'

Malcolm leaned across and took his daughter's hand. 'My daughter and I haven't seen eye to eye for a while, but I think we've sorted it out now.'

'It was Mark who stole the money, was it?'

'Yes, but I put him up to it. He'd do anything for me and I used him. Not a very nice person, am I?' she said sullenly.

'Why did you need the money?'

'It wasn't for me, it was for the baby. I knew Sebastian wouldn't pay any maintenance and it was his child, after all. I didn't want to bring it up in some slum.'

Malcolm spoke up again, 'I'll pay back any money Sebastian might have lost as a result of what's happened, just let me know the amount.'

Farmer nodded and continued with the interview. 'You say you never saw Mark that night?'

'No, he never turned up.'

'But Bird did?'

'Yes, we thought we would be safe at the station. It seemed like a good place to meet, out of the way, no chance of any of Sebastian's friends spotting us.'

'What makes you think he killed Mark?'

'He'd obviously been out looking for him and he knew where I was, that was no coincidence. He was in a violent mood too. I've never seen him so angry. I thought he was going to kill me.'

'And that was when he hit you?'

Frances nodded.

'Did he get his money back? They certainly didn't find any with Mark.'

'I don't know. He's never really mentioned it since.'

'So he hasn't gone out looking for Mark or tried to get his money back?'

'Not that I know of. No.'

'Any idea how much Mark stole?'

'Not exactly, but it must have been a few thousand, he took it from Sebastian's safe at the club.'

'Right, well I think we've heard enough. I'll get a police officer in here to take your statement and if you tell her what you've just told me, that should be fine.'

Frances looked across at her father who smiled at her encouragingly.

The queues were as long as ever outside Bird's club. Farmer looked along the line of young faces, recognizing several of them. She decided it looked like a Who's Who of Cambridgeshire's young villains. She glanced at her watch. 'Where the bloody hell are the wooden tops?'

Adams, sitting next to her in the driving seat, looked at the clock on the dashboard. 'It's only just eleven, ma'am, give them a chance.'

Farmer wasn't in the mood to give anyone a chance. 'They're supposed to be professionals which means they should have been here at eleven, not a few minutes past.'

Adams judged she wasn't in a reasonable mood and decided not to continue the discussion, sucking on his cigarette deeply instead and blowing the smoke out of the car's open window, watching it disappear into the cold night air. The sound of a vehicle braking behind him made Adams glance up at his rear-view mirror. A white transit van had pulled up behind their car and a number of large police officers in heavy blue overalls were jumping out on to the street. Adams looked across at Farmer, 'They're here.'

Farmer and Adams climbed out of the car and walked across to the nine Special Operations Unit officers who stood by their van awaiting orders. Farmer walked up to the sergeant, who was quick with his apology, 'Sorry we're late, ma'am. Bit of trouble in . . .'

Farmer cut him short, 'Have you been briefed?'

The sergeant nodded.

'Then let's get on with it, shall we?'

The unit followed Farmer and Adams across to the club. The jeers from the people waiting to get in had already begun by the time they reached the door. Adams, together with two of the SOU officers, walked across to the large wind chime hanging outside the club's main entrance. Adams examined the long brass tubes and quickly discovered that at least two of them were missing. He nodded to one of the officers with him and they began to take it down, dropping it carefully into a large black exhibits bag.

The two doormen had been slow to react, not entirely sure what to do. Finally one of them, deciding that it was his job to stop unwanted intruders entering the club, stepped forward, putting himself between Farmer and the club door. She stopped and looked up into his large imposing face, her eyes meeting his and fixing on them. Despite his bravado he was nervous. She could see it at the back of his eyes. 'Are you going to move, or am I going to have to move you?' He hesitated, uncertain what to do, almost transfixed by her penetrating stare. He stayed a moment too long. When it happened, it happened quickly. For a brief second Farmer's eyes seemed to drop and she appeared to look away from him, it was a relief and he could feel his body begin to relax, it was a mistake. Farmer brought her knee up into his groin with all the power she could muster, making him double up in pain. As he bent over she brought her fist crashing down hard on to the back of his neck sending him sprawling to the floor. His partner made a move to support him, but a fierce glance from Farmer stopped him in his tracks and he thought better of it.

She looked down at the moaning, prostrate figure on the floor. 'Arrest him.'

The SOU officer was confused. 'What for?'

Farmer wasn't used to being questioned and disliked it. 'Breach of the peace. Now get on with it.'

The sergeant gestured to two members of his unit and they dragged the moaning figure towards their van. Farmer and Adams climbed the stairs into the main club with no further opposition and made their way to Bird's office. She didn't bother with the formality of knocking, just pushed it open. When she entered, Bird was sitting behind his large oak desk working on some papers. He looked up.

'Who the fuck are you?'

Farmer walked across to the desk pulling her warrant card out of her coat pocket and showing it to Bird. 'I'm Detective Superintendent Farmer and this,' she indicated to Adams who was standing by the door together with two SOU officers, 'is Detective Inspector Adams. Are you Sebastian Bird?'

Bird looked first at Adams and then back to Farmer. This was his office and he didn't welcome the intrusion. 'What is this, some kind of game? You know who I am. What's this all about?'

'Sebastian Bird, I am arresting you on suspicion of the murder of Mark James. You are not obliged to say anything unless . . .' She droned the rest of the caution out in her normal style.

Bird could feel a rising sense of shock and anger pour through his body. 'This is a joke, right? you're not the police, you're bloody Jeremy Beadle.'

Farmer looked across to the door and nodded. Adams stood to one side to let the two SOU officers into the room. They walked across to Bird and pulled him out of his chair, forcing his hands behind him and clicking on a pair of ratcheted handcuffs. Bird felt unsure of himself and his composure began to leave him. It wasn't a feeling he was used to and he didn't like it. 'This is crazy, I've done nothing, I haven't killed anyone!'

Farmer smiled at him as he was dragged from the office, still protesting his innocence. Adams lit up another cigarette and drew in a deep lungful. He looked slowly around the office. He was, despite himself, impressed by Bird's style. Everything looked expensive and was beautifully co-ordinated; wallpaper, rugs, even the numerous pot plants surrounding the room seemed to blend in with the general look of the office. The only object which looked strangely out of place was an ancient sepia photograph of two black men dressed in Victorian farming garb. The photograph sat above a large, green ivy plant whose vines trailed on to the floor. The two men were standing side by side outside a thatched cottage. Behind them, with a large white beard, was an elderly white man dressed in similar style. Adams studied the photograph for a few moments wondering who the men were before his thoughts were invaded by Farmer barking another order.

'All right, let's have this placed cleared and turned over. I want some SOCOs here as well, let's have the job done properly.'

She glanced across at Adams with a questioning look. Adams understood, he'd seen the look enough times before. He moved away from the photograph and began to search through Bird's desk drawers.

Malcolm Purvis tapped lightly on his daughter's bedroom door and gently pushed it open. Frances was lying on the bed, her hands tucked under her head, staring thoughtfully at her bedroom ceiling. Malcolm walked across to her.

'Saw your light was on. Can't you sleep?'

Frances pulled herself up on to her elbow and looked across at her father. 'No, I can't help wondering if I've done the right thing, going to the police. Perhaps it would have been better left.'

Malcolm sat on the bed next to his daughter. 'You did exactly the right thing. If he did murder Mark, then he wants locking away for a very long time. I know Mark wasn't the most perfect human being but

I quite liked him. He thought the world of you, and he certainly deserved better than that.'

Frances fell back on the bed clearly unconvinced. 'I didn't exactly see him do it.'

'No, but the circumstantial evidence is pretty strong. It's up to the police and courts now, you've done your bit.'

'But what will happen when he gets out?'

'He won't be coming out for a very long time, and when he does, he'll be so institutionalized he won't be a danger to anyone.'

Frances sat back up again. 'I thought barristers could see the good in everyone.'

'That's social workers, different profession. I don't like most of my clients.'

'You liked Mark.'

'Despite my better judgement. Probably because he'd been so good to you.'

Frances smiled and held her father's hand. Malcolm leaned down and with his spare hand searched inside a small plastic bag he had brought into the room. From it he produced a small, blue baby's jacket, holding it up in front of her. 'What do you think?'

Frances giggled, taking the jacket with her other hand. 'It's beautiful but a bit presumptuous, isn't it? How do you know it's going to be a boy?'

Malcolm put his hand back into the bag and this time emerged with a pink jacket which he also handed to Frances. She looked at them both. 'This is going to be one mixed-up kid.' Throwing her arms around her father's neck, she hugged him closely. 'I don't know how you put up with me, Dad, I'm nothing but trouble.'

Malcolm put his arms around his daughter. 'You're my daughter and I love you, that's unconditional. All for one, just like when your mother was alive.'

Large, hot tears slowly trickled along Frances' cheek before dropping down on to the top of her father's shirt.

Farmer spoke into the tape recorder which was on the edge of the table in the police interview room. At the table Farmer and Adams sat opposite Bird and his solicitor, Mr Colin Lane. Bird sat impassively, casually leaning back in his chair.

'I have to remind you that you are still under caution. Do you understand?'

Bird raised his eyebrows in a dismissive gesture of acknowledgement.

'For the tape recorder, please.'

Bird leaned forward, 'Yes.'

Farmer continued, 'I am making enquiries into the death of a man by the name of Mark James. I believe you can help me with those enquiries.'

Bird failed to respond and maintained his impassive stare.

'Did you know Mark James?'

'Yea, I knew him, he worked for me sometimes.'

'What did he do?'

'Barman.'

'How long had he been working for you?'

'Off and on for about two years. It was pretty informal.'

'We've had information that he stole several thousand pounds from you. Is that right?'

Bird nodded, Adams pointed to the tape recorder.

'Yes, that's right.'

Adams asked the next question, 'Why didn't you report the theft?'

'What's the point?'

'We might have been able to get it back.'

Bird leaned forward across the desk and looked straight into Adam's face. Adams didn't move,

'I can't get insurance any more, do you know why? Because my club has been broken into seven times over the past year. I've had over twenty thousand pounds' worth of kit either stolen or smashed up and you lot did nothing. That's why I didn't bother reporting it.' Having had his say Bird leaned back in his chair.

'But you knew who it was this time.'

'I knew who it was the seven times before that but you still did nothing.'

Farmer came back into the interview. 'So you decided to take the law into your own hands and went after James?'

'That's right, I wanted my money back.'

'Is that why you killed him?'

'I didn't kill him.'

'You went after him.'

'Big difference between going after someone and killing them.'

Bird leaned forward on his seat again. 'Frances has been telling you all this, hasn't she? Look, she's got her own axe to grind with me so I wouldn't take too much notice of what she tells you, she's a bit . . .' He indicated with his finger to the side of his head.

Adams joined in the interview again, 'So what happened when you found him?'

'I never found him. I searched, went to all the usual places, clubs, pubs, the streets where the pimps and tarts hang out, but there was no sign. Then one of me mates said that he'd seen Frances walking up towards the station. Well, when I left her she was supposed to be at death's door so I went to see. She was there all right but Mark was nowhere to be seen.'

'What were you going to do if you'd found him?'

'I was going to give him a bit of a slap, he'd got it coming, but that was all. Anyway he never showed, so that was that.'

'So you took it out on Frances?'

'Yea, maybe. I went a bit too far. I didn't really mean to hurt her though, she hit her head. I told her I was sorry, tried to make it up to her. I felt bad afterwards.'

'It wasn't just the money though, was it? You thought he was going to run off with your girlfriend. You'd have lost a bit of face if he had.'

'Nobody kills anyone over a woman.'

'Hundreds do each year, why should you be different?' interjected Farmer.

'Frances is a free agent, if she wanted to run away with the creep then she was welcome to him, they just weren't going to use my money to do it with.'

'Is that why you killed him?'

'You can keep asking the question but you'll keep

getting the same answer. I didn't kill him. I didn't even find him. And if I had found him he wasn't worth doing life for. You've got the wrong man.'

'Why didn't you keep searching for him after you found Frances?'

'I asked around but he'd just vanished. Thought he was sitting on some beach somewhere laughing at me with my money under his arm.'

Farmer placed an exhibits bag on to the desk containing the wind chime and cord they found around James' neck.

'I am showing the accused, Bird, exhibit number twelve, the wind chime and cord used to garrotte James. This was used to strangle James and it's been identified as coming from the wind chime outside your club. Have you got an explanation for that?'

Bird picked it up and looked at it through the clear plastic bag.

'Yea, I might. A couple of the chimes went missing a few weeks ago. They're always going missing. I leave them out all night. Supposed to ward off evil spirits.' He looked into Farmer's face, 'Think I'll get my money back? They clearly don't work.'

A broad smile crept its way across Bird's face as he sat back in his seat and put his hands behind his head.

Bird sat calmly on the bed inside the bland prison cell and smiled arrogantly at Farmer as he watched her slam the cell door against him. The station sergeant chalked Bird's details on to a board by the side of the cell door and Farmer and Adams walked away.

Adams lit up another cigarette and looked across at his boss.

'Think he's going to have it?'

'He'll have it OK. Bloody psycho, just enjoying the control.'

'He isn't going to admit it, his sort never do. Think we've got enough to bang him up?'

Farmer looked back at him. 'Not sure. A few years ago there'd have been no problem, but now . . . Depends on the magistrate, you know what inconsistent bastards they can be. We need a bit more and I know just where we're going to get it.'

Farmer was interrupted by a shout from the station sergeant's office.

'Ma'am, the Chief Super' would like to see you straight away.'

Adams raised his eyebrow quizically, 'Want me to come with you?'

'No, he'll only want an update. He'll accept one of us bull-shitting, but not two. Thanks, anyway.'

Adams watched as his boss walked away from him. He knew the Chief Super' too well to believe that he'd turn out in the middle of the night for an update. He realised Farmer must know that, too. There was trouble and Farmer was going to face it alone. Adams walked back slowly towards the incident room.

CHAPTER FOUR

Detective Chief Superintendent Words slammed a pile of newspapers down on his desk in front of Farmer. Farmer disliked Words at the best of times but now at his arrogant, bombastic worst, she despised him.

'Tomorrow's papers, we're front page bloody news!'

Farmer picked up the well-known tabloid at the top of the pile and read the sensational front page,

BLACK MAGIC SEX SLAYING IN SLEEPY CAMBRIDGESHIRE VILLAGE

The article contained a full account of the investigation surrounding the unidentified, murdered body found in St Mary's churchyard, described in lurid detail, including a photograph sexton holding his dog and a complete description of the circumstances leading up to the discovery of the body by the sexton's dog. The rest of the papers were written in a similar style.

Words roared on, 'It's not good enough, Harriet! It's just not good enough. Where the hell did they get all their information from?'

'Probably slipped the sexton a few pounds?'

'The sexton could only have told them part of it, where's all this stuff about black magic sex slaying come from?'

'Dr Ryan, the pathologist, mentioned it in her report. Well, the ritualistic possibilities anyway, they've made the rest up.'

'Why these bloody people don't keep their bizarre ideas to themselves, I don't know. All we need to know from her is, yes he's dead and this is how he died. Then she should bugger off out of the way. I'll be having words with her Trust about this. So are you telling me that the leak has come from her?'

'No, I can't be sure of that.'

'Then where has it come from? Your team?' Farmer was beginning to get a little tired of his hysterical outburst and accusations. 'I've got no idea where the story's come from. I've got Adams looking into it.'

'Well make sure he does his bloody job. I want this leak plugged and if it has come from your team I want the bastard's balls on my carpet as soon as you know who it is.'

Farmer nodded, she could do little else.

Words continued, 'What about this suspect you've got in. Charged him yet?'

'No, not yet, but it's looking promising.'

'I don't want "promising", Harriet. I want a result and I want it bloody quick. The sooner this nonsense is sorted out and the people around here feel they can sleep safely in their beds again, the better.'

He calmed for a moment trying to make Farmer relax before his final threat.

'I don't want to fall out with you, Harriet, but if this job isn't cleared up quickly and the press don't get off my back, we'll find ourselves discussing your career and how you might look in blue!' Farmer breathed out deeply but remained silent. There was nothing she could do that would pacify him, except charge Bird, and she wasn't sure she was in a position to do that yet.

PC Sandy Wilson sat outside 42 Croft Lane with his partner Philip Troakes. He looked around at the various houses. It was a nice road, modern but nice. All the houses were large, four-bedroomed constructions with double garages and large driveways accommodating top of the range cars. It was just what he wanted, but couldn't afford. It seemed to Sandy Wilson that there was no limit to the price people were prepared to pay for these houses, there was always someone willing to buy them. They must all have bloody well-paid jobs or be on the fiddle to afford these, he thought. He turned to Philip Troakes.

'Think you could live here?'

Troakes, who had been leaning back in the passenger seat of the white Panda car dozing, pulled his cap away from the front of his eyes and looked around. 'Wife-swapping and orgy land? Yea, I'd give it a go.'

'How do you know that then?'

'Try reading the Sundays, there's stories in every week. Middle-class women bored out of their minds. They're gagging for it.'

Wilson shook his head at his colleague. 'You live in a world of your own, you.'

'Look at that murder enquiry at Bradthorpe last year. Middle-class estate right? Two of the lads got sent back to section for drinking on duty, six got sent back for shagging, and one of those was the local bank manager's wife. Caught them at it apparently, he still had his helmet on.' Troakes burst into laughter at his own joke before pulling his cap back over his eyes and sinking back into his seat.

'A real credit to the force.'

Troakes answered without moving, 'Look, it's this great new world of police accountability. We're expected to provide a service, right? Well, we are. Community policing at its best, that's what I call it.'

Sandy Wilson shook his head in disbelief and continued to watch the house. He hated jobs like this, domestics. They always ended in tears and no one ever came out with any credit. There were more coppers killed and injured through being in the middle of some stupid domestic dispute than for any other reason. As his thoughts began to drift towards the weekend and the football match on Saturday, a dark, grey Ford Escort pulled on to Bird's drive and stopped. Troakes, awaking from his slumbers, looked across as a blue-suited man emerged from the car and stared across at them.

'Is that him?'

'No, away colours, probably his brief. Sergeant said he'd be here.'

As they watched, Bird's solicitor walked up the drive to the front door and let himself in. A car drove past them slowly and stopped further up the road. They didn't noticed it. Even if they had, there would have been no reason for them to be suspicious. It was just another car on the road. Their inquisitiveness was satisfied and, as the object of their attention disappeared into the house, they relaxed back into their seats.

Malcolm Purvis stepped out of his Range Rover and looked across at the police car. If he hadn't known better he'd have sworn they were both asleep. He slammed the driver's door just to let them know he was there. The two constables sat up with a start and, after adjusting their caps, stepped smartly out of their police car. Malcolm had mixed feelings about the police. He realized that they had a difficult job to do, but he did wish they'd take a more professional approach sometimes, especially when it came to giving evidence in court. He'd lost too many cases to hold many of them in any great esteem. These two seemed big enough and ugly enough to get the job done, though. He hoped they wouldn't be needed. He walked around to the back of his car and opened the boot, removing a large, brown suitcase before following the two PCs along the drive to the front door.

They didn't have to knock, the solicitor had seen him arrive and had opened the door in anticipation. He led them up the stairs into the master bedroom and opened a wardrobe door. Malcolm Purvis nodded his thanks and began to load Frances' clothing into the suitcase he'd brought with him. Bird's solicitor stood over him, watching him closely and making a note of everything he took. Finally, the suitcase full, he closed it and clicked the fasteners shut. Bird's solicitor followed the small group back down the stairs and saw them safely out of the house, not taking his eyes off them for a moment. Once outside he locked the door and waited until he saw both Malcolm Purvis and the police drive away.

As the two vehicles rounded the corner at the top of the road he noticed another car pull away from the side of the kerb and begin to follow the small convoy off the estate. It was the deliberate nature of the car's actions that made him suspicious, as if it had been waiting for them. He wondered if it might be worth a quick but anonymous call to the police on his mobile phone. If Bird's friends had decided to take the law into their own hands he didn't want to be involved. He pulled the phone from its clip at the back of his trousers and pondered his decision. Although the car had been a good distance off he was sure the driver was both white and middle-aged, not the type of person who would readily associate himself with Bird. After a few more seconds' thought he clipped his phone back on to his belt and made his way down the drive to his car.

It was early evening when Sam finally returned home, her car overflowing with plants of every size and variety. Several of them protruded through the car's open windows giving it the outward appearance of a mobile greenhouse. She tried hard to keep her weekends free and, short of emergencies and the occasional on-call, she generally managed to do so. Weekends offered one of the few opportunities she had to shop, clean the cottage, and spend time in her beloved garden. Autumn was a busy time and there was always something to do. She adored the soft sleepiness which descended over nature at this time of year, and the necessary duties of planting, pruning, dividing and general tidying in preparation for winter's icy blanket were her joy and salvation.

Sam lived in a small, two-bedroomed, former game-keeper's cottage. Although she enjoyed its age – it was over two hundred years old – she also enjoyed its upgraded comfort. It retained many of its original features, like the large, open fireplace and the dark-beamed ceiling, but extensive, sympathetic renovation had been carried out to introduce all modern necessities. The only unfortunate thing about it was its name, 'Badger View'. As far as Sam could tell, all the badgers in the district had either been gassed or dug out by baiters long ago and during her year of occupation, despite catching tantalizing glimpses of the district's other wildlife, she hadn't seen a single badger. The cottage was remote and surrounded by woodland and fields with just a small dirt track leading to the front gate. That's why she'd chosen it, that and the fact that it had one of the most beautiful gardens she could ever remember smelling.

Although neglected, the garden had held its own against the invading weeds and was resplendent with old English roses, the scent of which has rarely been captured by modern hybrids, while honeysuckle and jasmine scrambled amongst the rambling roses over the side of the house and the wall which protected the garden from the east winds. Aromatic herbs and varieties of lavender were planted at the rear of the house, along the path leading from the kitchen door into the main body of the garden. Here the sun warmed the plants for most of the day and with each trip into the garden the leaves were lightly bruised, releasing their distinctive and pungent fragrance. Wallflowers had endured many winters and mingled with old garden pinks planted in light, free-draining soil in a raised bed in front of an old lilac tree and, as she was to discover to her continuing delight during her first year in the garden, there was no time of year which did not bring forth the delights of aromatic leaves and flowers in this remarkable garden. Sadly, as is the way with nature, some of the plants were diseased or too old to be rejuvenated and so she had spent both time and money taking cuttings, collecting seeds and searching catalogues in an effort to replace those specimens beyond help.

Her nearest neighbour, the farmer who had owned the cottage, lived over a mile away across the fields and she enjoyed the solitude. It gave her time to think, reflect and prepare for the following week. When not engrossed in the garden, Sam spent hours just rambling through the woods and tramping across the fields, breathing in invigorating lungfuls of the fresh, clear air and admiring the ever changing, living world around her.

She always drove slowly along the rutted dirt track leading to her cottage, pulling her car from side to side to avoid the large, water-filled pot-holes of uncertain depth which always littered the road. An absent-minded miscalculation could result in her plunging into one of the perpetually glutinous ruts from which she might never extricate herself, not to mention the damage it would do to the car. Sam viewed the tricky navigation of this track as a type of 'rite of passage' which separated her cerebral, professional persona from her spiritual, personal self. As she finally pulled her Land-Rover on to the drive she noticed a dark blue car parked just beyond her cottage and facing towards her. In the fading evening light she couldn't quite make out the faces of its two occupants but she guessed they were police officers. Despite their best efforts, police cars, even the unmarked ones, still looked like police cars. Sam walked to the rear of her car and began to unload the boot. The sound of Farmer and Adams' footsteps crunching across the gravel path alerted Sam to their approach. She put down the large witch-hazel she had just wrestled from her car and turned around to face the two police officers, eyeing them suspiciously and hoping they had a good reason for invading the privacy of her weekend.

'Didn't know you made house calls?'

The annoyance on Sam's face was apparent and made Farmer feel slightly uncomfortable, a feeling she didn't enjoy.

'Sorry, we don't normally, but this is a bit of an emergency.'

'You're going to have to talk to me in the garden, I want to get this in before it's too dark to plant.' She indicated the *Hamamelis mollis* sitting on the ground in front of her.

Farmer looked across at Adams, 'Give Dr Ryan a hand would you, inspector?'

Adams was clearly unhappy at the order but realized he had no choice but to comply. Sam looked across at him, smiling mischievously, before walking off with Farmer to the rear of the house, leaving Adams pondering how to lift the large, awkward plant without getting the contents of the pot all over his clothes.

It had been a long walk from the main road to the cottage and it had all been uphill. His progress hadn't been helped by the state of the track. He'd slipped and stumbled on several occasions by the time he reached the cottage and his hands and the knees and hems of his trousers were both wet and covered in thick dark mud. The large, white machine he clutched closely to his chest, rather like a child with a favourite stuffed toy, wasn't helping the situation as it kept him constantly off balance. When he finally reached his destination he was exhausted, and leaned heavily against one of the cottage's antique gateposts to recover. It wasn't until that moment that he noticed the blue Vauxhall. It was parked by the side of the track a few yards in front of him. He didn't pay it much heed at first, assuming it belonged to visiting friends. When the police radio suddenly crackled into life, however, with its familiar beeps and call signs, he began to panic. Abandoning his prized machine, leaning it against the side of the gatepost, he ran headlong into the dense woodland that abutted the cottage, disappearing quickly into the undergrowth and shadows until he felt safe.

Even as winter approached, Sam's garden was still beautiful and had the power to charm. Farmer, who was no great gardener, admired it. She was impressed by the amount of work which had clearly been necessary to create and maintain it. The borders were full and deep and had been planted in such a way that there was colour, shape and form, as well as perfume, throughout the year. At the far end of the garden, separated by a trimmed hedge and well-constructed trellis-work there was a small orchard of assorted fruit trees, the leaves of which had turned and now, even as they died, exhibited a Rembrandtesque blaze of reds and browns.

Sam made her way into the small porch at the back of her cottage and collected a pair of green wellingtons as Adams struggled around the corner with the witch-hazel, searching for a place to deposit it. Sam noticed his discomfort and called across to him, 'In the corner!'

Adams moved, but in the wrong direction. Sam was quick to redirect him, 'No, not that corner, over there.' She indicated to the far end of the garden. Adams glared across at her, clearly tiring of orders and becoming impatient with the menial task he had been given. Finally, reaching the area Sam had indicated and having had the royal nod of approval, he carefully dropped his parcel on to the ground.

Slipping on her pair of size-five boots and collecting a spade and a bag of rotted compost from the shed at the back of the cottage, Sam walked across to where Adams was standing and began to dig a large hole. Still unhappy at the two police officers' unwelcome intrusion and racing against time to get the plant into the ground before the light failed completely, Sam initiated the questioning.

'So, what's so important that it's dragged you two out on a cold, wet Saturday?'

Farmer looked across at Adams and then back to Sam. She found it a little disconcerting trying to interview a moving target.

'Mark James. We've got someone for it.'

Sam looked up but continued to dig, her laboured breath pouring from her mouth like fog into the cold evening air.

'I'm impressed. If you've got someone what do you need me for?' She finished digging the hole and emptied a generous amount of the compost into it, not waiting for Farmer's reply.

'The person we've arrested is a local club owner, a man called Sebastian Bird.'

Sam stopped working for a moment and leaned on her shovel. 'Has he got any sort of interest in the occult?'

'This has got nothing to do with black magic. One villain has fallen out with another and paid the penalty.'

'And the cross cut into James' chest?'

'These aren't nice people, it's the kind of thing they do to each other.'

'Sounds like you've got all the answers, what do you need me for?'

'We know James stole several thousand pounds from Bird's safe, and that Bird went after him on the night we think he was murdered. We've got a witness who confirms those two points. We also know that he was strangled . . .'

Sam interjected, 'Garrotted.'

Farmer accepted her mistake grudgingly, 'Garrotted, by a tube from a wind chime we found outside Bird's club. The trouble is, anyone could have stolen the chime, it hangs outside twenty-four hours a day, and that, unfortunately, is as far as it goes.'

Sam returned to her work. 'He hasn't confessed then?'

Both Adams and Farmer shook their heads in unison like nodding dogs at the back of an old car.

'So where do I come in?'

'I'm not sure we've enough to hold him, it's all pretty circumstantial.'

Sam evened out the compost at the bottom of the hole.

'We,' Farmer glanced briefly across at Adams in an attempt to share the responsibility with him, 'were wondering if you'd found anything else that might help the cause.'

Sam walked across to the garden tap by the side of the shed and turned on the water, dragging the long black hose-pipe across the ground to the hole, and began to fill it with water. She looked back up at Farmer. 'Sounds as if you've already got enough, circumstantial or not. I don't think I can add anything.'

Having watered the hole she turned off the tap and began to wrestle the plant from its holder. Adams, unsolicited this time, crouched down by her side and helped her to lift the plant from the pot and place it into the hole where it finally came to rest with a splash of muddy water.

Farmer, irritated by this domestic scene, persisted,

'With the exception of the wind chime which, considering its general accessibility, is not of much use, we've got no evidence putting him at the scene, nor have we been able to link any of the other forensic evidence we found to Bird.'

Sam looked at Farmer inquisitively and Farmer continued, 'So, we were hoping you might have spotted something.'

Sam wasn't quite sure what she wanted. 'Like what?'

'Anything. Anything that might link Bird directly to the murder scene would be handy.'

'Marcia Evans discovered some fibres on his body, they might be worth a look.'

Adams spoke up, 'We've checked those. We're pretty sure the horsehair came from James' car seat. And Doctor Owen sent us samples from his jacket. They match the ones found on the body. So they're not much help either.'

Sam raised an eyebrow disapprovingly,

'He has been spoken to. It won't happen again!' Farmer snapped. Sam wasn't convinced but allowed Farmer to continue. 'Are you sure there was nothing? Nothing that might perhaps, if it were interpreted in a different way, give us what we're looking for?'

As the sun finally went down, melting into the top of the cottage, Sam shovelled the last few spadefuls of dirt into the hole and heeled it down firmly while Farmer continued her verbal onslaught.

'If we don't find something soon we might lose him. Are you *sure* you didn't find . . . anything?'

Sam couldn't pinpoint what it was, something in the tone of Farmer's voice, the look on her face, but whatever it was, with the waning light came the clarity of Farmer's intention. Sam realized exactly what she was being asked to do, and she resented it.

'I can't find what's not there,' she snapped.

'Perhaps you missed it the first time, only just discovered it. Do you understand me?'

Sam finished raking the ground around the plant and looked Farmer full in the face. 'I understand you all right. You've got my report, everything's in there. I didn't miss a thing.'

Farmer's face flushed with anger as the two women stared into each other's face. The moment was broken, however, by Adams' quick intervention.

'Like me to bring the other plants around?'

Sam looked across at him, tearing her eyes away from Farmer's. 'No, I think I'll do those in the morning. There's been enough *planting* for one evening.'

She looked down at Adams' trousers which were covered in mud. 'Sorry about your trousers.'

Adams glanced down and, annoyed, attempted to brush the worst of it away. 'Shit!'

Sam glanced back at him on her way into the house. 'Probably.'

She opened the back door and walked into the kitchen, closing the door behind her and locking it with a decisive click, leaving the two detectives standing alone in the darkening garden.

It was clear from the moment they entered the room

127

what the rest of the class were thinking. A late middle-aged man with a pretty young girl on his arm, another case of mid-life crisis gone mad. She was young enough to be his daughter, which, of course, she was. Malcolm Purvis sat awkwardly at the back of the class with Frances, feeling a little embarrassed and looking forward to the moment when all could be revealed. The lecturer, a short, plump midwife with a round, kind face introduced herself and then asked each couple in turn to do the same. Each married couple reeled off their names, outlined the stage of their pregnancy and gave a brief family background. When Malcolm's turn came, the whole class seemed to turn and look at him with almost universal disapproval. Their unfounded assumptions caused a flare of annoyance within him and he was almost tempted to make out that Frances was indeed his girlfriend and that the baby was his. However, under the circumstances common sense prevailed and he heard himself blurt out, 'My name's Malcolm Purvis and this is my daughter . . .'

Frances spoke up, 'Frances, who is about to make him a grandfather for the first time . . .'

Malcolm quickly ended her sentence, 'And I'm looking forward to it.'

The class turned back to face the midwife, some smiling their approval, others looking slightly embarrassed by their mistake. Frances saw the contented look on her father's face and nudged him in the ribs with her elbow, smiling as she did.

The darkened figure watched as Farmer and Adams

drove away. He waited until he saw the car's brakelights flash on at the bottom of the lane and then disappear as it accelerated on to the main road. When he was certain they had gone he turned and began to make his way along the gravel path towards the back of Sam's cottage. Sam stood in the kitchen preparing dinner. She was hungry, having had no time to stop for lunch during the day. Bernard, her long-haired tabby, jumped up on to the kitchen worktop and sniffed around the pan. Sam picked him up gently and began to stroke him. Bernard was the only company she really had and she valued it. He'd been lost for a while after they'd moved. Being a city cat, the great outdoors had unnerved him for a while, but he gradually got used to it and now brought home a succession of dead rats, voles and fieldmice. As she put him back on to the floor she heard a tapping on one of the glass panes in the conservatory. She strained her eyes against the darkness but could see nothing. She flicked on the security light and the garden was immediately illuminated in its beam, but there was no sign of life. Slightly unnerved, she slipped on her boots and picked up her garden spade as a weapon. She unlocked the back door and ventured cautiously into the garden.

'Hello, Aunty Sam.'

The voice was familiar but it still made her jump. Sam spun around to be confronted by the smiling face of her errant nephew. Although greatly relieved, she was angry.

'Why don't you knock on the front door like every one else? You'll give me a heart attack!'

'Sorry, I was waiting for your visitors to go.'

Sam couldn't believe the state he was in. 'What have you been up to? You look like the creature from the black lagoon.'

Ricky looked down at his mud-covered clothes. 'Sorry, I fell down a couple of pot-holes on the way up here. It was dark!'

Sam had always loved her nephew but sometimes it wasn't easy. He was tall and slim with the gangling awkwardness that seems to come with the onset of puberty in boys. The one blessing was that he hadn't developed teenage acne, and his handsome face and crop of red hair were his redeeming features.

'Have you eaten?'

'Not recently.'

'Come on, you can share mine. I think there's enough.'

Ricky followed Sam back into the house, kicking off his muddy shoes by the kitchen door as he went. Sam moved across to the stove and examined the contents of the pot. She looked back at Ricky.

'A few more minutes and it'll be ready. How's the family?'

'Gran's much the same. Mum seems to be angry all the time, and David spends most of his time out with his new girlfriend.'

David was Wyn's older son and Sam's only other nephew. Despite Sam's fondness for Ricky, she'd never liked David. He was far too much like his father, self-centred and broody, and he lacked the youthful friendliness of his brother. Although Ricky was far from perfect, there was a basic goodness about him which Sam loved. She was glad that there might be a chance of David moving on. It would certainly give Wyn and Ricky the break they needed.

'We might be having a wedding in the family then?'

Ricky wasn't so sure. 'I doubt it, use 'em and abuse 'em is his motto.'

Sam could feel her hackles rising. It was typical of David. She changed the subject. 'Can you get a couple of plates out, Ricky? They're in the cupboard over there.'

As Ricky got up from the table he took his left hand, which had been concealed since he arrived at the cottage, out of his pocket. Sam noticed that he had wrapped a grimy white handkerchief around it. The handkerchief was covered in a mixture of dried blood and dirt. She walked across to him.

'What have you been up to?'

Sitting next to him, she took his hand and began to remove the make-shift bandage. He winced as she unravelled it, exposing a nasty gash that ran the length of his palm.

'How did you manage this?'

'I cut it on some glass, stupid really.'

She hadn't noticed before but now that her nephew was sitting close to her she could smell his breath.

'Been drinking?'

'Just a couple.'

Sam nodded sceptically and walked across to one of her cupboards, pulling out a first-aid kit before returning to the table. Splashing antiseptic on to a wad of cotton wool she began to clean the wound, making him flinch as she did.

'Sorry. Are you sure this is a glass cut? It doesn't look like one.'

Ricky nodded but Sam wasn't convinced. When she'd finished she wrapped his hand with a fresh bandage before securing it with a safety pin.

'There, that should do it.'

She put two plates out on to the table and began to serve up the pasta.

Ricky started eating almost before Sam had finished serving. Then he looked across at his aunt, trying to look as pathetic as he could. 'Can I stay here tonight? If I go home I'll only have to explain this.' He held up his bandaged hand.

Sam looked at him. 'Nothing to explain, is there?'

Ricky continued eating, talking between the pieces of pasta that filled his mouth, 'No, but try telling Mum that.'

Sam sighed, but her sense of duty and the genuine affection she had for her nephew overrode the irritation she felt at this further disruption of her weekend.

'I'll make up the bed. Better give your mum a ring and tell her where you are.'

Ricky looked sheepishly at her. 'Don't suppose you could . . .'

'No chance, you do your own dirty work and before you do that, you can wash up.'

Ricky leaned back in his seat and breathed out, loudly. Sam didn't really like upsetting her nephew so she decided to add a sweetener, 'Sorry I forgot your birthday, things have been a bit hectic recently.'

Ricky shrugged as if he understood. Taking her purse

out of her handbag Sam handed a twenty-pound note to her nephew.

'Spend it wisely.'

He smiled broadly as he looked at the note. 'Thanks, Aunty Sam, I will.'

She doubted it, but it was good to see him happy.

'How's the new job going?'

Ricky's head dropped and he looked down, morosely, at his food.

'What happened this time?'

'Bad timekeeping. It was a dead-end job anyway. I want to go back to college but Mum won't let me.'

'Well, you didn't exactly shine at school did you?'

'That was different. Anyway the teachers hated me.'

Sam smiled wryly. 'And with good reason as I remember. Do you think college will make any difference?'

He nodded enthusiastically. 'They treat you like an adult not a kid.'

'The question is, will you act like an adult?'

'You sound like my mum.'

Sam stopped eating for a moment. This comparison with her sister irritated her and effectively ended the discussion, and the meal.

'You start the washing up and I'll make your bed.'

Ricky nodded.

'And don't forget to ring your mum.'

Ricky looked uncertain.

'I mean it.'

After initially reacting to them with caution, Malcolm and Frances had become a *cause célèbre* within the group. The other couples were very impressed at the support Malcolm was giving his daughter. There was much talk about how he'd cope *the second time around*, and he and Frances were often called to the front for practical demonstrations. Frances was impressive and had an instinct for the tasks required. He, on the other hand, was hopeless. He dropped the doll at least twice, pricked both his fingers and the baby with a safety pin, and spilled the bath water down the front of his trousers. Frances cried with laughter but found herself loving her father all the more. At the end of the evening and despite his continuing disasters he received the congratulations of all the parents-to-be.

Apart from feeling embarrassed, Malcolm found he had actually enjoyed himself. As they walked back towards his car he was in a reflective mood, going over in his mind all the things the baby would need, making mental lists of the essentials. Frances, her arm locked firmly in his, looked up into his face reading his mind.

'I think we'll have to rely on disposables after your effort with the real thing.'

He looked down at her. 'I think you could be right. Still, it's only money.'

Frances laughed. They were too engrossed in their plans to notice the dark maroon car parked only a few spaces from theirs. The occupant noticed them, however. He glanced at his watch and made a note of the time they left the college before following them out of the car-park to check their route home.

It had gone nine by the time Sam came scurrying down.

The smell of the fried bacon had already registered in her nostrils before she reached the bottom of the stairs. She walked into the kitchen to find the table laid and her nephew standing by the stove preparing breakfast.

'This is nice.'

Ricky turned briefly to look at her. 'A good, healthy fry-up.'

'I don't know about healthy, think what it's doing to your heart.'

Sam grabbed her coat from the peg at the back of the kitchen door. Ricky looked at her.

'What about breakfast?'

She walked across and kissed him, sighing regretfully, 'Sorry, no time, I'm late.'

'But it's the weekend!'

'Work doesn't end for everyone on Friday afternoon you know.'

As Sam moved away from him towards the kitchen door, he called her back, 'Here.'

Ricky held out a bacon sandwich and Sam grabbed it taking a large mouthful.

'Thanks, it's great.'

Ricky watched her rapidly disappearing back.

'What did your mother tell you about speaking with your mouth full?'

'Are you going to be here when I get back?'

'Probably not, better go home and face the music.'

'Good luck.'

She moved to the front door and stooped to pick up her mail. Most of it was circulars, but there was one postcard which she read immediately She was still chuckling over this as she took another mouthful of sandwich and opened the front door. Standing in front of her was Detective Inspector Tom Adams. He was holding a large white cigarette machine on the back of which were large lumps of plaster from where it had been ripped from a wall. Around the edge of the machine its attacker's bloody fingerprints were still clearly visible. Sam swallowed hard trying to force down the last bit of her bacon sandwich. Adams smiled and gestured to the postcard in her hand.

'Family away on holiday?'

'No, just an old boyfriend. Apparently I'm to expect a visit from him.'

Adams' expression changed briefly and he pushed the machine towards her.

'Yours? I found it lying outside your cottage. Didn't know you smoked.'

Sam frowned at him, 'I don't.'

She looked at the blood on the side of the machine and suddenly realized how Ricky had really injured his hand. It was time he was taught a lesson she thought. Even if it's only not to lie to your aunt. Adams put the machine down and quickly disclosed the real reason for his early morning visit.

'Sorry about last night, nothing to do with me. There's a bit of pressure to get a result.'

'And Farmer's passing it down the line?'

'Something like that.'

'I appreciate your honesty. I'll take another look at him if you like, see if I missed anything, but if it's not there . . .'

Adams held his hand up, 'I understand, thanks.'

Ricky, having heard his aunt in conversation at the door, made his way inquisitively along the corridor. Sam, hearing the footsteps behind her, turned to see her nephew approaching.

'Ricky, let me introduce you to Tom Adams.'

Ricky put his injured hand out.

'Tom's a detective inspector.'

Even as she spoke, Ricky noticed the bloody cigarette machine leaning against the side of the door. He half withdrew his hand before beginning to sway awkwardly from side to side.

'He found this in the drive,' Sam indicated the cigarette machine. Ricky tried to look indifferent. 'Looks like a good set of prints to me, should get the culprit. What do you think inspector?' She winked at Adams and he nodded, looking straight at Ricky.

'We anticipate an early result.'

Sam gave Ricky a final smile before making her way to her car. 'Well, must go. I'm sure you two will have a lot to talk about.'

Ricky watched her go with a mixture of disbelief and betrayal. Adams looked at him.

'Shall we go in and discuss your latest "no smoking" campaign?'

Adams picked up the cigarette machine and followed Ricky back into the cottage, closing the door firmly behind him.

Half an hour later Sam was pulling into the small, cobbled car-park at the front of St Steven's College.

She made her way through the gate and into the porters' lodge where she was directed across Grand Court towards Simon Clarke's rooms at the far end of the court. Sam thought Grand Court had to be the most beautiful in Cambridge. A huge space surrounded by three gates and rows of rooms belonging to both students and Fellows alike. To the right of the court from the main gate was the college chapel, a tall impressive building where the great and the good had prayed for hundreds of years and where Roubiliac's masterpiece of the college's greatest scholar, Newton, sat looking out towards the college he never really left. At the far side of the court stood the hall with its beamed ceiling and long, stained-glass windows in which food was still eaten on large wooden tables, served by uniformed college servants to the few individuals privileged enough to be members of this very exclusive club. The focal point of the court and the most charming feature for Sam was the fountain. Erected by Italian craftsmen to an Elizabethan design it dominated the court. Its gently gurgling waters could be heard in almost every room around the court and created the calming, contemplative atmosphere that was so conducive to serious study.

Sam finally arrived at staircase M10 and climbed the wooden stairs which were smooth and worn by years of use. At the top of the stairs she came to a large, green, oak door. The outer door was already open and the white inner door ajar.

As she was about to knock, a voice shouted from inside, 'Come in, come in, I'll be with you in a minute, make yourself at home.'

Sam pushed open the inner door and entered the room. It was dark. The four windows that overlooked the court were covered in dense ivy which forced the light to fight its way through the vines to brighten the gloomy interior wherever it could. The room was dominated by a large Georgian fireplace with a wide mantle on which stood an assortment of jars, statues, and pots of all shapes and sizes. At the far side of the room was a sagging bookcase overflowing with books of all ages, many in a poor state of repair and looking as if they were about to fall apart. In the centre of the room was a wooden desk which was obscured by papers and books. The room had the faint, musty smell of old, damp paper, mingled with stale smoke and an air of having been closed for some time after a hurried abandonment. The walls were lined with pictures and prints depicting everything from the common to the totally weird. One thing that caught Sam's eye was a black death mask which hung precariously from a single nail above the fireplace. Its expression was almost hypnotic and Sam began to find herself increasingly drawn to it. Her concentration was broken by a sharp voice.

'Aleister Crowley's death mask. The great Warlock, the beast of the three sixes.' He marked the air with his finger. 'It's very rare.'

Sam raised her eyebrows and then returned to the mask. 'I'm not surprised.'

'You must be Samantha Ryan, Trevor Stuart's friend. Simon Clarke, pleased to meet you.' He extended a slightly tobacco-stained hand and Sam took it.

'Thanks for seeing me on a weekend.'

'All the same to me, weekdays, weekends, they all merge into one. I seem to work on all of them.'

Simon Clarke was about thirty, but looked ten years older. He was tall and thin with thick, wire-rimmed spectacles and a permanently dishevelled look about him, and smelt strongly of stale tobacco and sweat. He returned to the mask.

'He engaged in every debauchery known to man, and a few that weren't. Died during a drug-crazed orgy in France.'

'With a smile on his face no doubt.'

Simon burst into a quick, sharp laugh before walking briskly across to his desk and dragging off a large leather book. Dropping it on to the floor he sat cross-legged in front of it.

'Why did you choose pathology?'

Sam was a little surprised by his question but answered readily, 'I find the dead more interesting than the living. And they don't squeal so much when you prod them with a sharp instrument.'

He smiled briefly. 'I did three years at medical school; didn't suit me, couldn't get used to the operations, tying up bits of body. Still makes me shudder.'

Sam decided to ask her own question, 'Why criminology?'

'Liberal intentions at first. You know, put the world right, reform criminals, make them worthwhile members of the community, that sort of thing.'

'And now?'

'Just help catch the bastards. Most of them don't want to be reformed; they're quite happy being criminals. So if I can help put a few of them away so much the better.'

'Hang 'em and flog 'em, eh?'

'Bullet in the back of the neck actually; cleaner, quicker.'

Sam was a little surprised at his views. Simon was amused.

'You're shocked, obviously not bitter and twisted enough yet. When someone close to you is murdered or violently assaulted and all the system wants to do is get the perpetrator back on the street as quickly as possible to carry on their carnage, then you'll change. Come back and see me then.'

Sam remained silent and he quickly returned to the point. 'It's not the first time this kind of symbolism's been used in a murder.'

For moment Sam was confused.

'The upside-down cross – it's not the first time it's been used.'

Coming to her senses, Sam joined Simon Clarke on the floor.

'Really?'

Simon continued, 'It all happened around here actually. Well, in the fens anyway. Do you know anything about black magic?'

Sam shook her head. Simon opened the book and searched eagerly through the pages, finally letting the book fall open on the floor. Depicted on the pages were two women about to be burned at the stake.

'This whole area is steeped in it.'

Sam examined the pictures carefully. One of the

women was clearly screaming from the effects of the flames as they licked around her legs and body. The other, her face contorted in pain, her tongue hanging unnaturally out of her mouth, was being strangled by one executioner as the other began to light the fire at her feet. Sam pointed to the second woman. 'What are they doing to her?'

Simon looked at the picture. 'Garrotting her.'

'Why? Aren't they about to burn her?'

'If they admitted their guilt they were garrotted before they were burnt. Quicker, less painful. Merciful lot, weren't they?'

Sam continued to look at the picture. 'Yes, very.' She noticed something wrapped around the left wrist of each of the women and pointed it out to Simon. 'What's that around their wrists?'

'Ivy probably.' Simon grabbed a magnifying glass from the top of his desk and took a closer look. 'Yes, garlands of ivy. It was supposed to prevent the witches from using their powers against their enemies. Ivy's used in a lot of black magic ceremonies. The Romans used to make the Jews pray to it.'

Sam nodded, fascinated. 'But what's all this got to do with the Mark James murder?'

'I was coming to that.' He flicked through several more pages until he came to a picture of two black men in nineteenth-century farming garb. 'Here they are, Charles and Isaac Ironsmith.'

'They're black?'

'Yes, I think they must have been the only black men in the area at the time. They were quite an attraction. People used to come from miles just to look at them.'

Sam took the magnifying glass off Simon and studied the photograph closely. 'A sort of Victorian Ann and Nick.' Simon was confused and Sam reminded herself of his cloistered existence. 'Sorry. I'm just being flippant.'

He nodded and continued with his story, 'They turned up in Little Overton just after the turn of the century. They were only about ten at the time and couldn't talk a word of English. No one seemed to have a clue where they came from. Anyway, Joseph Ironsmith, a local farmer, took them in and raised them as his own, hence their name. He'd lost both of his sons in the Boer War and until these two turned up was desperately short of help on the farm. The association seemed to work well. When the old man died he left the farm to the two of them and although they kept themselves to themselves, there were never any problems that I'm aware of and they ran the farm well enough.'

'Did they ever learn to speak English?'

'Yes and no. No one ever heard them speak English but most people who came into contact with them were convinced they understood every word being spoken and they communicated with the old man well enough.'

'This is all fascinating stuff, but you still haven't answered my question.'

'Patience, I'm getting there. There were a lot of stories surrounding the boys, most of them nonsense but strange things did seem to happen when they were around.'

'Like what?'

'Wax impressions of people were found nailed to the

church door, graves and tombs were vandalized, cattle fell ill, all the usual things and none of them directly attributable to the brothers. I think some of the locals would have burnt them if they'd had the chance but the old man was fiercely protective.'

'Did anyone discover where they came from?'

'There were a few stories, the odd legend. It was rumoured that about a month before the boys turned up at the village a trader from Haiti was wrecked off the Norfolk coast, hence the voodoo connection.'

'Is that true?'

Simon shrugged, 'I've searched every archive there is to search and I've found no record of the wreck but that doesn't mean there wasn't one, not all the wrecks were recorded.'

'It all sounds a bit far-fetched to me.'

'Possibly, but voodoo certainly synthesizes a lot of African beliefs. It also owes a lot to Catholicism. The boys may well have been influenced by it during their early life. It would certainly explain a lot.'

'You still haven't told me what it's got to do with Mark James though.'

'A lot. One of the brothers, Isaac, was killed in a farming accident during the twenties leaving Charlie on his own. The farm was too much to work alone so he sold it to a local landowner and moved into one of the small farm cottages where he lived happily doing odd jobs around the farm until his early demise.'

'What happened to him?'

'He was murdered in the mid-sixties.'

'Murdered!'

'He'd been out hedge-cutting and when he didn't come back after dark they sent out a small search party. They found him on top of Primrose Hill just outside the village.'

'And the connection?'

'He'd been garrotted and a garland of ivy tied around his left wrist.' He looked into Sam's face for a reaction. 'More interestingly,' he paused for effect, 'a large upside-down cross had been cut into his body.'

Sam was relieved that her visit hadn't, as she had begun to fear, been a total waste of time after all. 'Was anyone arrested for it?'

'Not that I'm aware of. The person to talk to is John Shaw. He's been the vicar in Little Dorking for the last twenty-something years. He's a bit of a walking encyclopaedia on local witchcraft and the murder of old Charlie. He might be worth a visit.'

Sam stood up and looked at Crowley's death mask on the wall. 'Look, I don't mean to be dismissive but isn't witchcraft more to do with people having sex in odd places with funny hats on than anything else?'

'To some. But there are over a quarter of a million practising witches and warlocks in the country at the moment and most of them take it very seriously indeed.'

'Ghoulies and ghosties and long-legged beasties and things that go bonk in the woods?'

Simon smiled, not greatly amused. 'There is someone else who might be worth talking to, one of my old students. Wrote his dissertation on the Ironsmith case. Did a good job too, as I remember. Trouble was, he became so obsessed with the story that he forgot about the rest of his work and finally managed to get himself sent down.'

He began to rummage through the mountain of paper on his desk. 'Now what was his name? It's here somewhere.' He finally recovered the piece of paper he'd been searching for and waved it at her with a satisfied flourish. 'That was him, Sebastian Bird.'

Sam stared at him, hardly believing what he'd just told her.

Detective Superintendent Harriet Farmer stormed along the narrow corridors of the Cambridge magistrate's court, her heels clicking against the hard stone floor and echoing around the building. 'Bloody do-gooders, no social responsibility whatsoever. Where did he get those kind of sureties from? It's bloody ridiculous. If he kills again it'll be on *their* heads not mine!'

Adams, hard on her heels, tried to rationalize the situation, 'The evidence wasn't that strong, ma'am, you knew that when you went in. They've imposed conditions and we can always bring him back in later, when we've got a bit more.'

'Try telling that to the family of his next victim.' She stopped for a moment and turned to him, 'I want him followed morning, noon and night. If that bastard farts, I want someone there to smell it. Do I make myself clear?'

Adams nodded and Farmer strode off again making her way out of the building and into the low autumn sunshine. When she reached the top of the steps she suddenly stopped. The movement was almost unnatural, as if she'd walked into an invisible wall. Adams, who was close behind her, had to step smartly to the side, only narrowly avoiding a collision with her stiff, indignant back. Farmer was almost transfixed, staring towards the pavement at the bottom of the steps. Adams followed her gaze. Sebastian Bird was standing by his red Porsche, his solicitor by his side. They were clearly discussing the outcome of the hearing and had an aura of self-satisfaction about them. After a brief conversation the two men shook hands and separated. As his solicitor walked away Bird looked up and spotted Farmer. A slow, confident smile slowly crept its way across his face. For a moment Farmer didn't move, then a minute tremor ran through her as she realized that Bird's car was parked on double yellow lines. She turned to Adams, 'The bastard's on double yellows, go and book him.'

Adams looked at her despairingly. 'What's the point, ma'am?'

'The point is, he's breaking the law, Inspector, now do your duty.'

Adams sighed inwardly before setting off in Bird's direction.

CHAPTER FIVE

It had been almost a month since the last killing and he was ready for the next. He hadn't expected the court to come to the decision it had, but he was pleased. Although the time had gone quickly it hadn't been wasted. He pulled a green file from his cabinet and spread its contents on to the large oak table in front of him. Photographs, maps, information sheets; he'd left nothing to chance. He felt he probably knew more about the day-to-day movements of Frances Purvis than she did herself. In many ways murder was an intellectual challenge and one that he'd risen to. He'd selected alternative places to commit the killings, and to dump the bodies afterwards, in case the first locations proved unsuitable. He'd even walked around them, getting to know them intimately and assessing possible problems. He'd never felt more confident in his life. The James mission had proved how important planning was, and his death had gone like clockwork. It had been pleasant to discover how easy it had been to kill him. He'd felt no sense of remorse, no pangs of conscience; in fact, he'd enjoyed every moment, much as he imagined a general winning a well-planned battle might feel. Revenge, he decided, was a positive concept not a negative one and he fed off the emotion it generated eagerly. The elation he felt after the killing had lasted for days and was certainly better than any drug he'd tried. In fact the high was better than anything he'd ever felt before in his life and he was keen to repeat it.

He went through every detail of the plan one more time, making sure he'd memorized even the smallest detail. Testing himself, going over and over the plan in his mind. Once he was satisfied, he collected the contents of the file together and closed the folder, clipping the photograph of Frances to the front of it and after one last look at her face, dropped it into the section marked 'pending'. He was confident, but he didn't want to tempt fate. He leaned down by the side of his chair and picked up the small, black, leather bag. He pulled it sharply on to his desk and, unclipping the top, began to examine the contents. The black bag, he thought, added a rather macabre touch to proceedings. It reminded him of one of the three things which were the hallmarks of pictures of Jack the Ripper. His top hat, his cloak, and most of all, his small, black bag, inside which he kept his instruments of death. He pulled the dissecting knife from the dark interior and began to examine its edge. Despite having been used once, it was still sharp and well honed. He wondered idly how many times he would be able to use it before its cutting edge dulled and he would have to replace it with another. He flicked his thumb gently across the blade before slipping it back into its protective sheath and returning it to its rightful place inside the bag. He then examined his syringes and needles. They were fine, packed away inside their individual pockets. He couldn't use those twice but it didn't matter, he had plenty of them.

He considered the last two objects he pulled from his bag to be the most important. The small, bronze-coloured wind chime with its long cord stretching between the two holes at the bottom and top of the chime and the long garland of ivy which he had only recently cut. He ran it through his fingers admiring the leaves. He hadn't realized what a very attractive plant it was. It had grown around him for years, yet only now, when it had become such an important part of his scheme, had he begun to appreciate its beauty and subtlety. He dropped it back into his bag which he closed with a click before placing it back on the floor. He'd hesitated at the prospect of taking on two people at once but He seemed to be guiding him in that direction. He'd formulated a plan, of course, but two people presented particular problems, and had required a considerable amount of thought. He was going to enjoy this one for then it would be finished, and he could rest again.

Frances was sorting out her wardrobe when her father entered the bedroom. She'd already piled up her old clothes on the bed ready to hand in to the local Oxfam shop, whilst keeping back a few of her favourites, those with particular memories. She held one such article from of herself, turning to face her father, 'Remember this?'

Malcolm looked slightly bemused and clearly couldn't.

'It's the one I wore for Aunty Kitty's wedding. You

remember, when John got drunk and was sick down the front of it. Look,' she pointed to a small section at the front of the dress, 'that stain never did come out. Worn once and ruined, and he never offered to pay for another one.'

Malcolm nodded encouragingly but there was clearly something else on his mind. Frances remembered his moods and throwing the dress on the bed with the others, she waited for him to speak.

'I can't come to the good parenting class tomorrow night, sorry.'

Frances didn't disguise her disappointment. 'Why? You know this is important.'

'It's the last time, I swear. An old case has gone wrong and I've got to be in London to work on it.'

Frances folded her arms and looked away in disappointment.

'I'll stop off at Hamleys tomorrow and get you both something nice.'

She looked back at her father, 'Promise it'll be the last time?'

He held his hand up, 'Scout's honour.'

Frances scanned his face looking for the lie but it wasn't there. 'In that case you can drop off at Armani and get me something nice.' Malcolm threw his hands up in mock horror.

'But God knows what the class is going to do without its star turn.'

Malcolm laughed, 'I'm sure I'll more than make up for it next week.'

'I'm sure you will,' Frances agreed.

* * *

He had been surprised to see him leave. The fact that a taxi collected him and he was carrying an overnight case indicated that he might be away for a while, but the exact length of time couldn't be determined. After all his protracted planning, it appeared that they would be separated at the moment of retribution after all. With her father away, what would Frances' actions be? They really were making life very difficult for him, and they'd suffer for it. He realized there was nothing to be done, and he would just have to wait and watch and hope that he would not be too inconvenienced. The following week was going to be very busy and he wanted this sorted out quickly or it might be weeks before he could try again.

Marcia Evans looked up from her microscope and squinted at the clock on the laboratory wall while her eyes adjusted to the change in focusing distance. Two-fifteen, only ten minutes had passed since the last time she'd looked at the clock. She rubbed her eyes gently, trying to relax them and prepare them for the next assault. Even at twenty-four she was beginning to find the strain of long hours over a microscope taking its toll on her eyes. She hated the idea of wearing glasses, subscribing to the Dorothy Parker adage that men never made passes at girls who wore glasses. Still, she consoled herself, she could always use contact lenses. Despite her concerns, she placed her eyes back on to the top of the binocular microscope, adjusted the focus again and lost herself in a world of fibres and stains.

* * *

Sam paced anxiously back and forth across her sitting-room floor stopping occasionally to look for inspiration into the roaring log fire which crackled and spat, forming unearthly shapes within its hot flickering interior. After a string of late-night call-outs she had felt justified in taking an afternoon off, and besides, she needed time to think. Farmer would not be interested in her seemingly wild theories, so she would have to find some evidence in support of her ideas before approaching her. The problem was that no matter how she tried to dismiss the case from her mind, she felt compelled to follow up her theories. The dilemma was troubling. It was a lonely vigil with only Bernard, her cat, to share her turmoil. He watched her languidly from the sofa at the far side of the room, his head turning from side to side, like a spectator watching a tennis match on the centre court at Wimbledon, stopping only occasionally to preen himself and stretch indulgently. Finally, Sam stopped and, looking out of her back window through the rain towards the woods at the top of the hill, came to a decision. Walking quickly into the hall, she picked up the phone and dialled.

Marcia was in the process of replacing one slide with another when the phone rang at the far side of the laboratory. Even this was a welcome break for her aching eyes. She jumped off her stool, walked across to the phone and lifted the receiver. 'Marcia Evans . . .' She recognized the voice instantly. 'As I live and breathe, it's Dr Ryan. Whatever can a poor girl like me do for you?'

Marcia knew at once by the tone of Sam's voice that she wasn't in one of her lighter moods. 'Marcia, I know this might sound odd, but were any garlands of ivy handed in with the evidence from the James case?'

Marcia was slightly confused by the request but accepted it at face value. She dropped her humorous tone to match Sam's and scanned the evidence through her mind. 'I don't think so, would you like me to check?'

She walked across to a small pile of neatly stacked papers close to her microscope and began to search through them, carefully looking at a couple twice to make sure she hadn't missed the obvious, but there was nothing. She returned to the phone. 'No, no ivy, garland or otherwise.'

Marcia heard Sam breathe out in a disappointed sigh. 'Was it important?'

'I'm not sure. Maybe, just a hunch really.'

'If any comes in, I'll give you a ring.'

Sam replied with a sort of distant hum which told Marcia that her mind was already far away, lost in some complex thought pattern in an effort to resolve whatever nagging problem was bothering her. Finally, the problem having been resolved in her mind, she spoke up, 'I was wondering whether you were interested in going to the medics' dinner tomorrow? I've got a spare ticket.'

Marcia was tempted but, given the amount of work she had, was concerned that she would either be too busy or too tired to merit the expense. 'I'd love to, but money's a bit short this month.'

'My treat, there'll be lots of young, handsome . . .'

Marcia began to weaken, her mind racing as she tried to plan a way of reorganizing her work commitments. She felt like Cinderella wanting to go to the ball but being thwarted at every turn. 'I've got nothing to wear.' Sam realized Marcia was almost persuaded and pressed home her advantage, 'Richard'll be there . . .'

That did it, Marcia realized she'd have to go. 'OK, I'm convinced. Where and when?'

Sam knew she'd have to be careful with the next part and made the comment quickly, hoping Marcia wouldn't notice. 'Four o'clock in St Mary's churchyard for drinks at six in the Master's Lodge. Dress is smart, black if you've got it.' She wasn't quite quick enough though.

'Hang on, hang on. I'm sorry if I didn't hear you right but did you say graveyard?'

'Yes, I was wondering if you'd do me a small favour first?'

'Wear my glad rags to a cemetery? No chance, no chance at all.'

Although it was still early in the evening people had already begun to arrive at Bird's club. The two detectives watching the club guessed that they were employees arriving early to open up the place. Bird had been amongst the first to arrive. He parked his Porsche on the street outside the club before making his way inside. DC Jock McFadyed's camera clicked, taking two photographs in rapid succession. The first caught Bird as he climbed out of his car and the second was a strange back shot as Bird entered the club. While McFadyed took his photographs, his partner, Peter Morant, jotted down the time of Bird's arrival at the club, the car he was driving and any other details which he thought might be of relevance. When he'd finished he put the clipboard back at his feet, folded his arms, and continued his desultory stare out of the front windscreen of the car. He hated observations more than anything else he could think of. They were long, boring, normally fruitless and played havoc with his social life. He should, he thought, all things being fair, which they weren't of course, be down at the Dog and Bear with his missis, downing a pint and swapping a few lies with George and Glenda. Instead of that, he was watching some prat who was probably well aware that he was under surveillance and was very unlikely to drop litter, never mind commit a murder. He glanced sideways at Jock.

'I spy with my little eye something beginning with W.'

Jock looked back at him feigning interest. 'Windscreen.'

'Right.'

It was Jock's turn. 'I spy with my little eye something beginning with . . .'

Morant intervened, 'W?' Jock nodded, Morant continued, 'Windscreen.'

Jock shook his head at him, 'You're bloody good at this game, aren't you?'

'Practice.'

Jock agreed with him, 'I'm a bit like that with sex.'

'Especially when you're on your own I've heard,' grinned Morant.

Jock scowled across at him and the two men began to laugh. As they did, Morant noticed an attractive young girl walking towards them. She was carrying a tray with two glasses on it. She walked across to the passenger side of the car and Jock wound down the window, a sinking feeling in his stomach. Smiling, she looked in.

'Mr Bird said he thought you looked a little fed up so he's asked me to bring a couple of drinks across.'

The two detectives looked at each other, both suspicious and a little astonished. The girl continued, 'He said he'd have brought them across himself but he's had to go out.'

The detectives groaned in unison. Jock took the drinks and passed one to his partner. 'She'll have our balls on a pole.'

Morant raised his glass to the girl who smiled at him, 'What the hell, they can't hang us twice.'

The two detectives emptied their glasses in one.

Sam and Marcia looked at each other for a moment before Sam finally plucked up the courage to knock on the shed door. Almost immediately the door swung open and the church sexton, shovel in hand, and looking annoyed, stood before them. Sam spoke up, 'Dr Ryan, I rang the vicar.'

The sexton wasn't impressed by her rank or her connections. 'You're late. Vicar told me you'd be here at four, it's half past. I've got better things to do than hang round here waiting for folks.'

Sam was apologetic, she could be little else. 'Sorry, got caught in the traffic, you know what it's like.'

He stared at her for a moment without speaking, then threw his shovel over his shoulder and stepped out of the shed. As he walked towards Marcia she found herself stepping backwards and for a instant actually contemplated running. The only thing that stopped her was the sexton's Jack Russell. The small dog came running up to her wiggling his body and wagging his tail as he tried to establish whether she was friend or foe. Marcia crouched down and stroked him and he rolled over on to his back. 'Nice dog.'

Without speaking the sexton moved off into the graveyard followed by Marcia and Sam. As they walked between the ancient gravestones and tombs Sam couldn't help but contemplate what a beautiful place it was. Here, surrounded by death, was life in all its abundance. She'd never seen so many varieties of wild flowers in one place before. Rare ivies crawled along and through the old tombs while trees and bushes sprang up from the centre of ancient graves like the fingers of the dead searching for the light. With autumn had come the changes and, unlike the human remains she normally dealt with, here death was beautiful. As if in dying the leaves and the plants wanted one last chance to show how wonderful they had been in life. It was a place she thought she would visit again.

They finally arrived at the tomb they had been looking for and the sexton turned to them. 'Lot of trouble for no good reason if you ask me. You'll find nothing here, the police turned the place upside-down. And they didn't put everything back after them.'

Sam looked at him. 'They didn't know what they were

looking for.' She walked across to the tomb. The lid had a large section missing in one corner and Sam considered that she could probably squeeze through. She turned to the sexton. 'It was you who found him, wasn't it?'

He put his hand up to his nose and squeezed. 'Smelt him more like, right stink.'

Sam nodded, 'Better have a look then.' She pulled a small torch from the inside of her bag and pushed it into a pocket before handing her bag to Marcia and beginning to squeeze through the hole. It was a tight fit but she was just about slim enough to make it and was soon crouching inside the dark interior. Sam pulled the torch from her pocket, clicked it on and began to shine it around the interior of the tomb. The air in the tomb was heavy and damp with a muggy oppression. Despite the police search, spiders had already begun to re-colonize the crevices and there seemed to be dozens of webs. The floor was not as clean as Sam had expected as much of the debris had merely been stirred around rather than removed. Old detritus was forming a thin, slimy carpet overlain by fresh, dry, crisp autumn leaves. She began to run her hands carefully through the leaves, occasionally picking one up to examine it more closely. She tried to be systematic but it was difficult. The space was small and cramped and offered little room for manoeuvre. Every now and then a disturbed insect would scamper from under her hand or across her body in a bid to escape the danger she posed to its sheltered life. As she was resigning herself to abandon the search her torch finally picked up the shrivelled, but nonetheless distinctive, shape of an ivy leaf. She brushed the leaves away from her prize to reveal it fully before carefully picking it up and squeezing herself back out of the hole and into the fresh, sharp, night air. She shivered slightly, not so much from the cold, but more from relief and pleasure at having her expectation fulfilled.

The sexton looked at her. 'You've found something then?'

Sam smiled at him and holding the garland of ivy aloft, watched it lift gently in the breeze.

As the red-robed appeal court judges finished reading their judgment the court erupted. The defendant leaped to his feet and, looking across the court towards the public gallery where his friends were standing and cheering, threw his arms above his head and punched the air with delight.

A firm hand was placed on Malcolm Purvis's shoulder. Turning, he found himself facing his client's solicitor, who stood smiling with his right hand outstretched in thanks. The two men shook hands warmly before Malcolm looked back across the court towards the dock. His client, a smartly dressed, plump man in his mid-thirties, was sitting back in his seat, his head in his hands, crying like a small child, the initial euphoria of the verdict having deserted him. Normally Malcolm would have waited and spoken to his client and the family, basking in the praise which occasions like this always brought. On this occasion, however, the trial had dragged on, it was getting late and he couldn't wait to leave. He made his way quickly but quietly out of the court and into the cloakroom, slipping out of his wig and gown and making his way to the main entrance. At the bottom of the court steps was an army of journalists and television reporters. As he appeared, they surged forward towards him and he froze. Fortunately it was not him they were interested in, but his client, who had just emerged from the court-house behind Malcolm with his family and solicitor. As they were engulfed in a sea of cameras, tape recorders and notebooks, Malcolm was able to slip through undetected. At least, he thought, they were convinced of his innocence, which was more than he was. He hurried along the street towards his chambers which were situated about quarter of a mile from the court. When he finally reached them he dashed up their wooden steps, two at a time, emerging at the top exhausted and having to grip the banister tightly to stop himself collapsing.

'You'll give yourself a heart attack if you're not careful, Mr Purvis.'

The voice was that of his clerk, Michael Scott, who was waiting for him outside his office holding an attractive large royal blue pram which he gently rocked up and down with both hands, humming a lullaby to an imaginary child concealed inside. He waited patiently for his boss to regain his breath. Finally, having recovered sufficiently to stand up, Malcolm looked across at his clerk. 'Well done, Michael, just right, great.'

'We aim to please. Bit old-fashioned for this generation though, don't you think, sir?'

Malcolm was indignant. 'Rubbish. It's exactly the same make we bought for Frances.'

'Twenty odd years ago. Times have changed, and so have young women.'

Malcolm looked down at the pram and then back at his clerk. 'She'll love it. It will be just perfect for my grandson.'

'She's had the baby then, has she?'

'No, not yet, what makes you think that?'

'Grandson?'

'Well, granddaughter then. It's all the same as long as it's fit and healthy.'

Michael smiled and nodded as his boss took the pram from him and began to imitate his action by looking into the pram and rocking it gently. He decided he could take no more and retreated along the corridor towards his rooms.

There's nothing worse than an expectant grandfather, he decided.

Frances took a final sip of coffee from the mug on the kitchen table before grabbing her coat from the stand in the hall and pulling on her large woolly hat. She felt the cold, always had, even when she was a child. Her father had spent hours rubbing her feet in an attempt to keep the chilblains away. It hadn't always worked, but she enjoyed the personal contact with her father. She took one last look around to make sure everything looked its best. She had spent the whole day cleaning the house from top to bottom and filling it with freshly cut flowers. She remembered her mother doing that and had planned it as a surprise for her father when he got home, a token of her gratitude for his support and acceptance.

She glanced at her watch, she was late. Racing out of the front door towards her car she pushed the key into the lock of the driver's door and turned it. The car was as old as the one Bird had given her. It used to belong to her mother and Frances was convinced it gave her father immense pleasure just to watch her driving it. As she opened the door she was distracted by the sound of rustling from a bush close to the front gate. Frances turned and strained her eyes to see what had caused the disturbance and, although the drive was illuminated by street lamps, it was still impossible to recognize the figure which rose to standing as she watched. It was his voice, not his appearance, which gave him away. A cold shiver travelled down her spine; it was Bird. He slowly walked from behind the bush and stood only a few paces away from her. Frances' breath caught in her throat and her stomach churned within its confined space above her baby. Her hand moved instinctively over her stomach.

As Bird took a step closer, Frances fumbled wildly with the alarm she had, at her father's insistence, taken to carrying concealed in her coat pocket. Her fingers, without any conscious direction, triggered the alarm. The noise it made was extraordinary. It was loud, she had expected that, but as the sound bounced off the walls and bushes it seemed to fill the whole drive with a long, wailing cry. Frances was taken by surprise. She dropped the alarm and held her hands tightly to her ears in an attempt to keep the worst of the noise out of her head. Bird was caught completely off guard and spun around defensively, prepared for imminent attack from an unknown enemy or the arrival of a fleet of police cars. Lights along the road began to flicker on and doors opened. Frances' neighbour looked across his fence towards her, trying to shout above the din.

'Are you OK? What's the problem?' He looked across at Bird who glanced at him before his nerve finally deserted him and he fled from the driveway, jumping into his sports car and roaring off along the street towards the city.

Frances was freed from her inertia and retrieved the alarm, flicking it off. The sudden silence was almost deafening. She stood for a moment longer bringing herself back under control. Her neighbour, who had remained on the opposite side of the fence, shouted across again, 'Is everything OK, who was he?'

Frances felt that every nerve in her body was quivering but she turned to reassure the agitated man. 'Everything's fine now, thank you, Mr Miles, just a bit of a dispute with an ex.'

'Well, if everything's OK?'

Frances nodded and he walked back towards his house. Despite her best efforts she began to shake uncontrollably. She opened the car door quickly and sat inside grabbing hold of the steering wheel to support herself and breathing heavily. She felt sick and faint and for a moment contemplated going back into the house and missing the class for once. Finally, she decided that Bird had already affected her life enough and she wasn't going to be afraid forever. She wound down the car window and took in several deep gulps of air, wiping the tears which had forced themselves out of her eyes from her cheeks with the arm of her jacket. Finally, as she began to feel calmer, she straightened up in the seat, turned the key in the ignition and reversed out of the drive.

The disembodied voices of the choir singing inside the minstrel gallery, high above the Old Hall, floated majestically across the candle-lit tables. People waited, some with their eyes closed, absorbing the sounds which had been heard in this place for hundreds of years. Others looked about them at the peculiar shadows which danced across the portraits of the college's former masters hanging around the hall, making the forms shimmer and move for an instant, giving them life once more. When the singing finished the diners' attention was drawn to the High Table at the front of the hall. Professor John Watkins, the Master, stood, a crystal glass of wine in his hand, 'Ladies and Gentleman, the Queen.'

As he raised his glass the rest of the diners stood and in unison echoed the toast, 'The Queen!'

After the loyal toast was drunk the assembled crowd sat back on to their long oak benches and the room immediately filled with the buzz from the chatter and laughter of dozens of people. Sam sat looking exquisitely elegant in front of a portrait of one of the more severe-looking masters. During the short trip between Mary's churchyard and the college, Sam had somehow managed to slip into a short, black dress, brush the cobwebs from her hair and touch up her make-up, so that in the subdued and soft candle-light she was as perfectly turned out as all the other guests.

Marcia had become separated from her as they'd filed into Hall from the Master's Lodge, and now sat opposite a rather handsome man of about twenty-seven. Their body language as they executed an animated conversation revealed that were clearly getting on well. Sam smiled to herself, feeling slightly jealous of their youth and promise. She remembered rather wistfully the brief liaisons she'd enjoyed during her university days. Relationships then were light and very fluid. It was difficult for anyone outside her immediate circle of friends to determine which of the group had formed particular attachments; all were demonstrably affectionate with each other. She couldn't pinpoint the precise time at which relationships had begun to be more demanding and an encumbrance in her life, which was increasingly focused upon her career and her ambitions.

'Make a handsome couple, don't they?'

The comment burst into her reverie like an echo from those carefree days. It had come from the woman sitting opposite her. Sam looked across at her. 'Yes, they do, don't they.'

'Oh, to be young.'

'Sometimes.'

The woman put out her hand. 'I'm Janet Owen, I think you know my husband, Richard?'

Sam nodded. 'The police surgeon?'

'Well, he tries to be, I think he's getting a bit old for it to be frank.'

Sam smiled reassuringly across the table at her, trying not to show her complete agreement. Janet, however, wasn't so easily fooled. 'I see you're in complete agreement with me.'

Sam's embarrassment was masked by a slight commotion at the far end of the table. Trevor Stuart was sitting further down the table next to a young and attractive blonde girl. His hands were all over her and she was giggling with delight. He was making it quite clear to the assembled green-eyed men that she belonged to him. Despite her general liking for Trevor, Sam felt herself more than a little disgusted by him.

Janet looked back at her. 'How does he do it? If they get any younger they'll be wearing nappies.'

Sam remained focused on the lewd actions of her colleague. '"Now, how do we see ourselves getting that first-class degree, my dear?" I should think it probably goes something like that.'

Janet looked back at Trevor who was now nibbling his girlfriend's neck. Finally, sickened by Trevor's openly lecherous behaviour, Sam returned her gaze to Janet. Although she was in her mid-forties she was still in wonderful shape with a beautiful face and athletic figure. Which was more, Sam thought, than could be said for her husband, Richard. She couldn't understand why so many of her friends continued to look so good while their partners went to seed.

'Where's Richard this evening, not on call surely?'

'No, he's around here somewhere, looking to expand and probably chatting about the latest murder he's dealt with.'

'The James case.'

Janet looked across and seemed to be surprised for

a moment that Sam knew which one it was. Then her face relaxed as she remembered, 'That's the one you're working on as well, isn't it? That's why he's so worried.'

'Worried?'

'After you made a fool of him in court the other day.'

Sam was taken aback. 'I didn't make him look a fool.'

'He thought you did, especially over the cadaveric spasm.'

'There was no reason a GP, even one of Richard's experience, should have recognized that.'

'You did.'

'I was lucky, that was all. I don't want to fall out with him over it.'

Janet smiled, 'You won't, just pricked his male pride, that's all.'

Sam smiled, appreciating but not convinced by Janet's reassurance. She changed the subject. 'Richard tells me you're retired?'

'Semi-retired, if you please, I'm still doing a bit of locum work.' She held up her right arm. Her hand looked swollen and bruised and a number of her fingers appeared bent and unnaturally twisted. Unfortunately, this prevents me from doing more. Nothing to be done, about it, though, arthritis just does that. Too many years of delving around in cold, unpleasant places. I've been offered a few good roles in Peter Pan though.'

Sam smiled at her bravery. 'How do you cope with work?'

'Not much I can do. The pills control the pain but another couple of years . . .' She shrugged. 'I'm considering turning to psychology.'

'Delving around in minds instead of bodies, eh?'

'Something like that.'

A commotion at the far side of the table attracted Sam's attention. Trevor Stuart had climbed on to one of the benches with his young friend. He was clearly drunk and enjoying the attention. Two bowler-hatted porters moved quickly towards him and pulled him down from the table. On the way down he slipped and fell sprawling to the floor dragging his young friend with him. Sam shook her head in disgust and decided to leave.

Frances was beginning to regret going to the parenting class. It wasn't just the effect Bird's visit had on her, or the lectures themselves, she enjoyed those, with or without her father. It was the weather. When she'd left home it had been as clear as bell but in only a few hours a thick fog had descended over the whole town restricting visibility to only a few yards. It hadn't been so bad in the city where the buildings broke up the fog a little and the street lights combined with those in shop windows to penetrate the gloom. But the mile or so of country lanes which led to Frances' home were very different. They were dark with no artificial illumination and nothing to break up the swirling banks of fog that drifted across the fields and blanketed the roads. She leant forward over her steering wheel, straining her eyes to pick out the road in front of her. Even her headlights failed to penetrate the dense shrouds, which reflected white light straight back at her. She kept her speed down to below twenty miles an hour. She knew this road well and must have walked and driven it hundreds of times, yet in the fog it looked completely different. She tried to estimate how far from home she was but could discern no landmarks by which to judge it.

It wasn't a severe impact, just a jolt really. Fortunately Frances was sitting back in her seat at the time and her seat-belt held her firmly. She looked up into her rear-view mirror trying to distinguish who had collided with the rear of her car. She couldn't see much, just the dark outline of a long wide car. Although it didn't look like a Porsche, it suddenly occurred to her that the car might be Bird's. For a moment, and despite all the promises to herself, she was afraid again. She watched in her rear-view mirror as the driver's door opened and a figure walked around the car to the passenger's side. The figure crouched down and smiled in at her. She smiled back, leaning over the passenger seat and unlocking the door. He pulled the door open and stepped into Frances' car.

Standing by his study window, he watched as the white smoke disappeared over the village roof-tops. It was burning well. He knew he'd have to return to the garden later and pick up all the bits that the fire had failed to consume. Buttons, metal brooches; he'd always been slightly surprised at how many bits were left behind. Once he'd collected them he would dump them at various locations around the country so they would never be found, and even if they were, they wouldn't be linked to any of the killings.

He'd been disappointed that they hadn't been together, that would have saved time. Still, he had been lucky. He'd lost her for a while in the fog and thought he'd have to start planning it all over again, but then he'd quite literally bumped into her. He'd thought it was just good luck at first, but then he felt His hand guiding him through the mist to his ultimate destination.

'Two files completed, eighteen to go,' he murmured to himself. He reached forwards and pulled one down at random. He'd started to mix them up regularly so he'd have no idea who his next victim would be. After he'd selected his first three victims he'd decided that God should really be dictating the fate of the rest. They were all going to die, of course, but he felt he didn't have the right to decide the order, only God could do that. He opened the file, spilling its contents on to the desk and examined them. Most of the files contained basic details of a person's background, name, address, age and sometimes details of their place of work and car. The most important detail was the photograph. He'd managed to get one of every person. He was quite proud of that. He pinned the photograph on to the cork board by the side of the desk so he could look at it constantly and be reminded of what each one did.

He remembered this one; she'd been on the jury. He recollected the expression on her face when she saw him looking at her after they had announced the verdict. He hoped she'd remember him when her time came.

*   *   *

It was midday by the time Sam reached the village of Little Dorking. Although she'd set off straight after her morning list, the fog that had come down unexpectedly the night before still lingered and made driving both slow and difficult. By the time she reached the small Fenland village, however, the worst of the mist had been burnt away and the sun had begun to shine through its thin diminishing veil. She parked her car outside one of the local pubs, The Black Dog. It was a beautiful place, long and white with a thatched roof and small leaded windows. For all its beauty, however, Sam thought that the sign which swung gently outside its front entrance seemed strangely out of place. It depicted a large, snarling, jet black dog with bared teeth and red penetrating eyes. Sam couldn't help thinking that a picture of a black Labrador with a pheasant in its mouth would have been more appropriate. As she stepped out of her car she noticed two women watching her from the opposite side of the road. Their stare made Sam feel uneasy. There was something unusually intrusive about it, almost hostile. She decided to try a friendly smile but the moment she did the two women turned away and continued with their conversation, except that Sam felt sure that they were not really talking to each other, only waiting for another opportunity to stare at her. She turned and hurried into the hotel.

The reception desk was empty so Sam rang the bell on the desk and awaited a reply. The inside of the hotel was almost as charming as the exterior. Modern, but with sufficient of the original detail left to give the place a sense of age and interest. Opposite the desk was a large, open fireplace whose black sooty interior was clearly used regularly. At the bottom of the fireplace Sam noticed a series of interconnecting white rings. They reminded her a little of the Olympic emblem, only crude and slightly more spaced out. The receptionist, a short, plump, middle-aged woman finally arrived at the desk and smiled expectantly at Sam.

'Can I help?'

It was a warm smile and Sam appreciated it. 'Yes, I was wondering if you could give me directions to the Reverend Shaw's house?'

Still smiling, the receptionist walked out on to the street and Sam followed. With her arm extended like a mobile sign she gave her directions, 'Follow the road to the centre of the village and cross by the old memorial. Carry on following the road until you reach the old blacksmith's shop, then turn left on to Swallow Road and you'll see the vicarage on your right, about a hundred yards further along.'

As the woman began to move back towards the hotel Sam's curiosity finally got the better of her. 'Why have those white rings been painted at the bottom of the fireplace?'

'To stop witches coming down the chimney.'

'Ah.' Sam wasn't sure whether she was expected to smile or acknowledge the comment sagely. Finally, the woman turned and disappeared back into the hotel and Sam set off to follow her directions through the village.

Like many of the Fenland villages it was an old and

quaint place. A mixture of the old and the modern thrown together in a planning catastrophe. Whitewashed cottages with their small windows and doors leaned uncomfortably across uneven pavements and looked oddly out of place next to the modern shops and houses with their PVC windows and large glass shop-fronts. When she reached the market place she crossed the tarmacked road on to the cobbled surface. At the centre of the square was a large stone obelisk with several steps leading up to it. At first Sam thought it was a rather bland war memorial like hundreds of others in the area, commemorating the dead from two world wars. But as she got closer her curiosity was piqued. Etched on to the front of one of the base panels on which the obelisk stood was a crudely cut inscription:

IN SACRED MEMORY OF MABEL STEER
PUT TO DEATH BY BURNING ON THIS SPOT
IN 1722
THE LAST WITCH TO BE BURNT IN ENGLAND

Sam looked at the stone for a moment and imagined the screams of the woman as the flames began to lick around her body and burn her flesh. She remembered the pictures she'd seen in Simon's room and hoped that her end had come before the flames had reached her. The poor woman's only sin had probably been to practise a primitive form of medicine, an early ancestor of her own profession. But clever women intimidated men, and still did, she thought. Worse still, they intimidated the church, that bastion of male supremacy.

After one final look at the long brown stone she moved off towards the far side of the village. The directions she had been given were impeccable and she soon found herself walking up the gravelled path of a large redbrick Victorian vicarage. She'd seen similar buildings before but they had almost exclusively been turned into old people's homes or office buildings. This one, although looking a little run down and neglected, was clearly still used for the purpose it was intended and had a charm all of its own as a result. It had been Sam's dream for many years to own a house like this, but she knew it wasn't practical for one person to live in such a large place. When, and if, she ever had children she could perhaps consider it. Though, given her terrible luck with men, she was becoming increasingly pessimistic about the likelihood of children. She walked up to the large white door and hammered loudly upon it. She heard her knock echo through the house but there was no response. The sound of soft padding on the gravel made her turn her head and look along the side of the house. Plodding towards her was an old brown Labrador bitch. Her head was down but her tail wagged gently from side to side in a friendly expression.

Sam crouched down and stroked her head and ears. 'Where's your master then, eh? Where is he?'

As if understanding her question, the dog turned and began to make her way towards the back of the house. Sam followed. As she rounded the corner she was confronted with a view of a striking garden. At first sight it had the appearance of wild disorganization but Sam could discern a plan and realized that a discriminating mind had been at work.

She watched the labrador as it plodded its way across the garden to a figure in a thick Aran jumper kneeling by the side of the vegetable patch and lay down beside him. Sam made her way towards the figure, admiring the skilful combination of wild and cultivated plants. As she approached, the figure spoke without turning, 'You must be Dr Ryan?'

Sam was taken aback, 'Yes, but . . .'

Continuing to pick snails off his vegetables, he answered her question, 'Don't be so surprised. Simon Clark told me you might visit, and as no one else ever visits me in the middle of the day it wasn't a very clever deduction.'

Sam chuckled, impressed. 'Oh, I see.'

'I understand you're interested in the murder of old Charlie Ironsmith?'

'Yes.'

'Let me just get these last couple of . . . there that's got them.' He dropped his last two victims into a large bucket of salt water. 'Only way to kill them really. Tried pesticides; they kill the slugs all right but just about every other useful creature in the garden as well.' He looked into the bucket. 'The evenings are the best time, of course, but I was away last night. Fortunately the day's damp enough to tempt them out at the moment. Got over a hundred one night, quite a record, eh?'

Sam looked into the bucket of dead molluscs. As she looked up she noticed the Reverend Shaw looking at her closely. 'Simon described you very well.'

Sam felt slightly embarrassed by the vicar's attention and could feel her face begin to colour. He wasn't what she'd expected. Although he looked younger, Sam estimated he must have been at least in his mid-forties, tall and slim with a handsome chiselled face and a crop of curly black hair. Although her mouth didn't actually fall open she felt that it should. She also felt a sense of guilt at being attracted to a vicar. He noticed her discomfort and smiled at her. 'It's been a few years since I brought a flush to a woman's face.'

'There's no Mrs Shaw then?'

'She died.'

Sam felt embarrassed. 'I'm sorry.'

'Thank you, it's been a while now. Car crash, drunken driver. Still miss her.'

For a moment his face became sad and tense. Then he smiled and his face calmed again. 'Fancy some tea?'

'That sounds nice.'

They walked off towards the kitchen at the back of the vicarage discussing the finer points of cottage gardening and closely followed by the faithful Peggy.

Tom Adams was driving his car along King Street when he first noticed the commotion. He'd been forced to stop behind a queue of traffic which had, in its turn, been stopped by a coach full of Japanese tourists taking endless photographs of King's College. Patience was a virtue in Cambridge; it was a small town with enough activities for a large city and student life seemed to dominate everything. At times he found himself resenting their presence, but would then remember how important they were to the economic life of the city. They provided work for thousands of people, they used the local shops, restaurants and cafés, and the tourists who came to see the colleges and experience their ambience added millions to local coffers. For now, however, his concentration was taken up by a group of drunken youths who were staggering their way down King Street towards him. He thought they were students at first, but as they drew closer they didn't look quite right; wrong clothes, wrong attitude, these were local kids who'd had too big a sniff at the barmaid's apron. Suddenly, one of the youths leaped on to the bonnet of a nearby car and began to jump up and down on it, crumpling the thin metalwork into the engine. Adams jumped out of his car but before he had time to intervene, two uniformed police officers, helmets in hand, came running along King Street towards them. The group of youths standing on the pavement cheering their friend on spotted them in time and, sobering up quickly, turned and ran. The youth on the car, however, was not quite so lucky and in his haste to jump down from the car slipped and fell. Before he had time to scramble to his feet, the two police officers were upon him. They lay him face down in the street and handcuffed him before picking him up roughly and pinning him up against a wall whilst they radioed for help. Adams hadn't had a clear look at the youth until they picked him up, then as he struggled and shouted abuse at the arresting officers he turned his face towards him. It was Ricky, Sam's nephew.

As Sam walked through the house to the sitting-room

she was surprised at how bright and modern it was. Victorian fittings and fitments which were an integral part of the structure of the interior remained but everything else she saw, from the curtains to the prints on the walls, was boldly contemporary and strikingly colourful. Even the crucifixes and other religious *objets d'art* scattered around the house were modern and highly stylized. Only one object looked slightly out of place, a large photograph of Shaw in army uniform surrounded by some very tough-looking men, all of whom were leaning on an ancient Jaguar car.

'Tea.'

Sam turned from the picture to see the Reverend Shaw enter the room with a large wooden tray containing two china cups, an old brown teapot and plates full of scones and jam. He put the tray down on a small side table and Sam walked across to join him. 'It's only English Breakfast, I'm afraid. I'm a bit old-fashioned about tea.'

Sam sat in the large armchair opposite him. 'That's fine. I'm not a smelly tea fan either. Do I detect a female hand in the décor?'

The Reverend Shaw began to pour the tea using a silver strainer to catch the wet leaves. 'Indeed you do. My wife had a love of the contemporary and ran a thriving small business in interior design for like-minded individuals before she . . . Well, anyway, I'm happy to keep reminders of her around me.'

'I hadn't realized you'd been in the army?'

'Territorial, I was the padre for a local parachute battalion.'

'Bit of an odd profession for a man of God.'

'I was attached to the medical corps, first aid, that sort of thing.'

'You don't think you could kill anyone then?'

'I shouldn't think so, but who knows? Depends on the circumstances, I suppose.' He changed the subject, 'Now what do you want to know about poor old Charlie?' He finished pouring and handed a cup to Sam.

'As much as you can tell me,' she sipped at her tea, 'I'm probably barking up the wrong tree but there are certain similarities between the death of Charlie and a murder I'm dealing with in Cambridge.'

'The James murder?'

'Yes, as it happens.'

'I read about that, terrible business, awful, so young. Any closer to catching your killer?'

'No, not really, the police have a suspect, but I'm not sure.'

'Any evidence?'

'A few fibres, but that's about all.'

The Reverend Shaw sat back, still interested. 'What kind of fibres are they?'

'One's from a woollen garment of some sort, and the others are horsehair.'

'Horsehair, how peculiar.'

Sam began to feel a little uncomfortable with his questioning and feared she had revealed more than she ought. 'They've both been eliminated. You seem very interested in the case?'

'Bit of an Agatha Christie fan; I find crime fascinating. Don't get much chance to talk of such things in a backwater like this. The Ironsmith case was the only interesting thing to happen in the village for three hundred years.'

Sam brought the conversation back to the subject. 'Simon tells me you're a bit of an expert on the case.'

'I know something of it, much of it village gossip though. You know what places like this are like. Chief Inspector Romer was your man.'

'Where can I find him?'

'Graveyard next door, I'm afraid. You're a few years too late.'

Sam was intrigued, 'What happened?'

'Nothing sinister, cancer, poor man. I officiated at his funeral, first one I did after coming to the village. The murder became an obsession with him, even after his death. He insisted that he was buried in the local churchyard, sort of a permanent reminder to the killer that he was still around. Caused quite a stir at the time. Only case he failed to solve apparently.'

'What can you tell me about Charlie?'

'You know he was black? I think he and his brother must have been the first black people in the area. There are still not that many. Anyway a lot of people were afraid of him.'

Sam cut in, 'Because he was black?'

'Partly, I think, but they also thought he was a warlock. A male witch. There were a lot of strange things associated with old Charlie, a lot of stories too.'

Sam became increasingly interested. 'Like what?'

'Well, the strangest one is in here.' He picked a heavy leather-bound book off the table by the side of his chair,

Folklores, Customs and Superstitions of the Fenlands by the Reverend Clive Moulton, a predecessor of mine. He was the first person to write about the legend of the black dog. Didn't Simon tell you about it?'

Sam shook her head and remembered to take another sip of tea before it cooled.

'The hotel in the village is named after it.' Sam remembered the sign outside the hotel where she parked. Shaw continued, 'In 1910 a ploughboy came across a large black dog while working in a local field. He saw it at the same time, dusk, on eight successive occasions. The boy, who had been on his own when he saw the giant animal, told the other farm-workers of his experience but, of course, they just laughed and teased him. The following evening, however, the boy was visited again but this time instead of disappearing the dog turned into a headless woman. The apparition then proceeded to glide hair-raisingly through the youth's body causing him to faint. The same evening the boy's brother was killed when he fell under the wheels of a cart. Ever since that time the sighting of the dog has always been synonymous with a violent death of some sort.'

Although it was lunch-time Marcia Evans had decided to work on in the lab. It was the only time she could guarantee the solitude she needed to work on the ivy they'd found inside the tomb without the risk of being asked awkward questions. She examined it through a powerful magnifying glass. The main interest of her examination was the knot at the centre of the garland. As she looked at it she tried to draw its shape on a small scrap of paper. Once satisfied with her drawing, she put down her magnifying glass and took the paper along the corridor to George Bishop's office.

Her luck was in. George was sitting by one of the lab's work surfaces engrossed in this month's copy of *Yachting Monthly*, while at the same time trying to pull a small piece of his corned beef sandwich from between his teeth with his fingers. Although George was one of the lab's firearms experts he was also a keen yachtsman who'd written numerous books on the subject, the most important of which, for Marcia, was the definitive book on knots.

She knocked and entered the lab. George looked up. He was always pleased to see Marcia. She had to be the most attractive girl in the lab, he thought, certainly had the greatest legs. He watched her as she crossed the lab trying to imagine what she'd look like lying on top of him in the cabin of his boat. He'd invited her out for a day's sailing a couple of times but she'd always resisted. Although he was forty-three, overweight and married with three children, he still thought he was in with a chance. He finally pulled the piece of annoying meat from the back of his teeth and after inspecting it closely, wiped it on to his sandwich bag.

'You've decided to come sailing with me at last?'

Marcia smiled thinly, she'd often seen him watching her and when they had a conversation his eyes seldom roamed from her breasts. It didn't make her feel uncomfortable, just amused her. She was more than capable of handling the George Bishops of this world, but by occasionally flirting and acting the naïve innocent, she knew she was more likely to get what she needed from him. 'Maybe, depends whether you can help me with this?'

The merest hint that Marcia might be changing her mind about the trip had George interested. He wiped his hands down his lab coat and took the piece of paper on which Marcia had drawn the knot and examined it quickly.

'Do you recognize that knot?'

Bishop nodded. 'Good drawing, obviously good with your hands.'

Marcia raised her eyebrows at him, flirtatiously.

'It's a surgeon's knot. Developed in 1918 during the First War by a surgeon called William Speakman.'

Marcia continued smiling at him, eager for more information.

'It starts with a right over left, then a left over right . . .'

Marcia cut in, 'Sounds like a reef knot.'

Bishop looked impressed.

'I was a brownie.'

'Still got the uniform?'

Marcia gave a false laugh of amusement.

'Well, um, it's almost a reef knot but it does have slight differences. It's left over right, right over left, but the right over left again.'

'Do surgeons still use it?'

'Some. There are others, but this one's still in use.'

Marcia took her drawing from him and glanced at it again.

'Why do you need to know? One of your jobs?'

'No, but if I'm coming sailing with you I thought it might be a good idea to learn about a few knots first.'

She held both wrists together in front of her. At the sight of this Bishop's eyes widened and, thinking she might have pushed him a bit too far, Marcia skipped out of the lab, quickly returning to her own desk to ring Sam.

Sam reached into her bag and pulled out a small glass bottle containing a section of the ivy which she had found inside the tomb. She passed it across to Shaw. 'I found this inside the tomb where James' body was discovered.'

Shaw held it up in front of his face and examined it myopically.

'I'm told you're a bit of an expert on ivy as well.'

'Expert? I'm not sure about that, but I certainly dabble.'

'Can you tell me anything about this? It's not all there I'm afraid, the boffins have most of it.'

Shaw leaned back, lowering the sample. 'It's rather brown around the edges, but I think I can help. You say it was found in the graveyard?'

Sam nodded. 'Yes, I think it might have been tied around Mark James' wrist.'

'It would make sense if you think, and you clearly do, that there is some kind of ritualistic element to the James murder. Most of these rituals are carried out on consecrated land.'

'I thought Charlie was killed at the top of a hill?'

'Oh, he was, but Primrose Hill certainly comes under

that definition. It's been associated with witchcraft and devil worship for as long as anyone can remember. When was your man murdered?'

'We're not entirely sure, he went missing on 20 September.'

Shaw nodded sagely. 'The day after, the twenty-first, is the Autumn Equinox, one of the witches' eight great Sabbaths. They're periods well-known to occultists, a time of psychic stress and hauntings. It comes just before the end of the month of the vine and begins the month of the ivy.'

'When's the next one?'

'Thirty-first of October, Samhain, Hallowe'en to you and me. The beginning of the Celtic winter. The dark forces come out with a vengeance for that one.'

Sam suddenly straightened up. 'But that's today!'

'Has anything happened?'

'Not that I know of.'

'Looks like you've got away with it then.'

Sam looked at him, uncertain whether he was making fun of her.

Graham Dawes looked at the two young golden retrievers as they bounded about their compound in his back garden. Although they were only six months old they were already huge and almost impossible to control. He'd tried training classes but they'd been an abject failure; he wasn't sure if it had been his fault or the dogs'. He was too soft, but now he was left with only three options. To have them put down, to sell them, or give them away. He thought he'd try selling them first and if that didn't work, well . . . he shrugged to himself. The two adolescent dogs jumped up at the fence, their eyes bright and clear and their tails wagging furiously. He'd have to walk them soon. A swift pint down the local and then he'd give them the run of the park for half an hour; that should do the trick, he thought. He stuck his hand through the fence and let them lick his fingers for a few moments before walking off to fetch their leads.

It was a large greenhouse and very impressive. Inside were rare orchids of every description and the variations of shape and hue were wonderful. Shaw was clearly proud of his collection and boasted that he cultivated plants from the four corners of the world. Sam walked in to the greenhouse and was assailed by a heady aroma; she looked around her in delight and dismay and located the source of the aroma as a *stephanotis* plant nestling amongst the flamboyant orchids. Sam put her nose close to one of the trumpet-shaped blooms and breathed in deeply. The smell was overwhelming and delicious. It had to be because the formalin was beginning to take its toll on her nose just as it had on dozens of her friends' and colleagues'. When the effect became too pronounced her time as a pathologist would be over. For of all her senses, smell was, for her, the most important. Even if her sight failed her at some time in her life and she couldn't see her garden and plants she could at least smell them, and she wasn't sure that life would be worth living without that pleasure.

As Sam and Shaw made their way to the back of the greenhouse the look changed dramatically. Here was the most comprehensive collection of ivy plants Sam could have imagined. Every shape, size, and shade were represented. The Reverend Shaw emptied the small section of ivy on to the bench in front of him before turning to Sam. 'When did you lose your faith?'

Sam was totally taken aback by the question and her mind raced for an answer. Shaw answered for her, 'When someone who was close to you died.'

Sam could do nothing but nod.

'I thought so, it's normally the case.'

'How did you know?'

'I watched you examine some of my crucifixes. I'm a bit of a collector. There was interest but no passion. I even thought I detected a certain resentment. Sorry to embarrass you. I'm a great people watcher, comes with the territory.'

'My father, he was murdered when I was young, I saw it happen.' Sam couldn't understand why she was telling him this, she'd never told anyone else. He smiled at her as if he understood and then returned to the ivy, leaving Sam unsure and more than a little rattled. It was a feeling she didn't enjoy.

'There are ten species of ivy and you have managed to find one of the rarer ones.'

Sam stepped closer to him and looked down at the ivy on the bench. 'Really?'

'*Hedera Hibernica*. It's the wrong one, but it's rare. There's only one type of ivy associated with the occult and that's *Helix Poetica*, the poets' ivy. It was the one found around Charlie's wrist when they discovered him.'

'Are you sure?'

'Absolutely, your witches don't seem very well-informed do they?'

Sam raised her eyebrows at him.

'Let me show you.'

He reached up to a shelf in front of him taking down a large tray of ivy and putting it down on the bench. 'This,' he indicated to the tray of ivy, 'is *Helix Poetica*. Now, if you compare that with the example you brought me, the *Hedera Hibernica*, you'll notice several things.' He reached into his pocket and retrieved a magnifying glass which he had brought with him. He handed it to Sam who began to examine the leaves. 'You'll see that the veins on the *Hibernica* are far more pronounced and white in colour. The leaves are slightly larger too. The biggest difference will come later in the year when the *Poetica* will be covered with rather attractive orange berries.'

Without looking up Sam asked, 'What about the *Hibernica*?'

'That's only found wild in one area of the country, down by the Helford River in Cornwall. Although I understand that Kew has some fine examples.'

'Can it be propagated?'

'Oh yes, quite easily. As you can see it's an attractive plant.'

Sam handed back his magnifying glass and nodded. Shaw continued, 'I had a young man here a few years ago who was fascinated by the Ironsmith story. Even took cuttings of the ivy. He was going to write a book. Now, what was his name? Named after an animal of some sort.'

'Sebastian Bird?'

'Yes, that was it, Bird.'

Malcolm Purvis had arrived home early in the morning, having hired an estate car and driven back from London rather than catch the train the previous night. He wasn't sure how he would have managed going by train even in first class and the reports of thick fog had deterred him from attempting the journey until the morning. He lifted the pram from the back of the car before dragging it step at a time up to the front door.

He had become increasingly concerned about Frances. He'd left plenty of messages on the answer phone but she hadn't returned one. He unlocked the door and pulled the pram inside. The curtains were still closed and although the house was in darkness and he couldn't see them, the smell of the freshly cut flowers hit him at once. Their odour was everywhere, he hadn't smelt anything like it since his wife had died. This was Frances' work, he thought, and he loved her all the more for it. He turned on the lights and walked around the house calling his daughter's name. He even went into the garden, but there was no reply. Stepping down into the garage he noticed her car was gone too. Walking into the sitting-room he switched on the answer phone. The only messages were the ones he'd left, Frances had clearly never heard them. As the final message ended a dark apprehension began to descend over him. He picked up the phone and pressed in the numbers 999.

He'd enjoyed his pint, well three actually. The dogs had waited in the car for over an hour and now he felt guilty, so he'd driven on a few miles to give them a run across the Abbey grounds. It was an impressive sight, normally illuminated in the darkness by a dozen spotlights which shone their powerful lights upwards across the ruined walls. But the Abbey had been closed for some weeks now for urgent repairs and he had been forced to find a way across the fields and through a hole in a nearby hedge. He lit a cigarette as he watched his dogs race across the park towards the ruins, bounding and chasing each other in large circles. The nights were drawing in quickly now and the scene was gloomy. As the dogs moved further away from him he shouted to them, 'Pip, Max, here. Come here.'

They ignored him and raced towards the Abbey, jumping over a low stone wall and disappearing into the ruins. 'Bastards,' he thought, realizing he'd have to cross the park to fetch them. Dawes was a large man used to long drinks and short walks. He'd bought the dogs to provide an incentive to improve his fitness but he'd soon tired of them and as his inherent laziness took over, the walks had become shorter. As he made his way towards the Abbey the dogs began to bark furiously, frightened and confused at what they didn't understand. Their barking didn't sound natural and had a sort of hollow ring. For a moment Dawes was frightened but his curiosity got the better of him and he began to search for his dogs. He finally arrived at a set of steps leading down below the Abbey. The sound of barking was definitely coming from the bottom of the stairs. He called to them but there was no response. For a moment he was undecided but, finally plucking up the courage, he pulled a small torch from his pocket and slowly descended. He shone his torch on to a large oak door which stood half open with its metal lock hanging loose, having been forcibly ripped from its mounting. He squeezed his rather portly body through the gap between the wall and the door and found himself inside a large chamber. From its design it was clearly some sort of private chapel although in a poor state of repair. His dogs were both standing back from the altar at the far side of the chamber barking furiously at something lying prostrate across the top of it. Graham Dawes pulled their leads from his coat pocket and walked towards them. His approach didn't, as he had expected, calm them and for the first time he looked across in the direction they were barking to see what was causing them so much agitation. What he saw made him stagger back.

'Oh my God, oh my God!'

He grabbed the dogs by the collar and secured their leads, his eyes never leaving the awful sight by the altar as he dragged them backwards, finally turning and stumbling in panic back up the stairs.

CHAPTER SIX

The web covered her entire face like a grotesque veil refusing to reveal the beauty beneath. However, it failed to hide her agony. She had died hard, howling against her fate, her mouth open and fixed in a silent scream. Adams watched as the web's occupant, a large brown and cream spider, suddenly crawled towards its struggling prey. The fly had been caught directly over the girl's mouth as it had gone to lay its eggs in the deepest recesses of her dead body, and was now engaged in a life and death battle which it was bound to lose. Soon the fly was still and the spider began to wrap his web tightly around the paralysed body. He knew he shouldn't, nothing at the scene of a murder should ever be touched, but it was too much for him. He leaned down and plucked the spider from its web. It didn't come away easily and pulled part of the web away with it. Part of it had been attached to a long engraved silver ear-ring and as the web released it from its hold it rocked gently. Adams didn't want to kill the spider, he'd seen enough death for one day. He placed the small insect gently on to a nearby wall and watched as it scuttled off into a dark recess before returning to the scene.

Detective Superintendent Farmer arrived at the scene later than usual, in a vile mood. She'd been on the other side of the county on an enquiry when the call had come in, and her fool of a driver had not had the intelligence to mention it to her until she'd returned to the car. She consoled herself with the thought that she'd make sure he was back plodding the cold streets of Cambridge before the month was out. She gave no quarter; she had certainly received none during her career.

Logging in with the PC on the gate, she began to follow the taped path to the scene. Half-way towards the ruins she noticed Adams walking towards her. Without stopping for breath she started her interrogation, 'Who found her?'

'A chap walking his dogs.'

'I'm going to start a "man walking his dog" section, they seem to turn up more crime than we do.' Who is she?'

'Frances Purvis.'

The name made her stop for a moment as she began to feel the anger well up inside her. 'Bird's girlfriend?'

Adams nodded.

'Bastard. What did I tell you? There's going to be a lot of very awkward questions asked about this one. I hope the press hangs them out to bloody dry. I want him in, I don't care what you have to do, or who you have to do it to but I want him in.'

'It's all in hand. With a bit of luck they'll have picked him up by now.'

Farmer walked on without responding further, Adams followed. She descended the stairs quickly and was soon inside the chapel. She'd attended many murder scenes and seen more bodies than she cared to remember but despite that, this one still shocked her. Perhaps, she thought, it was because they'd met, she'd known her, although only briefly. It made all the difference. Most deaths, no matter how horrible, could be viewed with a degree of detachment and the only real grief was that of the family and friends, but that was expected and most members of the force learned to deal with it in this way. But when you've seen the difference between a vibrant life and an horrific death, it was brought closer.

She remembered Frances coming to the police station with her father to give them the information about Bird and James. Everyone, even she, had been struck by her beauty and zest for life. She had clearly slipped off the rails for a while and fallen in with an undesirable crowd, but she was intelligent and gave a clear and articulate account of what had occurred on the night of James' death; she'd have made a good witness, Farmer thought. Now all that was left lay at her feet, twisted and bloated like some dead animal carcass left in a field to rot. She watched Owen, the police surgeon, making his notes.

'How long's she been dead?'

'Couple of days, I think. Strangled. You'll have to wait for the pathologist to be sure though. I don't want to get into trouble again.'

Farmer looked across at Adams. 'Where is she?'

'On her way.'

'She always is.'

Farmer was secretly pleased Sam was late. She took a

perverse delight in displaying self-righteous indignation at Sam's inability to arrive promptly at a scene and she rather feared that one day Sam would arrive first. Still, by current evidence there was little chance of that, she thought smugly to herself. Farmer's thoughts returned to the body.

'This is a public park, why has it taken so long to find her?'

'It's been closed for the last couple of weeks for urgent repairs, some of the walls are in a bit of a state. The bloke that found her shouldn't even have been here. His dogs ran off and he followed them.'

Owen made his last few scribblings before packing his bag away. 'I'll let you have my report in the morning.'

Farmer nodded as Owen disappeared back up the stairs.

Sam had got the call as she drove back from Little Dorking. She had sworn at one time that she would never use a mobile phone but had slowly accepted its usefulness and felt she would now be lost without it. For once she knew exactly where the murder scene was. She'd been there with her mother the previous summer for a picnic. It had been one of the last occasions she could remember her mother still being her mother and not the rather sad figure she had become since her mind and memories had begun to decay. She remembered leaving her mother sitting in the warm sun while she explored the ancient ruins. Although still a majestic sight, the Abbey's decaying grandeur saddened her. She remembered standing on one of the last remaining walls and shading her eyes from the sun to look out across the ruins towards her mother who sat dozing happily under a large oak tree, relieved for the moment from the knowledge of the creeping inertia in her mind. She seemed to fit in well with the surroundings. The once consequential, now slowly decaying to the steady beat of time. Shelley's words floated into her mind: 'My name is Ozymandias, king of kings: Look on my works, ye Mighty, and despair!'

She spotted Richard Owen as she made her way towards the Abbey. He was at least wearing protective overalls this time. She had already made the decision not to stop and chat, she was late enough and nothing he could tell her was going to make the slightest difference to her own findings. When Owen saw her he waved and stopped, preparing to summarize his findings. She swept by him, 'Sorry Richard, can't stop. I'm late. I'll read your report later.'

Giving him a half wave Sam disappeared into the grounds leaving Owen feeling slightly bemused.

The moment she entered the chamber Sam had realized she was dealing with the same mind that had killed James. This time the cross, which had been cut deep into the front of the girl's body, was clear and vivid. By the side of the cord which had bitten into the girl's neck, was the long brass wind chime just as before. She looked across at the girl's left arm which was spread out by her side. Around her wrist and almost concealed by the clear plastic bag that had been tied over her hand, was a garland of dark green ivy. Sam crouched down and, gently pulling it clear of the bag, examined it carefully. At that moment she realized that whatever the murders were about, they had nothing to do with witchcraft. She laid the girl's arm gently back on to the ground and, opening her medical bag, began her preliminary examination.

PC Carver couldn't help feeling resentful that his lack of experience excluded him from most of the exciting events. When the body had been discovered the station had almost emptied as everyone went to help or just gape. Murder in this part of the world was still an unusual event and one not to be missed. He'd managed to get as far as the station yard before he'd been called back and told to cover the area car while everyone was busy. Still, he reflected, this was better than nothing. It was the first time he had actually been let out on his own in the car! Perhaps this was his big chance. Perhaps while the rest of them were stuck up at the Abbey he could make the big discovery and solve the case. They'd have to be impressed by that. He drove slowly along the main road feeling self-important and musing that he was probably the only effective law enforcement for miles. All those people relying on him for protection and he wasn't yet twenty-one; it made him feel good.

Whilst lost in his thoughts, his eyes picked up the shadow that moved rapidly across the front of his Panda. The dull thud and scream that came from the front of the car let him know that he had hit something. He braked hard and stopped, peering through the windscreen to see if he could spot what it was. He opened the car door just in time to see the vixen run, limping and screaming, through a farm gate into a recently ploughed field. The blood from her injured leg covered the ground by the side of his car and left a trail into the field. She's not going to get far in that state he thought, he'd have to try and finish her. He pulled his truncheon from his side pocket and began to follow the trail, using his torch to guide him. The field was large and black and there wasn't a sound, he'd never find her. She'd probably crawl into some shallow hole or under shrubbery and die quietly, he thought. He clipped his truncheon back on to his belt and was about to leave when he saw the car. It was parked tightly behind a hedgerow. He walked across to it flashing his torch across its length. At first he thought it might be a courting couple, but he soon discovered the car was uninhabited. He returned to the back of the car and flashed his torch across the number plate. Taking hold of his radio he held it close to his mouth, '1623 to Control, over.'

'Control to 1623, go ahead over.'

'PNC. Check please, Control.'

The voice at the other end seemed none too pleased at his request, 'Given the situation is the check considered necessary at this time?'

He thought it was. 'Yes, over.'

The voice was still exasperated. 'Go ahead, over.'

'Blue Renault registration number L, lima, seven eight four, Fox-trot, Yankee, Oscar. Over.'

'Stand by.'

While he waited he decided to examine the car further. From the impact damage at the back of the car it appeared to have been involved in a recent accident.

It worried him. Probably just pushed it in here while they arranged for it to be towed away, he thought. More stick when he got back to the station. His radio crackled back into life. 'No trace lost or stolen. Registered owner a Malcolm Purvis from The Gables, Fereham.'

'Thank you, control.'

He decided that at least he would pay Mr Purvis a call and see what was going on. He got back into his car and started it before turning the heater up to full blast and feeling the warm air drift over his exposed face and hands. He was about to pull away when his radio crackled back into life. This time it was not the control room operator but his inspector, 'Control 1623, are you still with the car, over?'

He called back, 'Yes, over.'

'Stay with it. We're sending up some help. It may have been used in connection with the murder up at the Abbey.'

PC Carver could feel the excitement begin to surge through his body. The radio crackled back into life once again. It was his inspector, 'And well done.'

PC Carver could almost feel his chest swell. He straightened his cap, pulled on his black leather gloves and returned to the field to guard his exhibit.

The preliminary examination finished, Sam packed away her tape recorder and pulled off her gloves. She glanced at her watch. 'PM at nine if that suits everyone?'

Farmer nodded, and as she was the only one who counted, Sam took it as an acceptance and left, closely followed by Farmer, eager for information. 'What can you tell us?'

Sam continued walking back along the taped path. 'I can't be entirely sure yet. I'll know more once I've carried out the PM, but I'd say she was almost certainly murdered by the same person that killed Mark James.'

'I guessed that much myself,' snorted Farmer. 'We should have Bird back in tonight.'

'You're still convinced it was him then?'

'Oh yes, it was Bird all right and if you'd come up with the evidence when I asked, that poor little girl in there would still be alive. I hope you can live with that.'

Sam stopped and turned angrily on Farmer, 'If the evidence had been there I'd have found it. It wasn't and I'm not going out on a limb for you or anyone else!'

Farmer quickly fired back, 'Even if it means an innocent young girl dies?'

Sam was equal to it, 'Don't you blame me for your cock-ups. You arrested Bird on nothing and then expected me to sort it out for you. Well, I don't work that way. Just try getting it right for once then perhaps that "poor little girl" *would* still be alive!'

Sam began to walk back along the taped path but stopped after only a few steps and turned back to Farmer, 'And for what it's worth, Bird didn't do it, you are wrong.'

For a moment Farmer was stunned and contemplated going after the rapidly disappearing pathologist but thought better of it, deciding to talk to her later after the PM when things had cooled down a little. She turned and walked slowly back to the scene. She was confident of her suspicions over Bird but Sam seemed equally confident and a small germ of disquiet was waiting to grow given a moment's weakness. She would not allow it to do so.

It had only taken Sam forty minutes to get home. She looked at her watch and sighed. It would be dawn soon. It had been very quiet when she'd arrived, only a high-pitched beeping filling the emptiness of her cottage. She walked across to the machine and switched it on. It was Marcia.

'I've made rather an interesting discovery about the knot in the ivy. Give me a call when you can. Oh, and thanks for the other night. I had a great time, I think.'

It was the only call and the machine switched itself off. Sam instinctively reached for the phone but then remembering the time stopped herself, writing a mental note in her head to ring Marcia the following morning. She decided it was hardly worth going to bed. Besides, she knew she wouldn't sleep, her mind was too active, full of calculations and theories. She changed quickly, slipping on her gardening boots before making her way out to the garden shed. It seemed the ideal time to finish planting the bushes she'd purchased a few days before. Switching on the security light which illuminated the garden, she collected her shovel and began to dig a large hole in the border at the far side of the garden. It was only here in her garden that she felt completely relaxed. Here she felt at one with her thoughts, emptying her mind of the day's rubbish and concentrating on the relevant. Although it was hard, she worked vigorously whilst her mind went over the circumstances of the two murders. She knew she wasn't just angry at Farmer but was also questioning herself and her own ability. What if Bird was the killer; perhaps Farmer was right, although the evidence was pretty circumstantial and weak. She wasn't a policeman after all, only a pathologist. Maybe this time she'd overstepped the mark. Had she missed something? Perhaps she could have made more of the evidence. If she had, then the murderer, Bird or whoever, might have been identified and the girl might still be alive. She bashed her spade into the ground in frustration and anger, breaking up the soil before shovelling it out and throwing it to the side. She decided the hole was big enough and began to drag the bush towards it. Suddenly a voice broke through the cold night air.

'Need a hand?'

Sam turned sharply to be confronted by the smiling face of Tom Adams. She was tired and in a bad mood. She didn't want to see Tom or any other policeman right now. She tried to make her feelings felt.

'You and Farmer are a double act, are you? Well, I've met the funny one so you must be the stooge.'

Adams smiled at the insult, he'd certainly been called worse. He walked up to her and started to help her pull the bush towards the hole she had just prepared for it.

'Stop me if you've heard this one, but do you know the story of the superintendent who's having to deal with two murders in a month and whose main suspect is walking around as free as a . . . Bird?'

Sam wasn't impressed. 'That's her problem.'

They reached the hole and dropped the bush into it.

'Thought it might be yours as well.'

Sam began to water the bush with the garden hose. 'Why should it be?'

'She's the first woman detective superintendent this force has ever had, and there's plenty of people that would like to see her take a fall. Some are already seeing this as their chance to give her a bit of a push. She might seem tough but she's still frightened of failing.'

Sam turned off the hose and looked at him. 'Aren't we all.'

Sam was suddenly pleased he was there. She looked into his face and wondered if he was as supportive of her as he was of Farmer. She found herself becoming slightly jealous of his relationship with his boss. Suddenly, realizing she'd been staring at him rather longer than was natural, Sam quickly turned her back to hide her embarrassment, beginning to fill the hole with soil. Adams was slightly nonplussed. For a moment he thought he'd detected a certain warmth but he was clearly wrong and realized that he was being dismissed. She was certainly no pushover, he thought. He hesitated for a moment, not wanting to end another encounter on a sour note.

'Do you need any more help with the Triffid?'

'No thanks, I've about finished.' She sighed and relented a little. She could tell by the tone of his voice that she'd made him feel awkward. She didn't really want him to leave quite so quickly.

'If you really want to help you could make some tea.'

'For two?'

Sam nodded and Adams disappeared into the kitchen.

* * *

Malcolm Purvis had searched everywhere. All her old haunts, friends, Bird's club and house and, although there was no sign of Frances, there was no sign of Bird either. It wasn't that he distrusted the police but they didn't know her as he did and he felt he had more chance of finding her. He'd even managed to get in touch with the woman in charge of their 'good parenting' class. She'd confirmed that Frances had attended the class and had left in good spirits, promising to drag her father there the following week, come what may. He parked the car in the garage, locked it and made his way inside. He looked at the pram, rocking it for a moment as he began to feel the weight of emotion take him over. The ring on the doorbell came as a welcome relief. He ran to the door and swung it open hoping to see his daughter's contrite face and to listen to her lame excuses, but he knew he wouldn't mind where she'd been. She would be safe, and that was all that mattered.

Policemen have a way of telling you everything without ever opening their mouths. He learned a lot about their facial expressions in court and prided himself that no matter how bland or disinterested they tried to make themselves, he could still read what they were thinking. So he knew what they'd come to tell him before they spoke and had to resist the temptation to slam the door against them. If he wasn't told then it wasn't true.

'Mr Purvis?'

'Yes.'

'I wonder if we could come in for a moment, sir?'

He stood for a second, barring their way. 'She's dead, isn't she?'

The inspector and the young policewoman by his side looked uncomfortable. 'Can we just come in, sir?'

Malcolm Purvis threw his head back, staring blankly through his tears towards the dark sky. The scream seemed to come from his very soul, its entire energy concentrated through his open mouth. Its intensity frightened the young, inexperienced policewoman and made her step back. The inspector had seen it all before and, wrapping his arms around Malcolm, held him firmly, like a father holding an injured child.

Sam was sitting on the small, wooden garden bench which she had sited at the back of her garden where it captured the view over the open countryside during the daylight hours. By her side Tom Adams sipped at his steaming mug of tea. Sam held her mug up to him.

'Nice tea.'

'Years of practice; you learn a thing or two in the police you know.'

Sam smiled, she enjoyed his sense of humour. 'I'm glad to hear it.'

Tom smiled briefly before his mood changed. 'I need to talk to you about Ricky.'

'You're not going to arrest him for the cigarette machine are you?'

'No, we came to an agreement about that one, but he has been arrested.'

Sam was shocked. 'Whatever for?'

'Criminal damage. He'd one too many and decided

to turn the bonnet of some poor unfortunate's car into a trampoline.'

Sam was exasperated. 'Are they sure it was him?'

Adams fidgeted in embarrassment. 'I saw him do it, sorry.'

Sam gazed across the darkened fields. 'Why should you be sorry, he did it. Bloody idiot.'

'He's young and he was pretty drunk.'

'That's no excuse. God knows what Wyn's going to say when she finds out. She's got enough on her plate without this. He's not likely to go to prison or anything is he?'

'I don't think so. I've had a word with the arresting officer, he's an old mate, I think I can probably sort it out. Depends whether we can square off the car's owner or not. Paying for the damage should do it.'

'You'll be lucky. Ricky's out of work and Wyn's having trouble making ends meet as it is. How much is it?'

Reaching into his jacket pocket, Adams produced an estimate and handed it to her.

'How much! What was it, a Rolls Royce?' She read it again. 'He's not a bad boy, you know, just having a bad time. If I pay up will it keep the little idiot out of court?'

'I can't promise that . . . But I'll see what I can do.'

'Thanks, Tom, I appreciate it.'

Adams had put himself out on a limb for her and having someone else take some of the responsibility she felt for her family was a welcome relief. He smiled and for a moment their eyes met. This time Sam didn't look away. Adams began to move his face slowly towards hers, giving her time to look away or pull back if she wasn't interested. She didn't move. It wasn't to be Adams' night, however, for just before their lips touched his radio suddenly crackled into life between them.

'Control to DI Adams, over!'

Adams pulled back slowly, not taking his eyes off her for a moment and answered the call. 'DI Adams to Control, over.'

'Superintendent Farmer's compliments, sir, and would you join her on the B784 about three miles outside Fereham. They've found the dead girl's car.'

'Twenty minutes, over.'

He slipped his radio back into his pocket and looked across at Sam. 'I've got to go.'

Sam nodded understandingly but disappointed.

'Oh, by the way, are you sure about what you said before?'

Sam was confused.

'About Bird being innocent.'

'I was angry, I'm not sure, but there are a few things that don't add up.'

'Like what?'

'The ivy around Frances' wrist; it's the wrong type, nothing to do with the occult.'

'There was an ivy plant in Bird's office.'

'Could you get me some? Might answer a few questions.'

'If I do, it's between the two of us. I don't want to find myself back in a funny hat walking some miserable beat.'

The sun was finally beginning to peep over the distant horizon, lighting up the fields and woodland beyond the edge of Sam's garden. Adams looked across at it. 'It's going to be a great sunrise.'

'The sunsets are pretty good too,' said Sam mischievously.

They smiled at each other in mutual understanding.

My, thought Adams, the Ice Maiden melts.

Adams arrived at the scene earlier than he had anticipated, the empty roads having hastened his journey. The scene was already basking in the beam of half a dozen mobile lights and the humming of their accompanying generators. Parked by the side of the road was a large, low loading lorry with two police officers preparing to lift the car out of the field and on to its back. He spotted Farmer watching one of the SOCOs take paint scrapings from the back of car. She looked across at him as he arrived, 'Good of you to come.'

Adams remained silent, keeping any excuses to himself. Farmer looked back at the SOCO who was examining the small slivers of red paint he'd managed to scrape from the car into a plastic exhibit bag.

'Are we sure we've got the right car, Bert?'

He lifted his large round face up in Farmer's direction. 'The registered owner is a Malcolm Purvis, who I assume is the dead girl's father, poor sod. And we found this.' He held up a long, patterned, silver ear-ring, identical to the one Farmer had seen swaying gently in Frances' ear.

'Anything else?'

'A few paint scrapings. Not as many as I would have

thought though. Our killer's trying to be clever, cleaned up after himself.'

Adams interjected, 'There goes the paint evidence then.'

'Oh, I don't know about that,' said Bert with a self-satisfied grin. 'He wasn't as clever as he thought, forgot the scene of the original collision. Managed to get a few good samples from the side of the road and the verge; should be enough to get a match.'

Adams walked over to the car and had a good look around it. 'Any attempt to burn it out?'

Bert looked across at him. 'No, I wouldn't be here if they had. Why?'

'If it's the same killer then I wonder why he didn't burn the car? He's been very careful up to now. He burnt James' car out.'

Bert looked across at Frances' car, 'They get careless, that's how we catch them.'

Adams nodded and walked back towards his two colleagues. Farmer began to follow the SOCO out of the field. 'When can you let us have something?'

'Give us a ring tomorrow afternoon, should have something for you by then.'

Farmer was not satisfied, 'Why is everything tomorrow with you people?'

'Ask me tomorrow,' chuckled Bert, as he walked away.

Farmer glared around at her team defying any sign of amusement.

Sam had arrived at the mortuary early for once. She wanted to go through Mark James' file thoroughly before starting the PM on Frances. She was already convinced it was the same killer and that he was either playing some kind of game or he really was a religious nut; Sam wanted to be sure that she wouldn't miss anything.

She hung her coat on the back of the door and walked across the room. There was a small brown envelope sitting in the centre of her desk with her name written in blue ink across the front. She opened it and put her hand inside pulling out a small piece of notepaper and a small section of ivy. She read the note.

'I normally buy ladies flowers, but I found this in Bird's office when we arrested him and thought you might find it interesting, Tom.'

She smiled, he'd come through with the ivy. She hadn't been sure that he would, she thought she might have been pushing their relationship a bit far. But she was wrong and pleased. Sam laid the ivy across the top of her blotter and took a magnifying glass. *Poetica*, she was right. She was convinced now that Bird had got nothing to do with these murders. If Bird was the murderer and trying to forge a connection with the occult, he would have known which variety of ivy to use, he even had easy access to some. However, trying to convince Farmer of her theories would still be difficult, she needed more evidence.

Malcolm Purvis was led gently into the mortuary, the inspector walking closely by his side. His face had lost all its natural colour and he was lined and aged. Inside he hung on to the final hope that a dreadful mistake had been made and that the poor unfortunate girl he was about to see wasn't Frances. For the first time since he lost his wife he prayed. Prayed that it wasn't Frances, that it was another girl, he didn't care who. He was aware of the selfishness of his thoughts but didn't care. As he entered the mortuary he saw Fred standing solemnly by the stainless steel trolley. The trolley was covered with a large, white sheet under which was hidden a human form. He stood by the side of the trolley, a rush of heat passing over him as his insides churned. The inspector spoke, gently, 'Are you ready, sir?'

Fred didn't move, awaiting the inspector's nod. Malcolm remained unmoving, trying to deny the moment that would change the rest of his life. The inspector tried again, 'Are you ready?'

This time Malcolm nodded. The inspector looked up at Fred who pulled the sheet away from the top of the trolley, exposing Frances' face. He didn't look down. He stared ahead, his throat swelling as the tears began to fill his eyes. Finally, the inspector gave his arm a gentle, persuasive squeeze and he lowered his gaze.

What he saw was not Frances but a bloated and blackened caricature of his daughter. He looked through the twisted distortions of her face at his lovely daughter who lay beneath. The tears from his eyes spilled down on to his face and he rubbed them away. 'Not now God, please not now. Don't leave me on my own.'

The inspector made a hushed request, 'Is this your daughter, sir?'

Malcolm nodded, 'Yes. It's my daughter.'

The inspector looked across at Fred who began to cover her face. Before he had a chance though, Malcolm grabbed his arm to stop him. He looked at Fred, the anguish clearly etched on his face. 'You will be gentle with her, won't you? She's suffered enough.'

For once there wasn't an amusing quip or thought in Fred's head. 'We'll take care of her sir, don't worry.'

Malcolm nodded and after one last look at his daughter's face, allowed Fred to cover it. As he turned to walk away Sam entered the mortuary. She was already gowned and ready for the PM. Malcolm saw her and understood what she was about to do. The horror of it finally made his legs buckle. The inspector moved quickly, throwing an arm around his waist, saving him from collapsing onto the floor and leading him carefully out of the mortuary. For a moment he looked up at Sam and their eyes met. Her timing had been bad and she knew it. She had a job to do and she was proud of her chosen profession but for the first time in her professional life she felt a sense of shame and lowered her gaze, unable to match his stare.

Although Sam found it difficult to remove the sight of Malcolm Purvis' face from her mind she was determined to put the experience to one side and throw herself into the PM. She had to banish from her mind that this had once been a person with people who loved her and were loved by her. Now she had an important job to do. The body could yield up the vital clues needed to catch the killer before he had time to strike again and she had to find those clues and find them quickly.

The body had already been removed from the bag and now lay still on the white marble slab while a group of white-suited SOCOs finished collecting samples. Sam looked around the room. As well as the usual array of people Adams was standing in the viewing gallery watching proceedings closely. She knew Adams didn't like watching the PMs. He'd told her that it wasn't so much the sights, as the smell, that really affected him. Well, there wasn't much she could do about that, that's the way humans were, smelly. Richard Owen was also in the gallery deep in conversation with Farmer. It was unusual for the police surgeon to attended the PM and she felt it was probably more to do with her than the body on the table. For a moment she wished she could be a fly on the wall but then changed her mind, who wanted to hear ill of themselves anyway. The SOCOs finished and Sam looked across at Fred, 'Everything ready?'

He nodded. 'There is one thing you ought to know. I think the body's been cleaned.'

Sam was annoyed and almost couldn't believe what Fred was telling her. 'Who the bloody hell's done that?'

'Nobody here, boss. I think the killer's done it. Trying to get rid of any evidence.'

Why? Sam wondered. Did the killer have a specific knowledge of forensics? Had something gone wrong this time so that the killer knew that he had left incriminating evidence? What sort of mind were they dealing with in these cases? She walked across with Fred and began her commentary as her world closed in around her.

'Post Mortem, 9 a.m., 1 November 1995. The body is that of a well-developed, and well-nourished, white female. She is sixty-seven inches tall and weighs one hundred and thirteen pounds.' She picked up her chart and examined the information. 'The remains are those of a Frances Purvis, twenty-four years old. She has brown hair and blue eyes. The body was discovered at approximately 11.30 p.m. yesterday, 31 October at Ruilex Abbey. Life was pronounced extinct by Dr Richard Owen, the police surgeon, at 12.42 a.m.'

She lay the board back down on a small table and began the PM. She'd done hundreds before, but despite this she tried hard to keep each one fresh and interesting, complacency only led to mistakes. After ensuring that the SOCOs had got all the photographs they required she cut the cord that was still embedded tightly into Frances' throat, being careful not to damage any knots. She did the same with the ivy around her left wrist. Both items were then dropped into exhibit bags and sealed by the SOCOs. She then scraped the nails, took swabs from the mouth, nose and vagina; examined the conjunctivae, the membranes connecting the inner eyelids to the eyeballs for the tell-tale bloodspots caused by haemorrhaging in cases of strangulation and asphyxia. Fred moved to the opposite side of the table and rolled Frances on to her side so Sam could examine the back of her body.

'There are no obvious signs of injury to the rear of the body.' She ran her hands through Frances' hair. 'The head also appears clear of any injury . . . what's this?'

She stretched the skin gently over a small puncture wound she discovered at the back of Frances' neck. She was surprised and slightly annoyed at herself for not noticing it at the scene. 'There appears to be a small puncture wound at the back of the neck, possibly caused by a needle of some sort.'

She looked across at the photographer. 'Can I have plenty of shots of this, please?'

The SOCO nodded and took several photographs from various distances and angles before Fred laid the body back on to its back. Sam then began to cut into the body. A large V-shaped incision was made into the neck and continued along the full length of the body. The cut was made slightly off centre to avoid interfering with the previous cuts that formed the upside-down cross. The neck muscles were then dissected off in layers, exposing the larynx, which were removed for examination together with the other neck and chest structures. Moving down the body she discovered the child. 'There is a well developed and apparently healthy, eighteen-to-twenty-week foetus present inside the uterus.'

Sam gently removed the child from its mother and passed its remains to Fred. She was saddened and wondered if the Reverend Shaw would still be so certain of his faith after seeing what his God allowed to happen to the innocent and the pure. She took a deep breath and continued with the PM.

CHAPTER SEVEN

Marcia Evans walked across the oil-stained, concrete floor of the laboratory garage. In the centre of the garage Frances Purvis' blue Renault sat covered with a large, clear, polythene bag. Inside the bag a white-suited SOCO, his nose and mouth covered with a face mask and his head with a disposable hood, prepared to evacuate the grey mist which filled the inside of the car, clinging to every surface. As Marcia watched, Alex Wood, the head of the unit, entered the garage and walked across to where she was standing. He was a short, stocky man tending towards the tubby with receding hair and a full beard. He was genial and hard-working but lacked ambition and the confidence needed to take him to the top of his profession.

'What are you doing here? Thought you were spots, specks and sperm.'

Marcia looked up at him, 'I thought I'd come and see how the other half live. What are they up to?'

'Just waiting for the super glue to clear. With a bit of luck it should cling to the sweat from any undetected prints.'

As Marcia watched, the glue's vapour slowly drifted

out of the car, dispersing through the air ducts in the roof of the garage.

'Lights didn't pick any up then?'

'None that we couldn't eliminate. This is our last hope.'

'We'll have to hope he wasn't clever enough to wear gloves then.' Marcia smiled but Alex did not respond. Marcia was well respected as a thorough and competent professional in her field and she was very friendly with Dr Ryan. Her presence made him uncomfortable and he didn't want his professional competence challenged. He stood supervising the activities of his colleagues who were by now back inside the car searching the interior's more inaccessible places with a high-powered light. Marcia crouched down to peep inside the car. The interior had been robbed of all colour and been transformed to a brilliant white, as if covered by a blanket of hoar-frost. The SOCO concentrated his light and magnifying glass on a small area of the interior under the driving column.

Alex spotted his interest. 'Found something, Bert?'

'Bingo, a couple of good ones. Have a look.'

Alex moved forward and Bert handed him the magnifying glass. 'Very nice, very nice indeed, better get the photographer in here.' Alex stepped out of the car with a smug look on his face and handed the glass to Marcia. 'Looks like our killer wasn't "clever enough". Want to have a look?'

Marcia took the glass and examined the two prints. They were clearly visible, sitting side by side, their white swirling loops and whorls starkly emphasized. When she had finished, Marcia stood up and passed the glass back to Alex. 'I'm impressed. This should help the evidence *stick*.' The SOCO took himself far too seriously and wasn't amused by Marcia's quip. She wasn't deterred though and continued, 'They're in a very unusual place though, aren't they?'

Alex was defensive and his reply was curt, 'I've found them in stranger places than that. Sometimes you're lucky, sometimes you're not . . .'

Marcia interjected, 'And this time you were lucky?'

Marcia's persistent scepticism was heightening Alex' discomfort. 'Yes, indeed, unless they can be identified and eliminated.'

She nodded uncertainly and walked out of the garage, leaving Alex seething with professional indignation.

The PM over, Sam stripped off her green gown and threw her gloves into a nearby bin before making her way into the small office by the side of the mortuary, closely followed by Farmer, Adams and Owen. The moment they entered the office Farmer began her interrogation, her voice sharp and to the point, 'Are we dealing with the same killer?'

Sam was tired to her bones with a weariness which had its roots in mental turmoil more than physical activity. She leaned wearily against the desk top and sighed, 'Almost certainly . . .'

Farmer, impatient for information, cut in, 'Just tell us what you've got and keep it simple.'

Sam was irritated by her attitude, 'The Jackanory explanation, just for you then, Superintendent.'

Adams and Owen couldn't help smiling at the professional conflict between the two women until Farmer caught their expression and turned to glare at them.

Sam continued, 'As you know, the injuries to the abdomen of both Mark James and Frances Purvis are unusual and identical . . .' She picked up several photographs from the desk and handed them around, keeping one for herself and indicating the injuries, 'and form this upside-down cross.' She outlined the cross with her pen on the photograph. 'By the way, your killer is left-handed.'

Farmer cut in, 'So was Jack the Ripper.'

Sam wasn't put off. 'The police didn't do very well then either, did they?'

Farmer scowled and Adams interjected, sensing a rising level of animosity, 'Any chance that it's coincidental?'

Sam shook her head. 'With identical cuts like those, I doubt it, but there's a bit more. Both victims were also garrotted, which in itself is interesting.'

Farmer cut in again, 'So they were both strangled, so are hundreds of others, I don't see what that tells us?'

'The fact that our killer has taken the time and trouble to make a garrotte might tell us quite a bit. Let me show you what I mean.' She opened the desk drawer and pulled out a length of string attached to both ends of a pencil. 'Here's one I made earlier. Can I borrow your wrist for a moment, Superintendent?' Farmer reluctantly agreed to it. 'It won't hurt.'

'Don't tell me, just a little uncomfortable.'

Sam slipped the loop over the outstretched wrist and

began to twist the pencil, slowly tightening the string and squeezing Farmer's wrist. 'Once the loop is around the victim's neck it doesn't require much strength to tighten it, a child could do it. All you have to do is twist the stick and the loop tightens, until, finally . . .' She twisted the pencil sharply turning the skin under the loop white and extracting a wince from Farmer. Her demonstration finished, Sam released the pressure and slipped the loop off Farmer's wrist. 'It was the main form of execution in Spain for hundreds of years.'

Farmer looked up at Sam, still rubbing her wrist. 'Remind me to cancel my holiday in Benidorm.'

'Although I'll have to wait for the lab reports for this one, I also think it likely that they were both drugged.'

Owen was surprised by this revelation. 'I don't remember your report on James mentioning drugs?'

'It didn't because there was no trace of any, but I think we'll find some in Frances' system.'

Adams cut in, 'What makes you think our killer used drugs?'

'Considering what our victims must have gone through before they were killed, I would have expected to have found some sort of defence injuries; bruises, scratches, or evidence of some form of restraint, rope burns around their wrists perhaps, but there was nothing. Given the time it took to find James' body the chances are that any drugs in his system would have had time to disperse and any small puncture hole would have been obscured as the body decomposed. However, there was a small puncture wound at the back of Frances' neck where I think she was injected. It would also explain why our killer went to so much trouble to hide James' body. By the time it was discovered all traces of the drug would have disappeared.'

Farmer wasn't convinced. 'Then why didn't our killer make more effort to hide Frances' body?'

Adams spoke up. 'He tried. The Abbey was closed for repairs. He wouldn't have expected anyone to be nosing around the old chapel for at least a couple of weeks. We just got lucky with the dogs.'

Farmer looked across at Owen. 'Bird's diabetic, isn't he?'

Owen nodded and Farmer continued, 'So he'd have easy access to syringes and needles.'

'Yes, but so have thousands of others, it doesn't necessarily make him a killer.'

Sam glanced across at him, she appreciated the support. Sam continued, 'There's something else you ought to know as well.' Her hesitation was barely noticeable, 'I found out that when he was at college Bird made a study of a murder that occurred in the Fens in the mid sixties. He did quite extensive research and later wrote a paper on it. The circumstances were identical to those of both Mark and Frances. The victim, an old man by the name of Ironsmith, was garrotted on holy ground and an upside-down cross was carved on to his body.'

Farmer's face flushed with anger. 'How long have you known about this?'

'Not long. I wasn't really sure it was relevant until now.'

'I'm the best judge of what's relevant. Not you. Any other evidence you're withholding?'

'I'm disclosing evidence not withholding it, that's my job, Superintendent. I found a similar garland of ivy to that found wrapped around Frances' wrist inside the tomb where they found James. There does seem to be a connection with the Fenland murder.'

Sam expected Farmer to explode but she didn't, she just sat passively, almost content.

'So, you came up with the goods in the end. Looks like we've got Bird bang to rights on this one. Well done.'

'There is one more thing I think I ought to tell you.'

Farmer looked at her suspiciously.

'It's the same thing I told you when we were at the Abbey. I don't believe Bird did it.'

Farmer's contented looked slipped and was replaced by one of enormous anger. 'Really, and why not?'

'The ivy, it was the wrong species.'

'I see. You've just given me enough evidence to get Bird convicted of two murders and now you're telling me he's innocent because some *plant* happens to be the "wrong type".'

'Bird wouldn't have made that kind of mistake; he would have known which variety of ivy to use to make it look like an occult killing. Christ, he had a pot of it in his office!'

Farmer glared across at her. 'How the hell did you know?'

Sam glanced, embarrassed, at Adams, realizing she'd just dropped him in it. Farmer picked up her look and realized immediately what had happened. She relaxed back in her chair, looked across at Adams and then back at Sam.

'So, there's a conspiracy is there? What else has been going on behind my back? I'll have both of you if there's any more tampering with the investigation.' Farmer knew she was being unfair but she felt betrayed by a close member of her team and she was finding it difficult to control her anger. Sam's face flushed with indignation and she prepared to unleash a tirade upon Farmer but, before either of them had chance to speak, Fred Dale entered the office.

'Sorry to interrupt but there's an urgent message for the Superintendent.' Farmer looked up. 'Can you contact the murder incident room as soon as possible, apparently they've matched the fingerprints they found in Frances' car with Bird's.'

Farmer's face was a study in triumph. She swung round to face Sam, 'Looks like we've got to arrest a killer.' She stood up and pulled her jacket from the back of the chair. 'In future, Dr Ryan, can I suggest you confine your "inquisitive mind" to your mortuary and leave the rest of the investigation to the professionals. You cut them, I'll catch them.' Farmer turned and left quickly without looking at Adams. As he followed her out of the lab Sam tried to catch his eye but he avoided her gaze, feeling angry and betrayed at Sam's indiscretion. He couldn't be sure if he had been used and discarded or whether Sam had made a genuine mistake in the heat of the moment. He would need time to think about this one and besides, there was Farmer to pacify. Sam turned to

Owen who shrugged nonplussed by what had just occurred.

Sam hated walking through the underground car-park, even now in the middle of the day it still had that feeling of impending danger and was the most oppressive place she knew. The sound of her every footstep echoed off the nearby concrete walls before bouncing back towards her, giving the impression of dozens of unseen people hiding in every dark recess and following her every move. As Sam reached her car she began to search through the rubbish which littered the inside of her handbag for her car keys. As she did, a sudden tingle passed through her as she heard the distinct sound of footsteps. Although they weren't close, they were certainly coming her way. An irrational fear overcame her. She tried to control it with the logic of her mind: hers was not the only car in the car-park, lots of people worked flexible hours at the hospital. Indeed, she had often had pleasurable encounters with colleagues she rarely saw during working hours in this very car-park. However, logic held no sway over intuition and pictures of the bodies of both Mark James and Frances Purvis filled her mind. She walked to the back of the car and strained every sense as she scanned the corridor to pinpoint who was there. She assured herself that it would only be another hospital employee making their weary way home but as she strained her eyes to break through the dark shadows filling the car-park's long corridors, the footsteps stopped, the silence spread like a blanket around her and she could see nothing.

She waited for a moment, controlling her breathing so that the air passed in and out of her lungs without a sound, waiting, hoping, to hear the sound of a car door slamming or the roar of an engine as it burst into life. She heard neither of those things and as she moved back towards her car the footsteps began again, only this time quicker and closer. Sam's search for her car keys now became a frantic scrabble, she began to throw things from her bag in her panic. Finally, she discovered them, hiding under a pile of crumpled receipts in a side pocket. She pulled them out of her bag and cursing, fumbled to find the car key before ramming it into the lock on the driver's door and throwing herself inside. She slammed the door behind her and locked it. Turning the ignition key she turned her headlights full on, forced the gear stick into reverse and accelerated blindly out of her parking place, cringing mentally in readiness for a collision. None came and she rammed the gear into first and raced along the car-park's corridors towards the exit. She couldn't be sure, it was just a fleeting image, but just as she accelerated away she thought she noticed a figure standing behind one of the pillars. As she passed it she glanced into her rear-view mirror but darkness had replaced the momentary light from her headlamps and she could see nothing.

She began to feel safe when she finally drove out of the car-park and into the well-lit hospital grounds. Her breathing slowed and she began to feel a little foolish, berating herself for letting illogicality take over. However, she persuaded herself that the incidence served to highlight the potential danger which the isolated, poorly lit car-park posed for the hospital staff, especially the female staff, and she decided she would make a fuss about it. It might have been nothing but then again . . . She'd get Jean to type out a report on the incident the following morning and insist that, at the very least, new lights should be installed.

As she pulled out of the hospital grounds the glare from a car's lights behind made her glance up into her rear-view mirror. The car behind was not only too close for comfort but had his lights on full beam. Sam put her hand up to the mirror in a vain hope of asking him to dip his lights, nothing happened, so she flicked her mirror down dismissing the glare. As she drove through the Cambridge traffic on her way out of the city the car remained with her, maintaining the same distance behind and keeping its lights on full beam despite flashes of annoyance from oncoming traffic. The car continued to follow her as she began to navigate the twists and turns of the country lanes which eventually led to her cottage. Sam could feel her mouth begin to dry as the fear she had experienced in the car-park returned. She accelerated, watching the needle on her speedometer increase quickly to a speed she knew was unsafe to drive at. Finally, the car behind made its move and began to overtake. Sam knew that if she allowed it to do so she would be finished. She pressed her foot down hard on to the accelerator but it made little difference; slowly but surely the car behind began to pass her. She glanced quickly to her right in a hope of seeing the other driver but although she could distinguish his dark shape at the wheel, she could make out nothing further. She knew little about cars but at this speed, and in her panic, she couldn't see this one clearly to identify its make. She could see that it wasn't new, it was too long and heavy and its lines had an old-fashioned feel, like one of the classic cars she occasionally saw driving around the streets of Cambridge. As it finally pulled ahead of her and began to brake, Sam saw her escape route, a small lane to her left. She braked sharply and threw the car around the corner before accelerating along the lane. As she reached a junction she stopped for a moment and looked back. The other car had reversed and was now racing along the lane towards her at high speed. With a sob of panic she pulled out of the junction and followed the signs back towards Cambridge. She looked down at her hands which, although gripping the steering wheel firmly, were shaking. In fact she felt as if her whole body had gone into spasm and had become uncontrollable. It was a relief when she finally reached the urban outskirts of Cambridge. She turned off the main road and travelled the side streets for a few minutes before heading back towards the centre of Cambridge. She knew she couldn't return to the cottage and decided to exercise her right to stay overnight at her old college, if there was a room available. She pulled up at a set of lights and was relieved when, looking into her rear-view mirror, the road behind her was clear. She put her head down on the steering wheel for a moment, trying to regain her composure.

The bang on the window made her jump and as she pulled her head off the steering wheel she screamed out. The windscreen washer who had, uninvited, begun to wipe down her front windscreen, jumped back in surprise. He'd had various reactions to his job but he could never remember making a woman scream before. He watched her for moment as she stared at him. He wasn't sure if she was mad or just scared. As the lights change from red to green she pulled away rapidly, sending the cloth he had abandoned on the windscreen, flying from the car and on to the road. As he ran to retrieve it, another car stopped at the lights. He turned and gestured to the driver with his cloth, but there was no interest. Pity, he thought, he liked doing the old classic cars; their owners were normally far more generous than most.

Sam was pleased she'd found Marcia on her own. Although she was still very shaken up by the incident she decided to keep it to herself for the moment as she knew Marcia would be horrified and worried by it.

Marcia was so lost in her work that she didn't even know Sam was there until she was standing by her shoulder.

'How did you get on with six-foot-two eyes of blue at the medics' ball the other night?'

Marcia jumped, and then smiled up at Sam. 'OK. Lured him back to my room with promises of seeing my collection of rare man-made fibres. He was sick all over my new carpet and passed out on the sofa. I haven't seen him since.'

Sam tried to hold back a laugh. 'Ah well, win some lose some.'

Marcia scowled at her, 'I'd just like to win *one*.

'Mind you, I haven't seen you with many, "to die for" men recently if it comes to that.'

'Wait, watch and see. I got a postcard only the other day from an old flame, Liam.'

Marcia was sceptical. She never had seen Sam with a man, which, given that she was an intelligent and attractive woman, was somewhat surprising. 'We'll see, we'll see.'

Sam smiled, 'I'm sure you will, soon. Thanks for the information about the knots.'

'You have no idea what I might have to sacrifice for that information.'

Sam felt it expedient not to probe too deeply into that remark for the moment. 'I thought we were on to something there for a while.'

'I take it you've heard about the prints then?'

Sam nodded. 'Farmer's like a dog with two tails. I was so sure.'

'These things happen.'

'But why use a surgeon's knot, why not a reef knot or granny knot or something.'

Marcia shrugged and crossed the lab picking up a report from a shelf on the opposite side of the room. 'I wouldn't give up hope just yet. I might have some good news for you.'

'She was drugged.'

'Who's a clever girl then?'

'Tubarine chloride, I found a concentration of it in her liver.'

'Tubarine, I thought that went out with Agatha Christie?'

'Apparently not. It's alive and well and living in

Cambridge. I had the toxicologists have another look at the samples from James, and do you know what? They found traces of the drug in some of the decomposed tissue.'

Sam was pleased with the result but they posed more questions than they answered. 'But why use Tubarine, why use any drug? They were both strangled not poisoned.' Sam quickly answered her own question, 'Tubarine doesn't have to kill, does it? Can't it cause paralysis if administered in the correct dosage?'

'Can do, but you'd have to know what you were doing. There's a fine line between paralysing someone and killing them.'

'So, a victim could still be alive when they were strangled, just unable to move. The ultimate nightmare. Where would our killer get it from do you suppose?'

'It's a curare alkaloid, comes from a South American plant, but most hospitals keep it. Couldn't be that difficult to get your hands on.'

Sam's thoughts returned to Reverend Shaw's greenhouse. 'Would it grow in an artificial environment, like a greenhouse?

'Perhaps, why, know someone who's got some?'

'I am not sure, maybe.'

Farmer and Adams looked across the interview table at a dishevelled and unkempt Bird. His arrogance had gone, he seemed somehow smaller. By his side, impeccably dressed as usual, was his solicitor, Colin Lane. Farmer began the interrogation.

'When was the last time you saw Frances Purvis?'

Bird remained silent for a moment. He wasn't being awkward, just confused. He'd spent the few hours before they'd come to arrest him just looking at a photograph of Frances. He hadn't really been aware of it before, but he loved her. He only knew that he had always been afraid of losing her, that fear had driven her away and now he'd lost her for ever. He finally replied, 'I can't remember.'

'Yesterday evening, wasn't it?'

'No, I don't think so.' Surely, he thought, it had been longer that.

'You were seen by several of the neighbours arguing with Frances.'

Bird realized he'd told a stupid lie and, although regretting it, continued, 'Maybe it was then, I don't remember.'

'In breach of your bail conditions.'

Bird shrugged, 'I wanted to talk to her, tell her it wasn't me, that I had nothing to do with killing Mark. She wouldn't listen, got upset. I didn't mean to do that, so I left. I wouldn't hurt her, I loved her.'

'You hurt her before, when you hit her, the night Mark went missing.'

'The one and only time, and I've got to live with that for the rest of my life. Love isn't easy, sometimes you do stupid things.'

'Did you know which was her car?'

'There was only one on the drive, a small blue Renault, I think. That must have been it.'

Adams asked the next question, 'Did you ever go inside Frances' car, the Renault I mean?'

'No, never, the first time I knew she was using it was when I saw it that evening.'

'So you've never accepted a lift or travelled in it?'

'No, never.'

Farmer jumped in, 'Then why were your fingerprints found underneath the dashboard?'

For a moment Bird was surprised, confused. 'They couldn't have been, I was never in the car.'

'Well, they were there and they're definitely yours. How do you explain that?'

'I can't, they must have been planted. You lot are good at that,' he accused.

'What, we took you to the scene at night and rubbed your fingerprints all over the car before we tucked you back up in bed? Come on, I think you'll find that not even Cambridge magistrates are going to believe that one.'

Bird just stared at her and didn't reply. Farmer continued, 'Where did you go after you left her?'

'Drove around for a while then went back to the club.'

Adams joined in the interview, 'What time did you get back to the club?'

'I don't remember, one, half past, look I was upset. Ask the doorman, Gerry, he might have a better idea than me.'

'We will. Were you alone during this time?'

'Yea, I needed some space to think things through, that was all.'

'Is that why you gave my men the slip outside the club?'

'Partly. Look they were never going to let me within a mile of Frances. I just wanted her to understand it wasn't me.'

Farmer interjected, 'Isn't it more likely that you went to see her to try and stop her giving evidence against you?'

'No, I just wanted her to know the truth.'

'But with her out of the way the main witness against you has gone and you're in the clear.'

'I'd rather do life than kill her, I loved her.'

'I thought you told us in the last interview that she was a free agent.'

'She is . . . was . . . but that doesn't mean I wanted to lose her, wasn't willing to fight for her . . .'

'Kill her?'

'No, no never! I'd never do that!'

'In your last interview you said that the wind chimes outside your club were there to ward off evil spirits.'

Bird shrugged.

'I understand you're a bit of an expert on the occult, written papers on it.'

'I know a bit, not exactly an expert though.'

'Come, come, I think you're being a bit modest; didn't you write a paper on some occult murders in the Fens? What was it, *The Fenland Murder and Enigma*.'

'That was a long time ago, I was nineteen. I wanted to make a name for myself.'

'Interesting though. Ironsmith was killed on consecrated ground, so were Frances and Mark. Ironsmith was murdered during one of the so-called witches'

Sabbaths, so were Frances and Mark. Ironsmith was garrotted and had an upside-down cross carved into his body. Surprise, surprise, so were Frances and Mark. Call me Ms Suspicious if you like but that's one hell of a coincidence, don't you think?'

'It's a well-known story, anyone could have found out.'

'It's not that well known. I'd never heard about it, you're the expert.'

Bird didn't speak. Adams continued, 'As the original murder was committed while we were all still kids, the chances are that the murderer of poor old Charlie Ironsmith is no longer with us, which leaves us with just one person who had the knowledge and motivation to commit the two murders.'

'Why would I murder them like that then, wouldn't it just draw attention to me?'

'Not if you thought we wouldn't find out.'

'You underestimate yourself, Superintendent.'

For a moment Farmer was caught off balance and she struck out, 'Did you kill her because you thought she was carrying someone else's baby?'

Now Bird was caught off balance. 'What baby?'

'Frances was pregnant when she was murdered. Your idea of an abortion, was it?'

Bird's solicitor, seeing the shock of his client, cut in, 'I must object to this line of questioning. It really is intolerable.'

Bird, tears beginning to run down his face, tried to defend himself, 'I didn't . . . she never told me. Was it mine?'

'She told her father it was yours, and she wanted you to have nothing to do with it.'

Bird became very still, staring straight ahead, not at anyone or, anything, 'I didn't know, I just didn't know.'

'Wouldn't you have cut her up if you had?'

Farmer was now on her feet leaning over Bird, feeling she was close to the confession she was desperate for. Bird remained silent. Bird's solicitor interjected again.

'My client is in no fit state to continue with this interview and I request it be terminated immediately so we can consult.'

'Interview terminated at 4.22 p.m.' Farmer moved her hand towards the tape recorder and clicked the machine off. She looked back at Bird. 'There'll be no bail this time. This time no one's going to want to know you.'

Bird looked through his tears into her face and slowly shook his head.

Sam and Marcia had moved to the opposite side of the lab where Sam's eyes were glued to a binocular microscope.

'What exactly am I looking at?'

'Paint flakes, the ones they found on Frances Purvis' car.'

'Any joy?'

'They're from a Jaguar saloon, Mark II, probably a three point eight 1963 to 66 vintage.'

'All that from a few flakes of paint? I am impressed, tell me more, Sherlock.'

'You see but you don't observe. It's all in the way the paint is layered. This one's metallic opalescent maroon.'

'Might be Inspector Morse then.'

'Wrong university, that's the other lot.' She changed the slide on the microscope and Sam took another look. 'If you observe the way the paint is layered you'll see that the first layer is dark brown, this is followed by red, pale cream and then green after which they spray the main colour, in this case, maroon, over the top. The combination was only used for metallic cars and then only between 1963 and 1966. They reverted to three undercoats after that. Except on the original "Knicker Ripper" itself, the old E-type, then they used it until 1968.'

Sam looked up. 'So why couldn't it be an E-type?'

'Elementary, my dear Ryan, because they didn't do E-types in opalescent maroon.'

'Brilliant! How rare are they?'

'There's still a few about, enthusiasts mostly. The police are trying to check on the owners but it's going to be a long job.'

Sam nodded. 'I've got to go. I've got an afternoon list.'

She rubbed Marcia's back affectionately for a moment before making for the door. As she opened it Marcia called across to her, 'By the way what's this I hear about you getting Owen a bollocking for not wearing his protective suit at the James scene?'

Sam smiled across at her. 'You should know better than to listen to rumours, Marcia.'

'He deserved it. You could have saved your breath. I don't know how the crime scene manager puts up with him.'

'No, I don't either.'

Marcia returned to her microscope and Sam closed the door quietly behind her.

Farmer and Adams sat opposite each other inside Farmer's office. It was a bleak place. The desk behind which she sat was old and had suffered years of misuse; they'd tried to change it several times but she'd always insisted on keeping it, calling it her lucky desk, whatever that meant. Grimy cream walls with the occasional black and white photograph of Farmer at some point in her career did nothing to lift the atmosphere. But the most bizarre object in the office was the large drawing of a tall, distinguished-looking chief superintendent in full uniform sitting behind Farmer's back, peering down menacingly into the room. It was new. Adams hadn't seen it before and kept glancing up at it.

'My father.'

Adams looked back at Farmer.

'The drawing you were looking at, it's my father. Didn't think I had one, did you?' Adams found himself feeling slightly embarrassed. 'They gave him that when he retired. He died a few years ago, it's been in my garage for ages. It started to go mouldy so I thought I'd stick it in here, brighten the place up a bit.'

'Hardly,' Adams thought.

Farmer continued, 'He was never the same after he retired. Lived for the job, it was more important to him than anything, even his family.' She knocked her fist on top of the desk. 'This used to be his desk, his office too. I think my mum was glad to see the back of him when he went. Heart attack on holiday in Yarmouth. They're all coppers my family; uncles, cousins. He didn't want me to join, though, said it was no place for a woman, he never forgave me for not getting married and giving him grandchildren. He was even more annoyed when I made inspector, not proud, you understand, just annoyed.' She turned and looked back at the drawing. 'I wonder what he'd think now, eh?'

For the first time since he'd known her, Adams felt a certain sympathy for her. Maybe it was something in his countenance which alerted Farmer that she had, perhaps, become too relaxed, but she quickly returned to the point.

'As soon as the paperwork's finished we'll charge him.'

'He did seem genuinely upset about the baby.'

'Maybe he was. Maybe he really didn't know, but maybe it was all an act for the tape recorder and jury. Even if he had known he'd still have killed her, no point being a dad and doing life. There'd be other women, other kids.'

'I suppose so but for a man with no previous to commit a murder like that . . .' Adams shook his head in disbelief.

'He'd got plenty of previous, it just wasn't on paper, we never caught him that's all. Do I detect a certain amount of doubt?'

'A bit.'

'Fancy it, don't you, Tom?'

Adams attempted to look innocent but knew exactly who she was talking about. 'Who?'

'Don't try and con a conner, Tom; the pathologist Sam Ryan.'

'Bit out of my class, ma'am.'

'You never know, she might fancy a bit of rough.'

Adams breathed out despairingly. 'Thanks a lot.'

'Look, you're a copper, if you want to get your leg over with the pathologist, fine, I hope you enjoy yourself, but you're letting it cloud your judgement.'

'I don't think so, I think I would have felt the same with or without her opinion.'

'Bollocks! Listen, don't let your prick rule your head, it's been the downfall of better coppers than you. The evidence we've got against Bird is overwhelming, we're all going to get a pat on the back because of it, so sit back, take the applause and don't spoil it by talking about bloody plants.' Adams realized she hadn't quite finished with him and remained cautiously silent. 'And just one more thing. If you do ever pull a stroke like the one with the ivy again, I'll not only have you off the case, I'll have you off the bloody force!'

'Yes, ma'am.'

'She's a service industry. She supplies us with information which makes it easier for us to catch the bastards that do these things, nothing else. If she and you remember that we'll all get along fine, if not, well, don't ever say I didn't warn you.'

Before Adams had time to defend himself or even explain his reasons for handing the ivy over to Sam, there was a knock on the door and a uniformed constable entered the office.

'Station sergeant's ready when you are, ma'am.'

Farmer nodded and the PC left the room. Farmer stood up and made for the door. 'Come on, let's get it done.'

Adams followed her along the corridor and down the steps that led from the CID offices to the station sergeant's office. Inside the office Bird stood with his solicitor. Adams couldn't help feeling what a pathetic figure he made. His eyes were red and swollen and his clothes crumpled and dishevelled. A feeling of loss and depression seemed to have pervaded him. The station sergeant passed Farmer the charge-sheet. Looking straight at Bird she began to read out the charge.

'Sebastian Bird, you are charged that between 20 September 1995 and 5 October 1995 in Cambridge you did murder Mark James contrary to common law.'

As Farmer read out the caution Bird just stared ahead at the wall behind her head. She continued with the second charge.

'Sebastian Bird, you are further charged that between 30 October 1995 and 1 November 1995, you murdered Frances Purvis contrary to common law.'

She repeated the caution. As she did Bird began to visibly shake and the focus of his attention moved from the wall to meet Farmer's stare. Suddenly with a half scream he came to life, leaping forward and grabbing Farmer by the jacket and screaming into her face, 'You've got the wrong man, you've got the wrong man!'

Adams and the station sergeant reacted and jumped between them sending Farmer crashing to ground and forcing Bird across a table with his arms held firmly behind his back. Adams knew Bird was a strong man who could handle himself, his reputation went before him, but as he held him across the table and handcuffs were wrapped around his wrists, Adams could detect no outward sense of aggression, just an inner rage, as if he was fighting against himself, trying to change what he was and put right what had happened.

Sam was only half-way through her list when Trevor Stuart entered the mortuary where bodies lay around in various stages of preparation.

'Got a minute?'

Sam looked up and waved her scalpel in acknowledgement of his request. She looked across at Fred. 'Put everything back and stitch up will you, Fred?'

Fred, who was just stitching together the remains of the last PM, waved his response and Sam made her way to the door.

'I hope this isn't going to take long, Trevor, I've got another ten to get through yet.'

They walked across to the small mortuary office and sat down.

'Farmer's on the warpath and threatening to go to the chief executive. Something about you withholding information.'

'Information that she wasn't bright enough to discover for herself. Who told you?'

'I have my contacts. Anyway, whatever the reason, I think you should be careful for a while.'

'What can she do?'

'She could certainly make life a bit awkward, depends how far she's willing to take it.'

'I could be in trouble then?'

'Not serious. She's not going to want to broadcast the fact that you found the information that led to Bird's arrest. But it might be worth watching your back for flying scalpels for a while.'

Although not happy, Sam appreciated Trevor's concern and judged it to be genuine. 'Thanks, Trevor.'

He smiled at her. 'All part of the service.'

As Sam prepared to return to the mortuary Jean Carr entered the office. 'Just a quick word, Dr Ryan, you haven't forgotten you're in court tomorrow with the Nash case.'

Sam had but she didn't want to admit it. 'Yes, yes, I'll be there.'

Jean could see by the expression on Sam's face that she had forgotten and was now finding it a serious inconvenience. 'You were warned.'

'I know, I know. Sorry, Jean, I've got a lot on my mind right now.'

Fred, still dressed in his mortuary gown and holding a stained needle in front of him with a section of twine hanging from it, stood by the door. 'Bad batch of gut. The bodies just burst open again.'

Sam watched as the colour drained from her secretary's face. She put her arm around her and squeezed her arm sympathetically.

*   *   *

Malcolm Purvis sat cross-legged in front of his television set, the hand control for the video recorder held tightly in his hand. He was watching a video of Frances with her mother. The film had been taken many years before at a local park and he had only just had it converted to video tape. As he watched, Frances hugged her mother tightly. The camera zoomed up to a close-up of their faces. Encouraged by her mother, Frances' small face looked right into the camera lens and, smiling, she spoke to her father, 'I love you, Daddy.' She put the flat of her hand against her lips and blew her father a kiss. He played the moment over and over, sometimes freeze-framing the picture, staring at his daughter's face.

Adams arrived at the house alone. He'd decided that perhaps Farmer's professionalism was not required in a situation like this. He knocked hard on the large oak door and waited. A few moments later Malcolm Purvis came to the door. Adams was careful and gentle, 'I'm sorry to bother you, sir, especially right now, but I need to take a statement.'

Malcolm Purvis stared at him blankly for a moment then stood to one side of the door and ushered him in. Adams followed him into the sitting-room where the video was still running. Adams sat on the sofa opposite the television and watched it. The picture had changed from the one Malcolm had been watching earlier. Frances, was playing on the Cambridge backs with her mother and a young boy. It was summer and they were rolling about in the grass, executing handstands and enjoying their young lives to the full.

'Is that Frances?' Adams indicated the television set.

'Yes, that's her. Took that eleven or twelve years ago now.'

'She was very pretty, even then.'

Malcolm sat by Adams' side and watched the screen with him. 'Yes, she was, took after her mother, thank God.'

'Is that her mother with her?'

'Yes, Anne. She died of cancer about a year later.'

Adams looked at Malcolm's face. He seemed to have aged since he'd seen him last. The lines on his face seemed more numerous and deeper and his grey hair had lost any distinction it may have given him. 'I'm sorry.'

'Frances took it very hard. And I was too busy and too depressed to cope. I let her down when she needed me, that's why it's my fault, you see.'

'I doubt it, life has a way of levelling things out anyway. She was home and she loved you, so you couldn't have got it that wrong.'

Malcolm looked across and gave Adams a half smile of thanks. Adams' attention was drawn back to the screen, 'Who's the boy?

'Mark James, would you believe. They'd been friends since they were young. Got him off a supplying drugs charge a few years ago. I normally wouldn't have taken the case but she was always able to get around me, and he seemed grateful enough.'

'Rather a tragic film, isn't it?'

'Yes, it is. I don't know why we've been singled out but there's been too much death connected with this family over the last few years.'

'We've charged Bird with both Mark's and Frances' murder. I just thought you ought to know.'

'Thank you, inspector, but it's all a bit late now, isn't it.'

Malcolm's face returned to the television screen and his daughter's laughing voice.

There was the usual scene of chaos surrounding Sam's kitchen, she was late as usual. As she scrambled to eat a slice of burnt toast while slurping down a mug of hot coffee and keeping one eye on the clock, she realized her car keys were not where they were supposed to be, on a small hook marked 'car keys' by the side of the kitchen door. Not that they ever were, but they were supposed to be. Giving up on the toast, she dropped it into the bin which was already overflowing with rubbish. It landed on the top, slid off an old can of beans and fell on to the floor. Sam was too busy looking for her keys to notice. Papers were lifted, pillows moved, even cat baskets emptied, but there was no sign of them. In her panic she decided to use the spare. Running to the drawer and opening it, she remembered that she was, in fact, already using the spare key. She slammed the drawer shut and was trying to create a mind picture of her movements since she last used the car when the doorbell rang.

Ricky stood in the doorway, a contrite look on his face. For once he was smartly dressed in jacket and tie and his hair was combed neatly; it was very out of character.

'Sorry, Aunty Sam.'

Sam stared at him for a moment, wondering what he was apologizing for. Then she remembered the dented car and the very large bill. 'I should think you are.'

'It won't happen again.'

'I'm glad to hear it. What was the outcome?'

'That friend of yours, Inspector . . .'

'Adams?'

'Yea, him. He got me a caution, that's why I've got me best Marks and Spencers on. Said there'd be nothing he could do if it happened again though.'

'You're lucky.'

'Yea, I know. He's a good bloke. I'll pay you back as soon as I've got a job.'

Sam smiled fondly at him and gave him a hug. 'Well, I've been thinking about the money . . .'

'You mustn't let me off, I will pay it back.'

'I wasn't going to let you off.'

It wasn't the reply Ricky expected.

'Come with me.'

She led her curious nephew through the kitchen and out into the back garden. She opened the shed door and emerged with a set of overalls, a pair of wellingtons and a spade, before continuing her journey to the top of the garden and a weed-covered wilderness of about half an acre that had once clearly been a much-prized vegetable garden.

'Well, here we are. Weeds go over there, you'll find the bags of compost in the shed but don't dig it in until you've cleared the ground and then make sure it's evenly distributed.'

Ricky's mouth almost fell open with the magnitude

of the job. He hated gardening at the best of times and had to be dragged screaming out of the house just to cut the lawn. This was in a completely different league.

'Nobody mentioned anything about slave labour.'

'Does your mum know about the caution?'

'No.'

'Do you want her to?'

'No.'

'Then get on with it, I'll be home about six. I'll run you back to your mum's then.'

She started to walk away from him. 'Sorry, I've got to rush. I'd have liked to watch you for a while, but I've got to call a taxi because someone's hidden my car keys. Should only take you a few days, then the debt's paid. It's a bargain if you ask me.'

Defeated, Ricky sat on the garden seat and began to undo his shoes. As he pulled up his foot, he noticed a set of keys lying next to him on the bench. He picked them up and called to his Aunt, 'Are these what you're looking for?'

Sam turned and, feeling slightly embarrassed, made her way back up the garden towards her nephew.

'The burglar must have dropped them as he fled across the garden, eh?'

Sam snatched them off him with an embarrassed 'Thanks.'

Tom Adams walked across the packed bar to the small brown table where Sam was waiting. He put her tomato juice down in front of her and, after taking a sip from his pint, sat in the chair beside her.

Sam raised her glass, 'Cheers.'

Adams responded before downing another mouthful of the clear brown liquid. Sam still felt annoyed with herself and embarrassed by dropping Adams in it over the ivy and was determined not to miss this opportunity to try and put things right,

'I wasn't sure you'd come.'

Adams sipped at his pint again, 'Nor was I. I must be going soft.'

'Then why did you?'

'Probably because I still think you're our best bet for finding the killer.'

'You don't agree with Farmer then?'

'She's the boss so I've got to support her decisions. But I've seen a few guilty men in my life, and I'm not convinced he's one of them.'

Sam sipped slowly at her drink giving herself a few seconds to summon the courage to make the apology. He certainly deserved it, but the words were difficult to say, 'I'm sorry, it just slipped out. I was angry and it was really stupid of me to let you down like that.'

As much as Adams liked and respected Sam, he wasn't yet in the mood to forgive, 'Yes, it was. Don't ask again.'

Sam had hoped it would be easy. It clearly wasn't going to be, 'It really wasn't deliberate.'

Adams thumped his pint down on the table, slopping some of its contents along the outside of the glass and onto the beer mat beneath, 'In this game, *Doctor* Ryan, trust is everything. Without it, you're buggered. Not only did you let me down, but you got me a bollocking from Farmer which I could well have done without. My entire career was under threat because I did you a favour.'

Sam had never seen Adams angry before and she didn't like it. Especially as she was the justifiable focus of that anger. 'Would it help if I talked to her?'

'No thanks. With your track record I'd probably end up inside.'

Sam was struggling, 'What did Farmer say?'

'Basically, that if I wanted to get you into bed then I should do it on my own time and at my own expense, not hers. She was right.'

Sam looked down and took another drink, nervous of asking the next question. 'Is that why you did it?'

Adams had no such reservations, and looked directly at her. 'Partially.'

Sam found herself in the peculiar situation of feeling both angry and flattered at the same time. Angry at his ulterior motive for helping and flattered because of his obvious and welcome interest in her.

Adams continued, 'It wasn't the main reason, though.'

Sam detected a softening in his voice, as if he felt that perhaps he had gone too far and was now trying to make amends. She looked up at him.

'You're a maverick, a one-off. You're the first and, I hope, last pathologist I have ever met who is willing to take their work outside the mortuary, and with the bottle to see it through. To be honest, if you weren't effective you wouldn't be tolerated.'

'Farmer doesn't think that?'

'Yes she does. But because of that, she also sees you

as a threat. When it comes to the credit for cracking this one, she wants it all.'

'I see.'

Adams turned towards her looking earnestly into her face, 'Sam . . .'

She was pleased that they were at least back on first name terms.

'Don't get involved any further, it could get dangerous and you're stepping on too many egos. If you push Farmer too far she'll react, and then we'll both be in the shit.'

Sam nodded, 'Ok.'

Adams smiled at her, pleased that at least she'd seen sense. 'Fancy another drink?'

Sam glanced at her watch. If she didn't go now it would be dark by the time she reached Little Dorking,

'Sorry, Tom, I've got to get back to the hospital, I've got a full list this afternoon.'

Adams was disappointed. Sam could see the disappointment in his eyes. He really was a very appealing man. She walked up to him and kissed him gently on the lips, whispering, 'You don't have to do me favours you know; you only have to ask.' She turned, picked up her bag from the table, and pushed her way back through the bar towards the door, leaving Adams flustered and frustrated.

CHAPTER EIGHT

He raged through the house. It had quite clearly been a big mistake, not in the original plan, not sanctified. These things took time. He appreciated that and had never skimped. The attempt to murder Dr Ryan had been rushed and had failed because of it. Now she was aware of possible danger, alerted and so on her guard. That would complicate the situation and could put at risk all the previous hard work; he would have to be patient. Frustration coursed through his veins like fire and it took a supreme act of self-will to remain rational. He gripped the edge of his desk and forced himself to be calm. Although Samantha would have to be killed, it would have to wait, he would have to return to the original plan.

With Bird out of the way his plans would have to change a little. The simulation of ritualistic killings had been a useful subterfuge and had served his purpose well. Two were dead and one would be lucky to see the outside of a prison cell until he was a very old and institutionalized man. Bird's release had been unexpected but had presented the opportunity to bring retribution in the same fashion a second time. Bird had even helped, behaving in a manner which perfectly complemented his purpose and assuring his eventual destruction. It was all quite wonderfully simple. Luck had been on his side, if that was a suitable description for His divine intervention.

New methods would have to be found to punish the remaining victims. A decision had been made at an early stage not to use the same method twice; with Mark and Frances it had been expedient and had worked well but now it was time to change. He lifted Malcolm Purvis' file and opened it, examining the scribbled note which he had written to himself outlining the type and method of Malcolm's nemesis. It was a good plan and should leave no clues as to the identity of those involved.

It was a very difficult thing for him to do but there was no longer any point in keeping these things. This time she hadn't gone away for a while, wasn't travelling the world or staying with her friends. She was dead and she wouldn't be coming home. He had his memories and his tapes and he treasured those, but they were all he had left. He'd spent the evening boxing up her clothes, her old toys and bric-à-brac. She would have wanted him to do that. He packed it all into the back of his car ready for his journey to the cancer research shop in town. The minutiae of a young, vibrant life was contained in only five cardboard boxes and two carrier bags. He had kept a couple of things, foolish sentimental items which she had loved and he couldn't part with. Her bear, Barney, which was the very first present he had bought her after she was born, and the black dress she'd worn to her mother's funeral when they'd offered and received love and support from each other. He shook his head in despair and grief. He'd had so many visitors since her death. People he'd forgotten existed. Friends from her past, old school friends, former boyfriends he hadn't seen for years, even people from the good parenting class they were attending. He'd welcomed them all and they helped him to retain her memory and remind him what a gentle loving child she had been. Many had said crass and foolish things, referring to life and death as if it was some game to be played by winners and losers. Others talked of His divine intervention and His will and plan for us all. They talked the platitudes of death, of peace and a better place. Malcolm listened patiently, understanding their difficulty and their fumbling attempts to comfort him, but he'd never believed; even now when it could have given him the greatest comfort, he still couldn't bring himself to compromise. For him heaven was here on earth in the pleasure he had derived from his love for his wife and daughter and now all that had been taken away from him. As he closed the boot of the car he looked up at the FOR SALE board outside the house. There was nothing left for him here. He'd decided to move into his London flat to see his remaining years out. Life could have little more of consequence to throw at him.

The FOR SALE board outside the house had brought proceedings forward. The original plan had to be scrapped and a new one would have to be made quickly. He'd watched as Malcolm loaded the back of his car with her clothes. He'd taken a perverse delight in having his own memories re-kindled. Bitter memories of undertaking the same tasks, of spending the entire night in her room packing away all her precious belongings and crying over every item until he felt himself teetering between sanity and madness. He hoped that *his* grief, *his* hurt, would be no less than his own. It was an ironic coincidence, he thought, but Frances would probably end up in the same graveyard as his daughter, 'united in death' he chuckled wryly to himself.

As soon as Malcolm's car pulled out of the drive and headed towards Cambridge, he made his way over to the house. Pulling a small notebook from his pocket he began to scribble intently. How many doors, where they were situated. The distance between the back door and the front drive, whether the drive was overlooked or not. How long the back garden was and where it led. He always liked to find at least two escape routes in case something went wrong. He worked very hard to avoid problems but God helps those who help themselves and so he prepared thoroughly. When he had finished and was satisfied that every eventuality had been covered, he made his way back to his car. The next stage was to drive around the area to familiarize himself with the layout of the roads, where they led, which were the dead ends, the short cuts. After half an hour, and assured that he had been thorough, he made his way home. As he drove into the Cambridge traffic he smiled to himself and thought, 'soon, very soon'.

They had been very grateful to receive the boxes and

had begun to unpack them at once. There was apparently a good market for the small-sized teenage clothes, especially in Cambridge. The elderly lady who took the clothes thanked him politely and asked him to send her appreciation on to his daughter. She had no idea who he was or what he was going through and he promised that he would. Once outside the shop he looked back into its busy interior. The clothes had already been supplied with wire coat hangers and were being hung on the long rails that stretched the length of both sides of the shop walls. As he watched, two girls walked up to the rack and took down one of Frances' dresses. He remembered it, she had bought it one summer on a trip to London. It hadn't been cheap but she'd looked so good in it that he had agreed to foot the bill. As he watched, one of the girls held it up against herself. It didn't look as good on her as it had on Frances, he thought. The girl noticed him looking and told her friend. She turned and they both stared at him as if he was a dirty old voyeur, lusting after their young bodies. Their stares penetrated his dulled senses making him feel uncomfortable so, turning away from the window, he returned to his empty car.

It was late afternoon by the time Sam finally managed to get to the village of Little Dorking and the Reverend Shaw's house. She was not entirely sure what approach she was going to adopt, it would be a case of playing the situation by ear. She parked her car on the drive, crossed the gravelled path to the front door and knocked. Although the sound echoed through the old house, there was no reply. Sam looked around the front garden half expecting to see Peggy's liver-coloured body marching up to her side to guide her once more to her master. This time, however, there was no sign of the affable dog and Sam made her own way to the back garden. She peered through several of the windows, looking for signs of life but there were none. She was quietly relieved, hoping that she could complete her task and go before the Reverend Shaw even realized she'd been there. She walked across to the garage and squinted into the gloomy interior through a gap in the old wooden doors. There were fresh pools of oil glistening on the concrete floor, indicating that a car was certainly still being parked there but the garage was empty and there was no sign of the car she had seen in the photograph on his sitting-room wall. The next source of her interest was the greenhouse at the far end of the garden. She cut across the garden and made her way along the damp, mossy path towards her objective. Even now, in the middle of her clandestine task, she couldn't resist pausing to stoop to catch the fragrance of the plants and flowers along the way. She had already decided that she was a smell junky and was convinced that one day it would probably get her into a great deal of trouble.

She slid the greenhouse door to the side and stepped in, carefully closing the door behind her. She wasn't entirely sure what she was looking for, a plant labelled *curare* would be helpful, she thought, or equipment of some description necessary for the distillation of illicit drugs, but unfortunately there were none of those things to be seen. Simply a large greenhouse with an abundance of plants and flowers of every description. She had at least taken the trouble to look at photographs of the plant she was looking for, not that it was much help in here. There was nothing particularly remarkable about it and it could thus be easily lost in this jungle of flora, something of a needle in a haystack. As she moved from plant to plant examining each in turn she began to fear that she would have to be there for at least a week to be able to cover all of the plants, then a voice shouted her name, 'Dr Ryan, Dr Ryan!'

It was the Reverend Shaw. Her immediate reaction was to jump guiltily and cast around for a hiding place but there was clearly little point as her car was parked on his drive and he was already calling her name. Her mind raced for a ready excuse as she slowly left the greenhouse. Outside, the Reverend Shaw was walking up the path towards her with Peggy, tailing wagging at the sight of her, leading the way. He gave her a cheery wave. 'Afternoon, and to what do I owe this pleasure?'

She waved back and then crouched down to stoke and fuss Peggy. A feeling of apprehension grew within her and she mentally berated herself for allowing herself to get into these situations in the first place. It was as if two sides of her personality were in conflict with each other for control of her spirit. One half that said, go to work, come home, lock the door and remain safe, and the other half needed to feel the adrenalin rush through her body to confirm her hold upon life. Despite her logic and her natural instinct for self-preservation, it was her more reckless half which frequently prevailed over the cautious side.

'I wanted another look at some of your ivies. I, er, thought it might tell me something I didn't know. I did knock but you weren't in, so I . . .'

'And did it?' His voice was fresh and energetic as if her interest in his subject had excited him.

'No, not really,'

He looked disappointed so, encouraged, she embellished her lie, 'It was very interesting though.'

He appeared to brighten at this and the two of them walked back down the path together towards the house companionably discussing his garden. Sam had already made a note of many of the garden's more interesting and unusual aspects and had decided to incorporate them into the plans for her own garden. It was well planned and well stocked with the kind of variety only a large garden such as this could support. As usual, talk of gardens had a relaxing, almost soporific effect upon her jangled nerves. As they reached the drive, Sam looked across at the car parked next to hers. It was an ageing Ford Escort which looked as if it had seen better days. Shaw remarked her interest, 'Bit of a wreck, isn't it, but it gets me from A to B and repairs are cheap.'

'A two-tone car.'

Shaw looked baffled as he stared at his car's dark blue paint.

'Blue and rust.'

He appreciated the joke and laughed heartily.

'Bit of an odd car for a man like you though, isn't it? I rather had the impression that you were more of the classic car type.'

'I used to be, but it had to go, cost far too much to keep.'

'Was that the one I saw you standing next to in the photograph?'

'The one in the photograph? Yes, that was it.'

Sam pressed him further, 'I'm afraid I don't know too much about cars. What kind was it? It was a beautiful colour.'

'Jaguar Mark II, in opalescent maroon.'

Sam felt her mouth suddenly grow dry as the adrenalin began to run. This time it wasn't fear, it was excitement.

'I bought it from a local farmer – the bodywork was in good shape but the engine was a wreck. I spent over a year renovating it. Ah, but it was worth it in the end.' Pride and affection were evident in his voice. Sam tried to control her excitement. After all, she considered, it didn't have to be the same car, there must have been hundreds produced in that colour but it was an exceptional coincidence.

'Who did you sell it to?'

'Some local man, about six months ago now. I miss the car but not what it was costing me.'

Sam was struggling to remain casual, 'Can you remember his name?'

'Well, no, not off the top of my head, sorry. Middle-aged chap, grey hair, knew a lot about the car. I felt sure she would have a good home.'

'Do you remember where he lived?'

'Cambridge, somewhere . . . hang on, if you're interested I still have the receipt, I'm a bit sentimental like that.'

He walked back into the house closely followed by Sam and Peggy. When he reached the sitting-room he began to rummage through an old sideboard drawer. After a few moments he emerged triumphant with a small scrap of white paper in his hand. 'Here it is. I knew it was around here somewhere. Old Simon Clarke put him on to me so I didn't have to advertise.'

Sam was almost beside herself with excitement. Her voice changed in tone with the stress. 'Who was it?' she squeaked.

He unfolded the paper slowly, if Sam hadn't known better she'd have sworn he was doing it on purpose to try and heighten her excitement. 'Yes, here it is, Dr Richard Owen, Owl Coats Farm, Swanham, Cambridge.'

There was an urgency in Brian Watton's voice when he called that had made Marcia drop what she was doing and react immediately. She wasn't quite sure why he'd called her, she'd certainly never had anything to do with fingerprints. She finally decided that he must have heard of her interest in the case and decided to pass any new information he'd discovered straight on to her. She hurried along the corridors until she reached Brian's lab and entered. Brian was a real ale drinking bear of a man. He stood well over six feet in height and was built like the proverbial brick privy with a thick, black beard and heavy glasses. However, Marcia liked him a lot. He belonged to the dying breed of happily married men and she felt genuinely comfortable with him. Despite having been around fingerprints for most of his working life he was still an enthusiast.

He ushered her to a chair before turning on the small slide projector situated on a stand at the back of the room. The image of four fingerprints close together were thrown up on to the wall.

'I wasn't sure at first, but the more I looked at

the prints the more convinced I was that they were wrong.'

Marcia looked intently at the prints but was unable to detect any obvious flaws. 'They look OK to me.'

Brian got up from his seat and, using the tip of his finger, pointed out the problems, 'Flatten your hand. The length of your fingers are uneven. Your index finger is smaller than your middle finger, your ring finger is larger than the index finger, but is smaller than your middle finger and so on. Now,' he said with a theatrical air, 'if you take a look at the prints found in the car, the tips of the fingers are in line.'

'So?'

'This only happens when a person is picking up a cylindrical object of some sort, like a glass for instance. Not when they've just placed their hand on to a flat surface.' Marcia pulled her chair up closer to the screen. 'The ridges are too heavy and spread as well. You only get this kind of pattern when pressure is applied to enable an object to be lifted.'

'So, are they Bird's prints?'

Brian nodded his head, 'They're Bird's prints all right, but I don't think he put them there. I think they might have been planted.'

Marcia was unconvinced. 'But how? I thought that sort of thing came within the realms of detective fiction.'

'Good fiction maybe; let me show you.'

He went across to the sink at the far side of the lab and filled a glass beaker with water before returning and handing it to Marcia. 'Now, just hold that for a few moments.'

After a few seconds he took the glass from her, took it over to one of the tables and, using a Zephyr brush, dusted it with aluminium powder. When he'd finished he showed Marcia her own prints, which the powder had revealed from the surface of the jar.

'Now, if we cut a strip of this tape,' he cut the tape from a roll on the desk before returning to the jar and rubbing the tape firmly over Marcia's prints, 'and press it against your prints making sure . . . there . . . are . . . no . . . bubbles . . . then I should be able to lift your print from the surface of the glass.' He peeled the tape back carefully, removing Marcia's prints. 'There you are, your prints neatly lifted off the glass.' He showed the print to Marcia who could clearly see the loops and whorls of her own fingers. 'Now, if I take this beaker,' he lifted another glass beaker off the work surface, 'and press your prints down hard on to its surface I should . . . be . . . able . . . to, yes, there you are.' He peeled the tape off the glass with a flourish and handed it to Marcia. 'One set of prints moved from glass A to glass B. Proving it was *you that did it.*'

Marcia looked at her prints on the jar, both impressed and concerned at the same time.

'Now, if you look carefully, you'll notice that the tips of your fingers are all even, just like Bird's. And to make absolutely sure there is no comeback, I just blow off any aluminium residue with my little brush.'

'Are you sure about this? I mean, you're an expert, is your average killer likely to know about this sort of thing?'

Brian shrugged, 'Depends whether we are dealing with

your average killer. I don't think we are. Perhaps Mr
Bird's made some very clever enemies.'

As Farmer and Adams walked along the corridor of the
police station one of the many blue-suited detectives
called out to her, 'Excuse me, ma'am, but there's a serious
problem, you're wanted on the phone in the control room
straight away.'

Farmer looked at Adams who shrugged. Farmer
turned and followed her subordinate officer back along
the corridor. He opened the door for her and she entered.
The room was pitch black and she strained her eyes to be
able to see inside. Suddenly the lights were switched on
and a dozen murder squad detectives began to sing, 'For
she's a jolly good fellow'. They were all wearing party
hats and most had either cans of lager or wine in their
hands. Draped across the top of the room was a large
banner bearing the words, WELL DONE BOSS. She
glanced at Tom with a quizzical look and he smiled
back, clearly having been aware of what was going on.
She turned to face the body of police officers with a
frown, 'Have you lot got nothing better to do than hold
parties when you should be out there nicking villains?'

Their voices came back as one, 'No!'

Farmer smiled, 'You bunch of lazy bastards, someone
had better give me a drink quick before I turn nasty.'

There were roars of approval, a can of larger was
pushed into her hand and someone turned on the music.
Adams looked at her and raised his can; she raised her
can in salute. They both took deep and long drinks.

*　　*　　*

Sam arrived home earlier than she had anticipated. She was caught on the horns of dilemma which she was having difficulty resolving. If she went to Farmer now she'd have to accuse Owen of being the killer and explain to Farmer why she was still involved in the case when she'd been warned to restrict her work to the lab. There had to be another way of establishing the truth. Her thoughts were disturbed by the sight of four youths, all in their late teens, walking along the lane towards the main road and all looking both dirty and exhausted. She concluded that they must be casual workers making their way home from the farm a further quarter of a mile along the track from her home. She pulled the car on to the drive and walked around to the back of the house to see how Ricky was getting on with the job she'd given him. She stared up the garden and, although she could see his spade leaning up against the garden shed, there was no sign of her errant nephew. She walked to the top of the garden to make sure he hadn't sneaked away for a quick cigarette in the small wild copse at the bottom end of the garden. As she reached the vegetable patch she was amazed to find that not only had it all been dug over and the weeds cleared but the compost had been forked in as well. She had to admit that she was exceedingly impressed.

Ricky's voice suddenly called across the garden to her, 'Tea's ready when you are!'

She looked back towards the house to see her smiling nephew waving at her. She waved back. Picking up the spade she scraped it clean and walked back to the shed, hanging it with the rest of the tools across one of the shed walls. As she did, she noticed that the smell in the shed was different, as if someone had been smoking in there. The obvious culprit was Ricky and although she objected to his smoking she was prepared to overlook it under the circumstances. She picked up a plant pot which was sitting on top of one of the shelves. It was full of cigarette stubs, thirty or forty of them. Unless Ricky had become a chain smoker of mammoth proportions he had not spent the day alone. She suddenly understood where the four youths she had passed on the lane had come from and she smiled to herself. Taking the pot down to the bin by the side of the house she emptied its contents before kicking off her shoes and walking into the kitchen.

The smell of curry hit Sam as she opened the kitchen door. It wasn't one of her favourite dishes but as Ricky had made it she decided it would be churlish to make a fuss. She walked across to the stove where Ricky was standing, stirring his evil brew with a large wooden spoon. Sam kissed him on the cheek and sniffed in deeply. 'Curry, one of my favourites. I'm surprised you've got the energy after all that gardening.'

'If you get stuck in and give it your best it's surprising how much you can get done.'

Sam nodded in mock agreement. 'I see you're still smoking?'

Ricky looked awkward. 'Just the odd one now and again.'

'I think you're being modest, there were at least thirty in the pot.'

Ricky was silent.

'So how did you get them all to help?'

Ricky decided to act the innocent. 'Who?'

'Those four friends of yours I saw walking down the path when I arrived.'

'Oh them, they just popped around to see if I was OK.'

'That was lucky, wasn't it?'

Ricky gave a short, false laugh, 'Yes, it was.'

'So they did it out of friendship?'

Ricky couldn't see the point of lying any further, 'All right. They owed me. They were with me when the car got damaged and I didn't grass them up. This was just their way of saying thanks. Sorry.'

Sam didn't want to detract too much from his efforts, especially as they had all been made on her behalf. 'Very enterprising, I'm impressed. You're obviously going to go far, my boy.' She rubbed his back gently. 'Well done.'

Ricky smiled at her, began to stir the pot with renewed vigour.

To Sam's surprise the meal wasn't that bad and she actually found herself enjoying it and the company of her nephew, who talked almost non-stop as he served up the curry. Sam opened a bottle of red wine and sat listening to Ricky discuss his plans for the future. He still wasn't sure what he wanted to do. Sam suggested being a chef and, although he wasn't entirely against the idea, had to admit that with the exception of curries and having worked in a fast-food restaurant for a while, his culinary abilities were limited. At the end of the evening Sam phoned to order a taxi for him and he left. She suddenly felt very lonely. She'd never experienced it before, preferring her own company and thoughts but now, without Ricky's exuberance, the cottage felt cold and empty. As she began to pack the dinner plates into the dishwasher the phone rang. She hesitated for a moment, letting the answer machine take it so that she could see who it was before committing herself to talking to them. She recognized the voice at once and ran to the phone.

'Sorry, Marcia, I was in the bathroom.'

Marcia's voice was excited and Sam realized something had happened. 'The prints they found in the Purvis car, they were planted.'

'What! are you sure . . . does Farmer know . . . are they releasing Bird?'

'They're double- and triple-checking before they tell the police but they seem pretty convinced.'

Sam's mind was still racing as Richard Owen's connection with the murder came to the front of her mind again. 'That fibre, the one we think came from Owen's jacket, have you still got access to it?'

'Which one, the one from the James murder or the one from the Purvis murder?'

Sam was confused, 'Which one from the Purvis murder?'

'I found some more fibres on the cord around her neck, the same as the ones we found at the James scene.'

Sam felt herself getting annoyed with her friend. 'Why didn't you tell me?'

'I did when you came to the lab the other day. I asked you how the crime scene manager coped with him.'

Sam remembered the flippant remark and its importance suddenly became apparent. 'Did you manage to match them with Owen's jacket?'

'It was the same type of fibre we found at the James

scene.' so I just assumed it was his. Obviously didn't bother wearing his protective suit *again*.'

'But he did he was wearing his protective suit at the Purvis murder!'

Sam arrived at Owen's house early, hoping to catch him in. There was something wrong, a nagging doubt at the back of her mind. She needed samples from his jacket, if only to allay her worst suspicions. Neither Richard's nor Janet's cars were anywhere to be seen but still, she knocked loudly on the front door to be sure. She waited for a few moments but there wasn't a sound.

She walked to the rear of the house and peered through the back windows, there was no sign of life. Although she might not be able to get samples from Owen's jacket, it seemed stupid to miss an opportunity to have a good look around. She knew if she got caught she'd be in trouble, but she decided it was a risk worth taking. She crossed the neatly trimmed lawn to the greenhouse. The garden was one of the most boring and predictable she had ever seen. It was mainly laid to a rectangular lawn with a selection of plants and shrubs in narrow borders around the edge. It was a garden designed to give its owner a minimum amount of work and a minimum amount of pleasure. The greenhouse, like the garden, was small and uninspiring, mainly full of tomato plants in grow bags and very little else. She crossed the garden again, this time towards the garage and peered in through one of the small windows at the side of the building. It was only a small garage, but crammed inside, swathed in a dark-coloured tarpaulin, was a car.

Sam began to feel her heart beat a little faster. She had been surprisingly calm up to that point, only half believing her suspicions. Sam walked to the front of the garage and grasped both doors, giving them a violent shake. But they were securely locked and offered no prospect of entry without considerable effort and inevitable damage. The two small windows at the side of the garage were also firmly closed and so she walked round to the other side where there was a single door. Without much hope she pulled at the handle and, despite her expectations, the door was unlocked. After catching momentarily where dampness had caused the wood to swell, it gave way and the door flew open throwing her off balance. With one last glance along Owen's drive she took a deep breath and entered the garage. Whatever the make of the car, hidden under its heavy covering, it was certainly long. She moved slowly to the front of the garage and, crouching down, lifted the front of the tarpaulin to reveal the front end of a maroon Jaguar. She stared at it for a moment as if it were a living thing, wondering what stories it would reveal when the SOCOs began to work on it. A coldness crept over her as she pictured the fear and pain of Mark James and Frances Purvis and tried in vain to connect the bumbling, affable Owen with the cold, cruel persona of their killer. Pushing her thoughts to one side, she began to examine the front of the car. The middle half of the nearside wing was crumpled and bore a number of deep scratches which had ripped the paint from the bodywork across its front. Sam could also see that the front bumper was missing. It looked as if one half had been ripped from its mounting while the other had been carefully removed.

She ran her hand along the smooth, dark paint checking for an area from which a scraping would not be noticed. She decided that one more scratch by the side of the already damaged area would be hardly noticeable and so, taking a penknife and a small plastic bag from her handbag, she began to scratch away at the paint until she was sure she had enough for a comparison. Then, dropping her penknife and the paint back into her bag, she replaced the cover over the front of the car. There was new little doubt in Sam's mind, Owen was the killer.

Sam pushed the garage door firmly closed behind her and she had just got back to the side of the house when she heard him call.

'Samantha!'

She whirled round. Owen's voice sent a shiver down her spine and for a moment she found herself unable to move. Willpower and an inbred survival instinct finally made her turn and, smiling, she gave him a cheery wave. Owen made his way up the garden towards her. She noticed that he had on the same smart blazer he'd been wearing the night James' body had been discovered. Now, in the bright sunlight it seemed far more vivid than she remembered and there could be no doubt, it was unquestionably blue.

'What a pleasant surprise! What are you doing here?' She could feel her body tense and a slight tremor begin. She knew she had to relax, it was important for her to appear normal if she was to bluff her way out of this situation. Drawing on all her mental reserves she affected a matter-of-fact air, 'I tried the front door, but there was no reply. I thought I might find you pottering around the back.'

'Well, you've found me. I had to pop down to the shops; my car's in the garage so I had to walk. Still, I'm sure it did me good. Coffee?'

All she wanted to do at that precise moment was run screaming into the road calling for help and pointing out to the world that friendly old Dr Owen was in fact a homicidal maniac and should be locked up for ever. Instead she found herself dumbly nodding her acceptance, 'That sounds lovely.'

She followed Owen into the house through the front door. She had never felt so alert in her life. Her eyes darted from place to place, continually looking for the quickest escape route, or some object which she could use as a weapon. By now her heart was pounding so hard that she felt sure Owen would notice it, even through her clothes. She tried desperately to remain calm.

'I only half expected you to be in, thought you might be at your surgery.'

'I get Thursdays off. Janet covers for me, she likes to keep her hand in. Now, let's see about that coffee.'

He made his way into the kitchen taking off his jacket and dropping it carelessly over a chair. Sam saw her opportunity and began to make her way carefully towards it. She had only gone a few steps when a shout from the kitchen stopped her.

'Black, no suggar, is it?'

Sam called back, 'Yes, that's right, thanks.'

Taking in a deep breath she plucked at the jacket with

her fingers, pulling away whisps of fibres and dropping them quickly into a white paper tissue she pulled from her bag. As she began to close the tissue Owen returned from the kitchen with the two steaming cups of coffee. Sam quickly brought the tissue up to her nose and pretended to sniff.

'Got a bit of a cold coming by the sound of it, like me to give you something for it?'

Sam shook her head. 'No, I'll be fine. Thank you.'

Owen put his coffee down on a small table and walked across to one of the window blinds. 'You'll have to forgive my back for a moment but I've got to get this thing restrung, the last cord broke.

While his back was still to her Sam slipped the tissue into her handbag. Now, as I take it this isn't entirely a social call, perhaps you'll tell me what I can do for you?'

Sam swallowed hard.

'I've come up against a bit of a brick wall over those last two murders. I thought you might have some ideas on the subject?'

'I thought they'd got that man Bird in for it?'

'They have, but I'm not convinced.'

'Really, might one ask why?'

Owen turned. He had a long white cord in his hand which he continually wiped across his palms. The movement seemed to have a hypnotic effect on Sam and she found herself becoming transfixed by the movement like a snake's prey waiting for the deadly strike.

'Too many holes.'

'Like what?'

The movement of his hands seemed to increase as he clearly became more agitated.

'The fingerprints, they were planted.'

'Planted? How can you tell?'

'The technician at the lab discovered some inconsistencies.'

'First I've heard, when did all this happen?'

'Yesterday evening.'

'Will they be letting him go then?'

Sam's breathing began to imitate the rhythmic movement of the cord through Owen's hands. She sipped at her coffee, affecting normality, trying to calm herself. 'I've no idea.'

'Well, let's hope they at least shut down that club of his.'

Sam nodded her false approval. Owen stopped pulling the cord through his hands for a moment and excused himself, 'It's too long, I'm going to have to cut it down a little. Back in a second.' He disappeared into the kitchen. Sam considered bolting for the door, she wasn't sure she could take much more. She realized, however, that if she did it would alert him and he might slip away before the police could stop him, he might be lost for ever. He returned to the sitting-room after only a few moments but this time instead of walking across to the blind he stood behind her. Sam glanced back. He had the cord wrapped tightly around one hand while he cut the other end with a scalpel. He looked at her, 'Sharpest thing I've got in the house, cuts through almost anything in a moment.'

Sam gave him a nervous smile and forced herself to turn

277

away in a parody of casual interchange, whilst expecting at any moment to feel the cord being looped around her neck or the sharp cut of the scalpel as it forced its way through her neck.

She continued with the conversation estimating that at least the sound of his voice would tell her where he was. 'I didn't know you had an interest in Bird's club?'

The reply came back sharply and with a hint of anger, 'I don't, but one hears stories. Bad influence on the young, deserves to be closed.'

Sam noticed a photograph of a young girl on the top of the fireplace and seized upon it as an excuse to stand up and cross the room, moving away from Owen. 'She's pretty, who is she?

'My daughter, she was eighteen when that was taken; she'd just got into Trinity Hall to read law. Her whole life was before her.'

'Where is she now?'

'Dead, she was killed a few years ago.'

Sam felt embarrassed and surprised. She suddenly realized how little she really knew about Owen. She'd always liked him as a friend and a colleague but they had never been close and she'd certainly never pried into his personal life. She doubted that anyone else had either. He was very adept at simulating intimacy without revealing anything of himself. Owen suddenly turned towards her and from the look in his eyes Sam could tell he was about to make his move, about to finish a job he had started days before when he tried to force her off the road.

Farmer was in the interview room when the call came

in. The place was winding down, computers were being removed, staff were clearing their drawers as they prepared to return to section. The DC who answered the phone did so in a very disinterested manner, 'DC Parker, murder incident room.' He listened for a moment, then called across to Farmer who was sorting through a stream of witness statements with Adams, 'It's for you, boss, forensic lab, I'll put it through.'

As soon as the white light began to flash on the phone Farmer picked it up. 'Detective Superintendent Farmer, can I help you?'

The voice on the other end of the phone was unmistakably that of Brian Watton. She knew it well, and she knew how good Brian was; he'd been the inspiration behind the resolution of more than one case in his time. What he told her this time, however, she didn't want to hear. Adams looked up as the room went quiet.

'Are you bloody sure? . . . Do you realize what you're doing? . . . Yes, I'm sure.' Farmer slammed the phone down hard on to its cradle. 'Shit, shit, shit, shit, shit, shit!'

Adams and the rest of those in the room remained silent, waiting. Farmer finally stood up and looked across at the remaining detectives. With a deep sigh she addressed them.

'Well, there's good news and bad news. We're back to square one. The prints on the Purvis car were planted and we've all been made to look a bunch of tossers.'

One of the DCs spoke up, 'And the good news?'

She snarled across at him, 'That was the good news,

the bad news is, all leave and time off is cancelled until we catch this bastard.'

She looked up at her WELL DONE banner which was still draped across the ceiling, 'And get that down before I strangle – sorry, garrotte – someone with it.'

Sam felt convinced that Janet Owen's timely arrival had been her salvation. She had apparently finished her surgery early and come straight home. Her arrival had broken the spell of the moment and taken the glaze out of Owen's eyes. She couldn't remember being more relieved to see someone before in her life. She hadn't wasted any time and despite the look of surprise and bemused incomprehension, Sam had made feeble and hurried excuses for leaving and fled the house. She tried desperately to control her rising panic but her hand was shaking so much that she had serious difficulty in getting the key into the lock. She pulled her coat around the side of her hand trying to hide her panic. Finally, the door opened. She jumped inside and pulled the car out of the drive, accelerating quickly along the road, leaving Janet waving earnestly from the front door. She hadn't travelled far before the tears which were filling her eyes and blurring her vision forced her to pull into the side of the road and stop. She pulled her mobile from her bag and dialled, desperately trying to see the numbers through her tears. Finally she managed to get through.

'Marcia Evans, please.' Sam tried to control her voice which threatened to fail her as the ache in her throat reached a crescendo and paralysed her vocal cords,

'Could you find her please, this is Doctor Ryan at the Park, it's very urgent.'

Marcia's concentration was almost tangible as she looked hard down her microscope. She changed the slides several times before finally looking up. Sam was sitting on a bench at the far side of the lab. Although several hours had passed since her encounter with Richard Owen, she still hadn't managed to regain her composure completely. She looked back at Marcia expectantly.

'The paint layers and colours are identical. I'm ninety per cent sure it's the same car. Where did you find it?

'It was parked in Richard Owen's garage.'

'The police surgeon?' Sam nodded. 'So I was right all along!'

Sam gave a forced half smile. 'What about the fibres from his jacket?'

Marcia walked across to a plump young girl working on the bench next to hers. 'Any joy, Jenny?'

The girl looked up. 'Well, I'll need a bit more time to be sure, but I'm almost certain they're *not* the same.'

Sam felt she should have been surprised but she wasn't. 'How are they different?'

The girl placed the fibres Sam had collected from Owen's jacket under an ultraviolet light. 'If you look hard, you'll notice that under the light it shows up bluey-green.'

Marcia and Sam examined the fibre closely as Jenny changed the sample.

'The samples we retrieved from the scenes are a much

more intense, flat blue. These are definitely not from the same garment.'

Marcia looked up at Sam. 'Are you sure it was the same jacket?'

'Yes. Well, it looked the same. It was certainly blue.'

'It was dark last time you saw it, you might have made a mistake. He's bound to have more than one jacket, and they're all bound to be dark. Can't see Owen buying a red one.'

Sam had been so sure. 'No, I suppose . . .'

'He's hardly likely to give us evidence that's going to incriminate him, is he?'

'No, I'm sure you're right.'

'We've got enough with the paint samples anyway.'

'I hope so, I'd hate to lose him now.' Sam looked back at Jenny, 'I didn't manage to pick anything else off the jacket that might help, did I?'

'Not much, a few plant hairs, that's all.'

Sam suddenly found herself becoming interested again, her optimism returning. 'What kind of plant hairs?'

Jenny shook her head. 'I'm not sure. Have a look.' Sam walked across to the microscope and peered in. She examined the hairs for a few moments then straightened up, a look of triumph on her face. 'I know what they are, *Hedera Hibernica*. They come off in the hundreds when you come into contact with it. They're difficult to get off as well.'

Marcia walked across to Sam and put her arm around her, 'Time to call Farmer, I think. This thing's getting a bit too dangerous for country girls like us.'

CHAPTER NINE

It was almost over. He knew the moment he walked up the drive and saw her coming out of his garage. The involuntary tightening of her grip on her handbag as she saw him was so revealing. She had worked it out, she had come looking for evidence and had found the car. He was sure paint scrapings would be inside her handbag. Scrapings which would match samples collected from the damage caused when he had collided with Frances' car. She had wrestled hard to act calmly, but it hadn't been entirely successful. He knew her well enough to be aware of her agitation. He could see it in her eyes, in her body language and the taut lines of her face. He'd even watched her from the kitchen as she had taken samples from his jacket and concealed them in a tissue and her feeble pretence of a cold. Even after she had fled from the house he had seen her hands shaking so much that she couldn't get the key in the lock of her car. He'd almost pitied her, so locked inside her fear, and contemplated offering to help her. Perhaps he should have killed her when he had the chance. If Janet had not come home he probably would have but what would have been gained from that? She'd probably already told someone where she was going and the game would have been up anyway. Besides, killing her now was not what He had ordained. And departing from His clear intentions would have made him a common murderer, and he had never been that. He wasn't convinced he had the stomach for it. Despite his anger and frustration at the way she'd thwarted his plan, he still liked Sam. She was honest and diligent and would undoubtedly do more good in this world than he, once his mission was complete.

He didn't know why but God had quite clearly decided that his mission was nearly over and that he had done enough. Mercy was, of course, within God's gift but not his. He had one more score to settle before he could feel any sense of justice. What was important now was to buy time and cover his tracks as much as possible so the mission could continue. He felt remarkably calm for a man who knew he must spend at least the next ten years in prison. They called it life; he supposed for man of his age they were probably right.

He walked outside and to the top of the garden where he pulled a large box of matches from his pocket and began a fire. He watched as it took hold of the dried wood and leaves and the grey whisps of smoke drifted into the damp, windless atmosphere over the adjoining gardens. He waited until the flames had taken a firm hold before piling more wood and leaves on to the top. When he was convinced that the fire was established he collected a spade from the shed, walked to the line of bushes at the back of the garden and dug the ivy bush out of the ground. The plant had blended in well with the evergreen bushes, and was difficult to spot unless you knew it was there.

He had to wrest its long tendrils from their anchorage points on the fence before throwing it on to the fire. It didn't burn well, but it did burn. Then he returned to collect the fallen leaves and any remaining branches and roots before filling the hole and levelling the ground and returning to the house.

Malcolm Purvis watched as the removal men carried item after item of furniture out of the house and into the back of the removal van parked in his drive. He planned to put most of it into storage, sell those items which he no longer needed and give the rest away to local charities. The flat in London was fully furnished so he had no immediate need for most of his furniture, but much of it held memories and each piece had been chosen with care, much discussion and good-natured banter with his beloved wife. He waited for them to bring out the large piano and watched them struggle down the steps with it before he went back into the house and up the stairs to Frances' room. It looked so forlorn now with her bed stripped and all her toys gone. He stood for a moment while memories engulfed him, glimpses of past Christmases, birthdays, tears and joy, grief and illness. He wondered if those memories and his grief would be etched into the very fabric of the house to reappear as unwelcome ghosts to future generations of owners. He tried to empty his mind for a moment to see if he could sense her presence but she wasn't there, even her smell had gone. The fragment of comforting words she had once spoken to him drifted into his mind, 'Wherever you are Daddy, so am I.' He was comforted. He decided that this would be the last time he entered this room. It was only an empty shell with no life. Finally, he walked across to the window, drew the curtains and left the room, closing the door quietly behind him.

The liquid was measured precisely into the syringe. When the vial was almost empty the plunger was gently depressed sending liquid squirting into the air to fall on to the carpet. The calculated amount of drug was sealed inside the clear plastic tube and it was dropped back inside the black bag which was closed and locked. The phone rang twice before it was answered. After a short conversation the bag was pushed under the desk and the room vacated.

The fire was burning well when Owen returned to it, his arms full of files, photographs and notes. Even the ivy seemed to be burning well now. He spilled the contents of his arms on to the fire and began to poke at the ashes with a long stick, trying to stoke it up. There was something about fire which he really enjoyed. It was created of strange pictures and images. He found the crackling and spitting comforting too, but most importantly it was a purifier. They'd known that almost since time began. It destroyed only to renew. Now it would destroy most of the evidence against him and renew his chance of finishing his work. He picked up one of the files which had slipped out of the reach of the flames and examined its contents. He remembered this one, Michael Kemp, 64 Denning Lane, Cambridge, a 43-year-old self-employed builder. Lived with his wife and one son. The other son was at college in Nottingham. He had two vehicles, an old, blue Ford van, registration number LLD 453E and a series three BMW, black, registration number M256 PDR. He looked at it one more time before throwing it on to the fire. It caught light almost at once. The edges of the file turned black and curled inwards before bursting into flames. He really didn't need the files any more but they had become like old friends, comforting and familiar. He'd spent so much time researching them, reading and re-reading every detail that the information was almost a part of his very being. He would miss them but he didn't need them.

After giving herself a final cursory once-over in the mirror, she pulled down the jacket of her suit, flicked the last strands of hair away from the side of her face, marched quickly out of the ladies' lavatory and headed towards the chief superintendent's office. Although she always endeavoured to look smart, she wasn't normally so precise about her appearance, but on this occasion she knew that not only was her position as head of the enquiry in doubt but her future career with the Cambridgeshire Constabulary.

The large, black plaque bearing the inscription, DETECTIVE CHIEF SUPERINTENDENT. MARK WORDS QPM, covered the entire top third of the door and confirmed her arrival at her destination. She wondered, facetiously, whether the plaque was there in case he forgot who he was. She took a steadying deep breath and knocked. A loud but firm voice echoed imperiously into the corridor from inside the office, 'Wait!'

He was on his own, of course, and the only person he was expecting was her but they had to play these little power games and she was in no position to prevent them. It had been like this during her whole time with the force. If they weren't trying to touch her up or persuade her that an episode between the sheets with them would increase her promotion chances, then they were putting her down, making light of her success, and blowing up out of all proportion her failures. She'd seen so many women join full of ambition only to have it knocked out of them by the system. And if one did beat the system and exhibit some success, then of course they had to be a dike. She knew that was the common denunciation of herself, and her lifestyle afforded ample affirmation of the presumption. Late thirties, unmarried, living alone; what else could she possibly be? Well, she wasn't, and she was damned if she was going to indulge in a pointless defence of her sexuality with any of them.

'Enter!' The voice boomed into the corridor once more. She breathed in again, pushed down the handle on the door and entered the office. It was typical of the style of office preferred by senior officers and could be summed up in one word, plush. Thick carpet on the floor, an oak desk, drinks' cabinet, television and video, a couple of large comfortable chairs for cosy, chummy meetings and the shelves and walls covered in mementoes and trophies from police forces around the world. He eyed her carefully, making his annoyance felt, and setting the tone of the meeting immediately, before directing her to one of the not so comfortable chairs in front of his desk. They were strategically placed. Not close enough to be too intimate, but not so far away that he would have to raise his voice above a reasonable whisper to be heard. They took a pride in sounding reasonable, she thought, they never were, but they liked to sound it.

'Well, we're in a right bloody mess, aren't we?'

Farmer watched him, resenting everything about him, but she remained silent.

'You've managed to make this force look complete bloody fools and you've done it all by yourself. We'll just have to hope he doesn't sue us for every penny we've got. God knows what your father would have said if he'd been alive. He wasn't the soft touch I am . . .' She waited for it. 'He was my detective inspector when I first joined the CID.' She mouthed the next bit in her mind, she'd heard it so many times before. 'He was the best boss I ever had, hard you understand, but fair, you knew where you were with him.' She knew for a fact that her father thought Mark Words to be the biggest prat who had ever been allowed into uniform. She'd tell him one day, hopefully at his retirement party when she'd got his job and he could kiss her arse. For now she settled for sounding reassuring.

'We've still got him for breaching his bail conditions.'

'Clutching at straws a bit, aren't we?' Farmer knew she was but couldn't think of anything else to say. 'That is, if you haven't managed to cock up that one as well?'

For a moment she fantasized about leaning over the desk and punching him in the face. He stood up from his desk and began to pace around the room, his hands behind his back with his 'let's have the cards on the table' conversation look on his face.

'I took a chance when I appointed you, Harriet. It was a sort of thank-you to the memory of your father really, to pay him back for all he did for me . . .'

Would that be when he tried to get you thrown off the job? she thought.

'I really believed that you, above all people, especially given your background, could handle the job.' He stopped for a moment and looked at her. 'I was wrong.'

Farmer couldn't remember hating someone so much in her entire life. She'd often heard it said that anyone was capable of committing murder, but until that moment she hadn't really believed them. After that, everything else the sanctimonious old bastard said just sounded like a distant echo.

'You've let me down, Harriet, you've let the force down and more importantly, you've let yourself down. I really do not have any other . . .'

The loud knock on the door stopped him mid-flow and he told the unknown intruder to wait but it was too late, Adams was already in the office.

'Excuse me, sir, but there's been a bit of a development.' He looked across at Farmer. 'Those paint scrapings you managed to find, ma'am, well, they've come up trumps, you were right all along, it was Richard Owen.'

Farmer was as surprised as Words but tried not to show it. This time it was Words who began to look uncomfortable.

'Do you mean the Police Surgeon?'

Adams glanced across at him. 'Yes, sir.'

'Good God, I had dinner with him and his wife on Saturday! Are you quite sure?'

'Yes, sir, very sure.'

Words returned to his desk and sat down. 'Looks like you might have the opportunity to redeem yourself. Better go and sort it out and make sure you keep me informed. I'll wait here and have a heart attack.'

Farmer nodded and made her way to the door which was being held open for her by Adams. She looked up at him as she passed. Normally she wasn't very good at thank-yous but this was the exception. 'You're a prince, do you know that? a bloody prince.'

'All part of the service.'

They exchanged wry smiles briefly before disappearing down the steps to the car-park.

Sam and Marcia were waiting outside when Farmer and Adams arrived supported by at least a dozen other uniformed and CID officers. They'd heard the sound of the police sirens as they raced through the rush-hour traffic for almost five minutes and so, presumably, had Owen. The white smoke which the two women had seen drifting over his house had lent an intensity and urgency at the sound. All Sam wanted to do was to rush into the house and prevent him from destroying any more evidence. She had experienced one frightening episode with Owen and she wasn't keen to experience another. Next time she might not be quite so lucky. The police cars came to a screaming halt outside Owen's house and dozens of police officers piled out. They moved into action like a flock of birds, responding instinctively to information and directions undetected by mere onlookers. Two sealed off the driveway to the house, several ran into the gardens of the adjoining properties, while others rushed up to the front door and smashed it in with a hydraulic ram. As Adams and Farmer dashed from their car, Sam and Marcia followed. They ran up to the back gate which led out into the garden and pulled on the handle, but it had been securely locked. Two hefty kicks from Adams' boot, however, sent the door crashing off its hinges and the small party spilled through.

As Adams ran towards Owen, he desperately threw the last few files on to the centre of the fire. Adams launched himself at Owen and, pulling him to the ground, forced his arms behind his back, handcuffing his wrists together.

Owen laughed and screamed hysterically as he was restrained, 'You're too late, you're much too late!'

Adams shouted to the uniformed officers who had followed him into the garden, 'Get some water – get this bloody fire out!'

The two officers rushed towards the kitchen as Sam and Marcia, shielding their faces against the heat, attempted to rescue as many of the smouldering files from the edge of the bonfire as possible, stamping on them to smother the creeping ribbons of fire which threatened to engulf them.

Finally, one of the police officers returned with a hose-pipe and began to douse the flames. Adams pulled Owen to his feet and, deferring the privilege, pushed him in front of Farmer who had now entered the garden from the back of the house.

Farmer stared coldly into his eyes. 'Dr Richard Owen, I'm arresting you on suspicion of the murder of Mark James and Frances Purvis. You are not obliged —'

Owen suddenly lunged forward to within a few inches of Farmer's face, 'Prove it!'

Farmer, unflinching and with contempt, continued to stare into his eyes and finished the caution before getting two of the uniformed officers to drag him out to her car.

The fire was extinguished and teams of SOCOs were already arriving to search and clear the house. Sam and Marcia carefully sifted through the charred remains around the fire trying to rescue anything that might help build up the case against the former police surgeon. Marcia found several ivy leaves and showed them to Sam who confirmed its species before Marcia dropped them into a small brown envelope. Sam found several metal buttons which looked as if they might have come from a girl's jacket, as well as a small piece of black cloth. Of the files they had managed to pull off the fire, only two were of any use. Adams and Sam flicked through them: flakes of black, shrivelled paper breaking off and swirling into the air.

'Look at this, they must have been his next victims.'

Sam stared incredulously at the files.

'Places of work, where they drank, the routes they took,' said Adams. 'Look, even where they shopped. Talk about "Who Dares", it's like an SAS operation.'

Sam took the file off him and looked at the photographs. 'I wonder how many we missed?'

'Doesn't really matter, they're safe now, they'll never let him out.'

'But why? Why would someone like Richard Owen turn into a homicidal maniac?'

'He'd obviously been thinking about it for a while. These must be the best laid plans for murder I've ever seen.'

Farmer approached them, taking the file off Sam and handing it back to Adams. 'Well done, Tom.'

'It wasn't me. It's Dr Ryan you've got to thank, she found the paint samples, not me.'

Farmer looked at Sam then back to Adams. 'Give us a minute, will you, Tom?'

Adams walked away and joined Marcia who was still hunting through the remains of the fire in the hope of finding something extra. As soon as they were alone and Adams out of earshot Farmer began, 'What did I tell you about getting involved in this enquiry?'

'I didn't have any deliberate intention to interfere, circumstances just dictated it. I handed over all the information as soon as I had it. I don't see what else I could have done. If you want to make an official complaint, then that's up to you.'

'Oh no. Not even I am that stupid. Have the world know that it was you who cracked this case and not me? I'd be a laughing stock. He'll be locked away, in a nice secure hospital where he belongs, and this will be our little secret. A perfect ending for all concerned.'

'Fine.'

'Look, I'm not very good at this sort of thing, and part of me still feels that you were in the bloody wrong, but well done – and thanks.'

Sam knew how difficult such a statement must have been for Farmer and appreciated it all the more.

Farmer continued, 'To be quite honest, if you hadn't stuck your nose in where it wasn't wanted not only might I have been off the case, I might have been off the job.'

Sam was conciliatory, 'Thank you. I *am* a bit of a nosy cow; it comes with the job.'

'Well, I think we can both be grateful for that.'

'What will happen to Bird?'

'We've still got him for the breaking the terms of his bail. I expect we'll drop that if he decides not to sue us. It normally works something like that.'

For the first time since Sam had known Farmer there was a hint of mutual understanding.

Shouts and screams from the front of the house sent them scurrying to the front gate. Standing at the bottom of the drive and struggling with two police officers was Janet Owen. She was angry, confused and crying bitterly as she watched her house being searched by a team of white-suited SOCOs and armfuls of her clothes and belongings being unceremoniously removed.

'My clothes. Where are they going with my clothes?'

Sam looked across at Farmer. 'I'll tell her. I've met her before.'

'She'll have to come in for questioning.'

'I understand, but if it wasn't for her I might be dead now, so give me a chance to calm her down first and I'll drive her in to see you after that.'

Farmer nodded, 'OK, I've got her old man to interview first anyway.'

Sam made her way back down the drive and through

the cordon. Janet recognized her at once. 'What the hell is going on, Sam?'

'It's Richard, I'm afraid. They've arrested him.'

'For what?'

'Let's go to my car and I'll explain.'

'No. If you know something, tell me now.'

'I'm sorry, Janet, but they've arrested him for murder. He's responsible for the deaths of Mark James and the Purvis girl.'

The effect of Sam's words on Janet was total. The colour drained from her face and her eyes glazed over. As she fell forward in a dead faint, Sam caught her and with the help of one of the nearby police officers laid her gently on the pavement, slipping off her jacket and using it as a cushion under her head. She shouted at the young PC by her side, 'Get an ambulance!'

She picked up Janet's left hand and began to stroke it rhythmically while she waited for help.

Adams watched Owen closely as he signed all the appropriate forms and disclaimers in the station sergeant's office. After he had finished he was escorted to an interview room in the company of his solicitor. The two video cameras had already been turned on. One showed a general view of the room revealing Farmer and Adams sitting opposite Owen and his solicitor. The second camera stood back from the table but showed a close-up of Owen's head and face. In the murder incident room a closed-circuit television showed the interview to the rest of the squad. Farmer began.

'We are making enquiries into the murder of Mark

James and Frances Purvis. I believe you can help us with those enquiries.'

Owen remained silent for a moment, scanning the two officers' faces. 'If you mean did I kill them and then cut them up, yes I did.' He smiled into the camera close to the table. 'And, what's more, I don't regret a thing.'

Mr Robertson, his solicitor, leaned across and spoke quietly to him, 'Do you realize the full implication of what you are saying?'

Owen looked back at him. 'Oh yes, I do, it's time for the truth I think, don't you?'

Sam had been joined by Trevor Stuart as she waited outside the busy casualty department at the Park Hospital where Janet had been taken for treatment. She was glad to see him and was surprised to find herself throwing her arms around him and hugging him closely. They sat down together and Sam outlined the situation. For the first time since she'd known him, Trevor had lost his humour and listened intensely to every word she said. When she'd finished he took her hand.

'I think I might understand his motivation at least.'

Sam was surprised. 'Why didn't you say something before?'

'It didn't seem relevant, not until now anyway.'

Sam waited expectantly.

'I think it has something to do with his daughter, Claire.'

'I thought she died in an accident?'

'Well, it was an accident of sorts. A drugs overdose at a party.'

'How long ago did all this happen?'

'Three years ago. Claire wasn't the angel Owen liked to portray her as. She was a bit of a bad lot actually. Ran around with the wrong crowd, got involved in drugs and started stealing to feed her habit, even from her parents. How they put up with it I'll never know. I think Janet was aware of what was going on but Richard wouldn't hear a word against her. Claire's death hit him hard. Janet did what she could, she's the strong one in the relationship, but it was still over a year before he went back to work. I don't think he's ever fully recovered. He found God as well and became a *bore*-again Christian.'

'Any other children?'

'No. She was all they had.'

'Where did the party take place?'

'I seem to remember it was in a local club.'

'Bird's Nest?'

'Yes, that was it, Bird's Nest.'

Marcia's laboratory was filling rapidly with the clothes and other paraphernalia from Owen's house. Each item had already been carefully bagged and labelled and now awaited the attention of one of the white-coated technicians. While some lifted fibres off the clothes with taped hands, others organized the fibres on to slides and began to examine them. Everyone knew it was going to be a long job but it didn't blunt their enthusiasm to ensure that nothing was missed.

Trevor had left by the time Janet emerged from the cubicle where she was being treated. The doctor had wanted her to stay in for the night, concerned about her condition, but she persuaded them that her husband's needs were greater than hers and assured them that if she experienced another bout of fainting she would return. Finally, she signed the release form and rejoined her friend.

Sam had parked her car directly outside the department in a slot which indicated 'Casualty staff only'. She helped Janet into the passenger seat and they began the short drive to the incident room. Sam was at a loss to know what words might comfort her. An awkward silence descended over them, broken finally by Janet.

'I knew he was ill, had been for a while. He never got over the death of our daughter from a drugs overdose a few years ago, you see. But I never thought he could . . . kill anyone. I still can't believe he'd do such a thing; he's such a gentle man. You know him, Sam, you know he couldn't do a thing like this.'

'I think the evidence against him is pretty strong. You never noticed anything?'

'No, he had his den and I was banned from that, called it his little bit of liberty, wouldn't even let me dust in there.'

'Is there anything you can think of that might help his case, explain his state of mind at the time of the killings?'

'He kept a diary. Would that be of any help?'

'It might be, where is it?'

'He kept it in his safe at the surgery.'

'Will it still be there?'

'Unless the police have already searched the place.'

'Would you mind if we went and had a look?'

'Not at all if it helps. He's ill you know, not bad. If those people hadn't supplied Claire with those evil substances she'd still be alive and I would probably be a grandmother by now.'

Sam tried to be sympathetic but she remembered how Frances' body looked when she'd first seen it, and the hurt in the eyes of her father when she'd seen him at the mortuary. She found it hard to feel any real understanding for Owen's actions.

'There's just one thing, my dear, can I go in alone? I know where it is. I won't be a moment but I'd like to be the one who breaks the news to the staff. They're going to be upset enough when the police start taking the place apart. It'll be better coming from me.'

Sam nodded in agreement. A few moments later they were outside Owen's surgery and Janet was disappearing through the swing doors.

Farmer persevered with the interview. Around the monitor in the incident room there was standing room only and, in a normally bustling and noisy office, the silence had a tangible quality. Farmer leaned back in her chair; she hadn't expected the confession to come quite so easily and hoped the rest of the interview would go as smoothly.

'Why did you kill them?'

Owen was totally calm and in control of himself. 'It wasn't murder, more like an execution, devine retribution, they killed my daughter.'

'How?'

'Drugs. They gave her drugs. She overdosed, died in Bird's club. He knew how ill she was but he just left her to die.'

'So what was Mark and Frances' involvement?'

'They took her there, gave her the drugs, as many as she wanted; you see, she had the money, that's all they were interested in. She was a wonderful daughter until they got their evil hands on her.'

'Frances Purvis wasn't evil.'

'Oh yes, she was, she was the worst of the lot. Claire had no idea about the kind of people they were. Pimps, prostitutes, pushers. They introduced her to all that. Do you know where they found her? In the cubicle of a public toilet.'

Adams cut in, 'I thought you said she died in Bird's club?'

'She did, but that's where they dumped her.'

A PC knocked and entered the interview room, passing Adams a sheet of paper.

'According to the information we have, your daughter died of an overdose. The conclusion of the inquest was that it was accidental. Nobody murdered her.'

'They might not have stabbed her in the heart or shot her but they murdered her just the same. You didn't know her, did you? She was the sweetest thing you ever met.'

'This report here states that your daughter had convictions for theft, robbery, violence and prostitution. James never supplied your daughter with drugs. Bird and Frances had tried to get help for your daughter, they knew she was ill but, by the time the ambulance got there she'd climbed out of a window and disappeared. They tried to find her, they wished they had. They were as upset as you were.'

Owen wasn't listening, 'Lies all lies. You're just part of it.'

'Part of what?'

'The cover-up. Do you know what the coroner said when he gave his verdict, "A tragic loss of a young life." Tragic, tragic. I'll show you what's tragic.' He rolled his sleeve up exposing his arm. The bottom half of which was covered in the tell-tale puncture marks of a drug addict. 'I'm an addict just like she was. It's the only way I can cope, you see – to stop the memories pulling me down and tearing me apart. That's what the tragic death of a young life does to a family, it destroys them. I think I could have coped if someone had been punished, but no one was. James walked free from court. Frances wasn't even charged. It was one big cover-up because certain people didn't want their precious reputations damaged.'

'Who was that, Dr Owen?'

'That's for you to find out. You lot couldn't catch a cold, never mind a murderer. Something had to be done, so I decided to do it.'

'What about the people who loved Mark and Frances? Did they deserve to suffer?'

Owen looked indignant. 'Yes, of course they did. That was all part of it, they were responsible for the kind of people their children became. I hope they rot in hell.'

'What about your wife, Janet? Who's she going to turn to now you're locked up?'

'What difference will that make? We both died on the

same day as Claire; you can't do any more to either of us. You were lucky it was only three, I wanted to kill a lot more.'

Adams looked across the table at him. 'We only know of two bodies. Where's the third?'

'That's for you to discover.'

Adams could feel himself becoming agitated. 'Is there a third body, or hasn't it happened yet? What the fuck are you up to?'

Owen smiled confidently. 'Later, I'll tell you later.'

Jenny was staring intensely down her microscope. She looked up and shouted to Marcia. 'I've matched the fibres with the ones from the jacket.'

Marcia walked across the lab to her friend who was sitting next to a dark herringbone tweed jacket.

'I thought you said the threads *didn't* match Owen's jacket?'

'Richard Owen's jacket didn't match, but this isn't Richard Owen's.'

Marcia was feeling slightly confused and agitated. 'Whose is it then?'

'It's a small woman's. The label inside says Janet Owen, so I guess it must be hers. I've found traces of ivy hairs as well.'

Without waiting for any further explanation Marcia ran to the phone and began to dial.

Farmer and Adams walked away from the cell block where they had just incarcerated Owen. Despite Farmer's optimism, Adams was not feeling complacent. Farmer noticed. 'Look, if there *is* another body we'll find it sooner or later. We can't do the poor sod any good now. Besides, there probably isn't one, he's just playing games with us. You know what these bloody psychos are like.'

'I don't think there *is* another body. Not yet, anyway. But there's going to be. There's something very wrong.'

'Not while he's locked up there isn't, and that's going to be for ever.'

They walked into the custody sergeant's office and he handed the forms to Farmer. She filled in the sheets, making an accurate note of the time the interview with Owen had taken place. Adams leaned over the desk and watched her. Suddenly he burst into action and, grabbing the form and the pen from Farmer, scribbled three or four incomprehensible words across the front of the sheet before drawing a line through all four and shouting to the station sergeant to follow him. He made his way quickly back to the cell block and Owen's cell. The station sergeant opened it. Owen was lying prostrate on the bed, his eyes closed, looking perfectly relaxed. Adams spoke up.

'Excuse me, sir, I've made a slight error with the paperwork. I wonder if you would be good enough to have a look at it and sign to say you've seen the error and accept it.'

Owen pulled himself to his feet slowly and examined the detention sheet. Farmer reached the door of the cell and watched with interest as Adams passed him the pen. Owen signed the mistake slowly and handed the pen back to Adams before returning to his bed and lying down.

'You're right-handed then, sir?'

Without opening his eyes Owen replied, 'Most people are, inspector, it's a well-known fact.'

'Maybe so, but our killer isn't; the cuts on the body were made by a left-handed person. You've an accomplice, haven't you? Who is it? Who the fuck is it?'

Owen opened his eyes lazily for a moment, waved a dismissive hand, and then closed them again. As Adams pondered what to do he heard the sound of running feet coming down the corridor. Chalky White, one of the team's two detective sargeants, handed Farmer a note. She read it in a glance and looked across at Owen. 'It's your wife, isn't it? Your partner in these killings is Janet.'

Owen sprang up and looked at the policemen who filled his cell and applauded. 'Well done, gentlemen, well done.'

Farmer looked at Adams. 'Where is she?'

A horrible realization suddenly gripped him. 'She's with Dr Ryan.'

Owen smiled. 'Now you know who the third body belongs to.'

He was lying, but he guessed it would keep them away from Purvis long enough for Janet to finish the final part of their mission.

Adams spun around and grabbed the front of Owen's shirt, pulling him to his feet and slamming him against the cell wall.

'Where is she, you bastard? Where the fuck is she?'

'You're too late! You're *far* too late. It'll be over by now.'

Adams brought his fist back and punched Owen as

hard as he could in the stomach, sending him crashing to the floor before pulling his head back up by his hair.

'I'll ask you one more time, where is she?'

The station sergeant moved forward to pull Adams away but Farmer stopped him just in time to see Owen vomit all over Adams' shoes and trousers.

Sam was still waiting outside in the car. She looked at her watch, Janet had been gone for almost half an hour and she was becoming increasingly bored with listening to a Radio Four play about life in the slow lane. She'd tried to phone Marcia to see how things were going, but she'd forgotten to charge the battery on her mobile phone, and it was hopeless. She climbed out of her car and walked into the surgery. A pleasant-looking middle-aged woman was on the reception desk.

'Excuse me, I'm looking for Dr Owen.'

The receptionist smiled at her. 'I'm afraid you missed her, she left about twenty minutes ago.'

Sam couldn't conceal her surprise. 'But I've been parked outside for the past half hour. I'd have seen her.'

'She took the back stairs, said she had to get to some emergency.'

'Which is her office?'

The receptionist pointed to a blue door at the far side of the surgery. 'It's in there, but I don't . . .'

Before she had a chance to finish her sentence Sam was inside Janet's office. Lying on the table were several small jars of Tubarine, two of which were empty. Although the computer was on, the screen saver obscured the open file. Sam moved the mouse and brought up the information.

At the top of the screen was the name, Malcolm Purvis, followed by his address and everything a would-be killer would need to know. There was even a photograph. She recognized him from the mortuary. Undoubtedly the rest of their intended victims would be on the same file. Sam ran from the office into the reception. The woman she had seen earlier was on the phone. Sam glared at her.

'Who are you phoning?'

The receptionist looked frightened and replied nervously, 'The police.'

Sam grabbed the phone from her hand making her jump back with a scream. She shouted into the phone, 'Write this down. My name is Dr Samantha Ryan. I'm the forensic pathologist at the Park Hospital. Ring Detective Superintendent Harriet Farmer and tell her that Janet Owen is also involved in the murders and she has gone after Malcolm Purvis . . . Yes, she knows where he lives. For God's sake be quick, tell her I'll meet her at the house.' She slammed the phone down, apologized to the receptionist, who had retreated to a safe distance at the far side of the office, and fled from the surgery.

It had taken Janet longer than she had anticipated to reach the Purvis house. Road works and the late arrival of her taxi had slowed things down considerably. She paid the driver and walked across the road to the house, holding her small black medical bag tightly in her hand. She didn't bother with the front door but walked directly to the back. She climbed the few steps leading to the kitchen door and knocked; there was no reply. She tried the handle. To her delight the door opened and she stepped inside. Making her way slowly along the corridor she listened intensely for any sign of her prey. When she came to the phone in the hall she pulled the wire from its socket before crouching down and removing a syringe and a long white cord from her bag. It wasn't what she normally liked to use, it was from the blind in her front room, but it was handy and strong and she was sure it would do the job well. The house was barren, almost empty of furniture. She walked slowly into the sitting-room. She was impressed by its size and décor and admired the taste. Strange squeaking sounds, a little like a distressed mouse, filtered to her. She followed the noise to an old, white sofa. She couldn't help feeling that it looked totally out of place in such fine surroundings. Hanging over the edge of the furniture was a pair stockinged feet. She moved slowly and quietly around to the other side of the sofa before moving in. Lying in front of her was Malcolm Purvis. Pressed in his ears were two small headphones which led to a personal stereo finely balanced on his chest. He appeared to be asleep which was a great advantage to her. Raising her arm she plunged the needle of the syringe into Malcolm's neck.

Richard Owen was slumped on his bed crying, his face in his hands, while Adams watched him from the hallway outside. Their frantic efforts to locate Sam and Janet had come to nothing, though every policeman in the county had been alerted.

Farmer walked into the cell and sat by his side.

'One more killing isn't going to bring her back, it's not going to make the slightest difference to anything.'

Owen kept his face hidden in his hands. 'It will to us. It balances things up, puts our lives back together.'

'You might think it will, but it won't take the pain away or bring back Claire. There's no more purpose to it.'

Finally he lifted his head from his hands. 'Our *purpose* ended when Claire died. Revenge isn't a negative quality, it's a positive one. It's the only thing that keeps us both going. It's a powerful force. It has allowed us to achieve things we never thought possible.'

'Like murder?'

'Yes, just like murder.'

'Whose idea was it?'

'Janet's. She was always the strong one. She couldn't do it alone because of her hands, so we did it together, but she always liked to be there at the kill.'

'Who thought up the ritualistic stuff?'

'She did, it was so sweet. We found out that Bird had an interest in it and it went from there really.'

'Who did the actual killing?'

'We both did, a shared experience you might say.'

'Is that why you used the garrotte?'

'Yes, it was the only way she could do it, and it fitted in nicely with the witchcraft theme.'

'Is that why you used the drugs as well?'

'It made things so much easier. But they knew what was happening to them. They were conscious all the time. So we made sure they understood why before we finished it.'

The phone rang in the lobby and the station sergeant picked it up. He listened for a moment before slamming it down and running into the cell. 'Message from Dr Ryan, sir. She says that Janet Owen is going after Malcolm Purvis. She'll meet you at his house.'

Adams was half-way down the hall before the sergeant had finished speaking.

Owen screamed from the cell, 'You're too late, you're much too late!'

Sam arrived quickly at Malcolm's house, having driven like a maniac from the surgery. She hoped that the police, when they received the numerous complaints from the public, would be generous. She tried knocking at the front door but when there was no reply she ran around the back.

Climbing the steps to the kitchen door she found it was open. She called inside, 'Hello! Hello? Is anyone there?'

She stepped inside the kitchen, straining her ears for any sign of movement. As she walked along the hall she continued to call, not that she thought anyone was going to hear her any more, but it was somehow comforting. As she approached the sitting-room door she noticed the telephone lead lying on the hall carpet where it had been pulled from its socket. All her instincts told her to run, and she would have if she hadn't seen Malcolm's body lying across the sitting-room floor close to an old sofa. She ran across to him, her own safety dismissed from her mind for a moment. She rolled him over on to his side and felt his pulse, it was weak, but still there.

As she began to pull the shirt away from his throat a loop was passed quickly over her head and secured around her throat. She was pulled sharply backwards, the rope twisting at the back of her neck. She grabbed the cord and tried to pull it away from her throat but it bit so tightly that she was unable to get her fingers underneath. She threw her arms blindly behind her, grabbing at anything which came within reach, but it was futile. She could feel her strength ebbing away. Her lungs were screaming for air, her ears ringing and her eyes and face suffusing with blood. She pulled ineffectually at the cord a few more times but as her swollen tongue was forced from her mouth the darkness began to close around her.

The sight that greeted Adams as he burst into the sitting-room stunned him for a moment. Janet Owen was sitting behind Sam, her long grey hair dishevelled and thrown over her face as she pulled wildly at a white cord which was wrapped around Sam's throat. Sam lay in front of her, her body jerking unnaturally as spasms passed through her. He raced across the room. Judging the situation too desperate for reasonable force, he kicked Janet Owen hard in the face, sending her reeling backwards before collapsing unconscious on the floor, her jaw broken and blood pouring from her mouth. He knelt down by Sam and picked up her lifeless body. As the room filled with police officers he screamed at them, 'Get an ambulance! For God's sake, get an ambulance!'

Farmer knelt down by his side and put her arm around his shoulder.

Adams, his composure returned, looked down at Malcolm Purvis' unconscious body on the stretcher.

'Will he be OK?'

The paramedic nodded. 'I'm no doctor but I think so; he'll have one hell of a headache though.'

Adams turned to Sam who was sitting on the garden wall with a blanket around her. 'I thought I'd lost you.'

She could hardly speak, and whispered her hoarse reply, 'I thought you'd lost me, too. What about Janet?'

'She's gone. For ever I hope.'

'What will they do with them?'

'Lock them up and throw away the key with luck. But they'll probably get lots of care and consideration as well.' He said it with a sarcastic tone to his voice.

'Why did they go after Malcolm?'

'He defended Mark James, got him off. They never forgave him, or his daughter.'

A paramedic pulled up a mobile chair in front of her and helped Sam into it. She waved limply at Adams as they wheeled her into the back of the ambulance. He waved back. Farmer walked across to him.

'What are you doing here?'

Adams shrugged. 'Thought you might need some help.'

'Yes, I do. Go and get a witness statement off our intrepid pathologist. You might as well travel in the ambulance with her.'

Adams hesitated for a moment.

'Well, off you go then.'

Farmer turned and walked back towards the house.